THE
RINGS
OF
SODOM

E. THORNTON GOODE, JR.

THE RINGS OF SODOM

iUniverse books may be ordered through booksellers or by contacting:

iUniverse
1663 Liberty Drive
Bloomington, IN 47403
www.iuniverse.com
844-349-9409

Because of the dynamic nature of the Internet, any web addresses or links contained in this book may have changed since publication and may no longer be valid. The views expressed in this work are solely those of the author and do not necessarily reflect the views of the publisher, and the publisher hereby disclaims any responsibility for them.

Any people depicted in stock imagery provided by Getty Images are models, and such images are being used for illustrative purposes only. Certain stock imagery © Getty Images.

ISBN: 978-1-6632-5146-6 (sc)
ISBN: 978-1-6632-5149-7 (e)

Library of Congress Control Number: 2023905016

Print information available on the last page.

iUniverse rev. date: 03/14/2023

IN APPRECIATION

My friend, Galen Berry, has allowed me to use his picture, so the reader may get an idea as to the appearance of the character, Bruce Livingston, who is a detective kind of guy who also plays the piano. Galen also was incredibly helpful in the proofreading, editing and making suggestions for clarification as well as things that could help the storyline. He has been helpful on the last six of my nine published novels. In my last novel, <u>Saying Goodbye</u>, he suggested an alternate ending to the one I had. I liked it so much, I rewrote the ending as he suggested.

⸺⸺⸻➤◆◀⸻⸺⸺

I would like to thank my friend, Julian Green, for the use of his picture. I told him he was the image of the character, Peter Solvinoski, in this novel. I wanted the readers to get an idea as to what the character would look like in real life. This book was completely written before December 2017, and Julian was aware of it before his passing on Christmas Day of that year. You are sorely missed, my friend.

⸺⸺⸻➤◆◀⸻⸺⸺

Thank you, Mario Figueroa, for letting me use your picture to show the image of the character, Captain Mario DeSilva, in this story. Thank you, Mario.

⸻

Terence Stokes is one of my friends from FaceBook. Originally from Barcelona, Spain, he is now a gym instructor, living in Austin, Texas. Terence is the spitting image of Shawn McAllister in the story. Thank you, Terence, for letting me use your picture. I gratefully appreciate it.

⸻

This is the first time this has happened. I am actually using one of my own pictures to represent one of the characters in my novels. This photo was taken back in 1985 when I was 40 years old. It would give a good representation of the character of Ethan Trendeau in the story. (Stop laughing. I know you are.)

⸻

Galen

Galen at his piano

Julian

Mario

Terence

Me

BIOGRAPHY

I can hardly believe it but this is novel number ten going to press. There are three more completed but they need some work. Here are the ones in print so far: The Old Lighthouse, The 2, Two Portraits in Oil, MURAROOT, The Stranger from the Sea, The Seashell, It Happened in Zihuatanejo, The Quake and Saying Goodbye. The first two books are available from this website: www.buybooksontheweb.com The others are available from this website: www.iUniverse.com

I guess I need to get to work on my next book to get it ready for publication. My goal is to get all thirteen of my novels and my short stories as a collection in print before I drop dead. If I do kick the bucket before that happens, maybe my good friend, Galen, will complete it for me. GRIN.

Mexico is great. Life is good here. Most everything is much less expensive than in the states. When you can go for an office visit to your doctor, who speaks English and is smart as a whip and the bill comes to 150 pesos which is around $7.75 right now, what can I say?

It's always summer here, too. If you don't like humidity, you might not like it here. I have to keep the house closed up because of the piano and the artworks. I had to buy a dehumidifier and keep it running to keep the strings on the piano from rusting. So you have an idea as to the humidity, with the house closed, the dehumidifier takes seven gallons of water out of the air every twenty-four hours.

That's right. Seven gallons, not quarts. I need to put plated strings on the piano but I can't find anyone who works on them here.

I know I should not put anything overly political in my books but I've been watching things happening in the states. I'm waiting for the IMBECILES in the Supreme Court to overturn same-sex marriage. They are trying to turn back the clock to the 1950s again. This is an issue that is obviously of importance to me and that's why I wanted to make a comment about it.

PROLOGUE

There are many who scoff at the concept of the forces of good and evil and the war between the two. Many think they are ideas instilled in the heads of people by the religious community to strike fear into them. Yes, I do believe the churches are guilty of the fear factor as a controlling mechanism but I also believe there ARE good and evil forces out there. It may be possible there's a devil who presides over a huge kingdom of satanic creatures and he's constantly trying to capture the souls of the dying. I'll reserve that conversation for another day. Some believe if bad things happen, they attribute it to the stupidity of the one involved and they should have avoided the situation bringing them the bad luck. It's the same for good fortune. Their comment would be 'they were just in the right place at the right time' or 'it was just a lucky guess or happening'.

Many will concur that stories of good people going bad with the issue of demonic possession, are only subjects for horror movies and are never actual events in reality. If so, why does the church have the rite of exorcism? Think about that.

For the purposes of this story, let's assume there really is a devil who is responsible for the evil in the world and conducts evil in the conflict between it and good. With that as the premise, here is something to think about. Would a good person intentionally sell his soul and do unthinkably bad things due to the influence of evil to be the most incredible individual in his profession, miles above all others? What if that person happened to sell his soul strictly by pure accident or happenstance? Would his soul have to spend all eternity in Hell due to a mistake he made without even knowing it?

CHAPTER I

The phone rang in the office of Peter's home. "Hello? Yes. Peter Solvinoski speaking. Don't worry. It's a mouth full. No one gets it right the first time. Sort of like General Custer trying to say Sacajawea's name in the movie, 'Night at the Museum'. No. Polish, actually. What can I help you with, Jerry? Oh. Your sheriff, Jake Banister, asked you to call me? What's it about? Wow. That's very interesting. Where? Small town in Maine? Just north of Portland on the coast. Thanks for the compliment and trust me, I'd love to help but I'm packing right now to leave the country very early in the morning on an assignment. Yes. The Amazon. Yes, it's way out in the boonies. It's a discovery they recently found and wanted me down as soon as possible. And here it's the end of August already. But I'll be back in about three to four months. Please, contact my office at the university here in Boston. If something urgent comes up, I'll see about looking into it when I get back. Oh, it will be warm there. Correct. I'll miss the beginning of cold weather here. I know. It usually hits around Halloween but that's just over two months away. Yes. Jerry, thank you again for calling and do keep me in mind for things like this in the future. Lord knows I love these kinds of situations. Thank you. I will. Goodbye."

He hung up the phone and continued packing. The information from the phone call was racing around in his head. "I just love it how the cops get hold of your phone number these days with no phone directories anymore. Guess my website online did help." His head tilted to the side and he gave a little giggle as he paused for a moment. Then, he shook his head. "No! I'm not changing my plans. I've been looking forward to this trip since the discovery. I just know I can get another book out of it, too."

Everything sitting by the front door, he went and fixed a cup of hot tea. After several sips, he went and sat at his 6-foot grand piano, placing the cup on the left corner of the music rack. A smile came to his face and he reached for the keys. The strains of *I'll Be Seeing You* filled the room. As the last chord faded, he removed his hands from the keyboard. He stared out as a distant reverie came to mind. After a few moments, he smiled again then quietly sang the last words of the song 'a cappella'. "'I'll be looking at the moon… but I'll be seeing…. you.'" There was silence for a few moments. He stared off into space and spoke softly. "I wonder where he is? I wonder how he's doing? I hope he's happy."

He reached for his cup, sipped and drank his tea in silence.

CHAPTER II

It was Wednesday, May 16th, 2007, and a real estate ad Ethan found on the computer intrigued him. There was a picture of a house as well as information about its location and description. Strangely, there was no price. Only a comment saying 'a ridiculously low price'. It seemed just too good to be true. He started talking to himself. "A house like that with its location couldn't possibly be selling for what they're calling 'a ridiculously low price'. I think the term 'ridiculously low price' is arbitrary and is according to whom? And of course, there were no numbers, stating that 'ridiculously low price'." But he couldn't help it. He just had to see it even if it was listed as a 'fixer-upper'.

For some time, Ethan and Shawn had been wanting to get a home of their own and they'd been looking for one online. Both were very successful. Everything was on the uphill and now they could afford to buy one.

———— ❖ ————

Shawn was one of the architectural firm's best. His career was assured. Not only was he brilliant with his ideas and concepts but his rugged swarthiness enhanced his appeal. Tall, muscular, dark wavy hair, neatly trimmed beard and mustache and piercing green eyes all added to his physical handsomeness.

As for himself, Ethan was no slouch. He had been booked for concerts across the country. The critics were calling him the 'Pied Piper of the Keyboard' because his technique, interpretations and absolute mastering of the piano made the instrument come alive. Several of his own compositions had won acclaim and were featured in his programs.

Everyone was amazed how someone with such a small frame, although well built, could deliver such a powerful forte. Yet, in an instant, could play a soft and delicate pianissimo. Some had said he was attractive looking with his dark brown eyes, dark brown hair, mustache and beard.

$$\Longrightarrow\gg\!\otimes\!\ll\Longleftarrow$$

Ethan went to the desk, reached for his cell phone and called the number shown on the ad. "Yes, may I speak with Marge Adams, please? Oh, Marge. Ethan Trendeau speaking. Yes. Yes, I'm that Ethan Trendeau. Well, thank you very much. I appreciate the compliment. Yes. I was calling to see about making an appointment to see the house you have listed. Right. That's the one. Off Schooner Head Road. We'd like to make arrangements to see the house. Yes. I read it's a 'fixer-upper'. I know. We're here in New York City but will take the train up to Boston on Friday morning and rent a car for the weekend. We can drive up there. It should only take a few hours. A little over five hours? Yes. I know we could fly into Portland but we have the time and wanted to see the countryside. But thank you for the suggestion. Okay. We'll come back on Monday. This Saturday, May nineteenth at ten o'clock? We'll meet you at the house. Fifteen hundred Schooner Head Road. Got it. That's great. We'll see you then. Yes. We will drive carefully. Thank you. Goodbye." He took the pen and wrote the agent's name on the pad and '10 AM Saturday, May 19' beside it.

He immediately made another call. "Hey, Brenda, Ethan here. How have you been? Yes. I'm working on a new program for the

4

upcoming season. Actually, composing a piece right now. You were? I hope you liked the music. Thank you. You're way too kind. Yes, I'd like to speak to Shawn. Thank you. Great talking to you, too. Take care."

After a moment, there came a deep masculine voice on the line. "Ethan! What's going on? I hope everything's all right there."

Ethan smiled. "Shawn! How's your day going? All's well here. I'm so excited and had to call you. I know we had planned to take this weekend as a little getaway to just relax but what would you think about us going to look at a most incredible house I found online? It sounds truly fantastic. Yes. Yes, I did. Called and made an appointment to see it this coming Saturday morning. I hope that's okay with you and you're not mad with me changing plans. Yes. Great! I thought you'd be happy. Wait till I show it to you. The picture is interesting and the description seems beyond belief."

"But… Well… It's out in the country. Like, way out. I mean, way, way out. Not a problem? Really? Fantastic! Price? Well, it's listed as 'a ridiculously low price' but I have no idea what that means and stupid me didn't ask. Damn! I'll call her back and ask. Oh. Okay. We'll just wait till we get there. Thanks. I really didn't want her to think me a total idiot. And even if it's too outrageous, we'll still have a nice getaway weekend."

"Yes. You know I love you, too. Yes. I'm still working on the new piece. I like it in adagio. It's more forlorn at that tempo. Okay. Talk with you tonight. Don't let anyone mug you on the subway." He chuckled. "Love you! Bye!"

After a quick bite, he put the sandwich meat back into the refrigerator, bread in the kitchen cabinet and headed to the piano. He was so excited he could hardly concentrate on the composition he was writing. He thought how wonderful it would be and so nice to have a place out of the city and out of an apartment.

Living in an apartment, his practicing was something he had to take into consideration with the neighbors. No one had ever made any complaints over the four years they'd been there. He did try to be considerate by keeping the lid closed and covering the piano with a thick blanket. But a home of their own would mean he could hear his playing without distortion.

When Shawn arrived home that evening, he was anxious to hear about the 'find'. Since he'd worked especially hard that day, he talked with his boss and was able to take off the next day, Friday, the weekend, Monday and Tuesday. He had a feeling that Ethan's comment about being 'way, way out' really did mean, not around the corner, so he was prepared and knew some traveling would be involved. When Ethan finally told him where it was and that it was by the sea, he was ecstatic. He and Ethan could spend the next day going up there then spend Friday, Saturday, Sunday and Monday doing some exploring, checking out the area before coming back to the city on Tuesday. They wouldn't be rushed. Of course, they would meet with Marge on Saturday at the house.

"Ethan, the picture of the house and its description are unbelievable but I may have to give a great pep talk to Jackson at the bank, so he'll loan us the money if it doesn't meet the appraisal. I have to admit, it should be interesting to know what they mean by 'a ridiculously low price'." He gave a big grin and flexed his eyebrows, looking at Ethan.

"All right. I know I get so stupid when I get happy." Ethan shrugged. "I'm so sorry for not asking Marge the price."

"Come here, you silly goose." Shawn pulled Ethan to him, hugging him. "You know I love you just as you are. I wouldn't have you any other way."

"Maybe the current owners would finance. Especially, if they want to unload it. Hey! You never know." Ethan clapped his hands. "If we're going to leave tomorrow, we need to get cracking with some packing." He and Shawn chuckled at Ethan's quick rhyme.

Both went to bed that night and could hardly sleep, thinking about the house on the cliffs, overlooking the Atlantic.

Driving down Schooner Head Road was like they had left civilization. It was two lanes and wound along the coastline. The area was not very developed with only a few driveways or roads leading toward the ocean.

"Well, one thing is for sure. We definitely wouldn't have to worry about noisy neighbors out here." Ethan began to chuckle as he looked out the windows on either side of the car.

Shawn searched along the road. "Did the agent say how far it was on Schooner?"

"No. Guess she knew we'd find it without much trouble. Just keep your eyes peeled for fifteen hundred."

Almost with the ending of Ethan's sentence, a wide driveway appeared with two square brick columns on either side. On the right column, cast in bronze, now with a heavy patina, were the large numbers. 1500.

"That's it!" Ethan was excited. "But I can't see the house." He looked at the many large shrubs hiding the property and growing along the curving driveway. He opened the window. "Can you smell that? It's the ocean!"

Slowly, they made their way up the drive. It reminded Ethan of the opening scene in the old black-and-white movie, 'Rebecca'. Before they knew it, they pulled into an open area right in front of the house.

"Are you sure this is right? The picture in the ad doesn't do it justice." Shawn stared out the front windshield of the car at the dwelling. "I can't imagine such a house, selling for 'a ridiculously low price', especially this close to the ocean. Maybe it's a ploy to get folks here before dropping the bomb as to the actual asking price."

"Maybe it's falling down? God, I hope not. But you're right. Something is really strange here." Ethan shook his head.

They both sat in the car in utter disbelief, looking at the structure in front of them. The very large, two-story Victorian was constructed of stone and brick with elaborate gingerbread woodwork placed in all the right spots. There was a tower with a pointed roof to the right of the center of the structure which was quite typical on many Victorian houses. The steep Mansard roofs were covered with dark blue slate and topped with an ornate railing. Several dormer windows made it evident there was a huge space if not rooms in the attic. Several tall chimneys spiked through the roofs in several places, adding to the exterior beauty and uniqueness of the house. Much of the shrubbery and lawn were unkempt and overgrown.

They got out of the car and walked closer to the house. "I wonder how long it's been vacant?" Shawn could see undisturbed leaves from the previous fall still on the large front stoop. "Wonder when it was last seen by anyone? Maybe they saw it and realized the work it needed and just drove off. Or maybe the asking price is not… 'ridiculously low'." He just shrugged his shoulders.

Ethan could hear the questioning in Shawn's comments. That was not a good sign.

Shawn started looking at the dwelling with the eyes of an architect and began calculating the cost of exterior repairs to bring the house back to its original splendor. He was surprised when it didn't seem to be as expensive as most with untrained eyes would think. Most needed improvements were strictly cosmetic. "I will say, once fixed up, it could be a showplace."

Ethan loved it when he heard Shawn's words. This dispelled his previous concern. It meant the possible purchase wasn't totally ruled out yet. But he knew everything would depend on the actual asking price.

The real estate agent arrived shortly but seemed in somewhat of a hurry. "Hello, I'm Marge Adams." She looked and smiled at Ethan. "Mister Trendeau, it's an honor to see you again. I was at one of your concerts as I mentioned on the phone and was amazed at your playing. It was absolutely beautiful." She turned to Shawn. "Mister McAllister, so very nice to see you again as well. When Ethan said 'we' on the phone, I realized he was referring to you. I know you don't remember me but I met you at the same concert reception for

Mister Trendeau when I heard him play." She extended her hand, shaking both Ethan's and Shawn's.

She looked up at the house. "I'm sure you've probably seen enough and aren't interested. I'm so sorry you came all this way to be disappointed. That drive up from Boston is a length. I do apologize for sounding so negative. I'm usually not that way about a house but those who have come in the past to see the house were immediately hit with the amount of work it needed and instantly lost interest even at the low price. I rather expected it would be the case with you. I always bring the keys but no one ever wants to go in."

"Well, speaking of the low price. What exactly is the asking price?" Shawn spoke up.

"Oh! Mister McAllister, I forgot. You have no idea. I forgot to tell Mister Trendeau. The owners want eighty for it." She shrugged her shoulders expecting to hear a 'thank you and goodbye'.

"Really!?" Shawn blurted out. "Eighty!? You mean like eighty thousand? Dollars!?"

"Yes, I know it would need a lot of work and cost a fortune. I didn't think you'd want it." Marge tried to sound understanding.

"Au contraire! Contraire! We would love to see it." Shawn could hardly hold back his enthusiasm. "What do you think, Ethan?"

Of course, Ethan was in shock, taken aback by Shawn's exuberance. "I think it's great! I'd love to see the interior!"

Marge stood there surprised and shocked. Her mouth opened agape. "Really?" She hesitated in her fluster. "Mister McAllister, please, forgive me. But I made another appointment at one, thinking surely you wouldn't be interested once you saw the house. I don't know what to say. Let me call them and let them know I'll be late."

"Nonsense. Not to worry. Is it possible we could use the keys, look at the house then drop them off by your office in town? Either later today or tomorrow?" Shawn gave his winning smile no one could seem to resist. "We're spending the weekend at the inn in Bar Harbor and not leaving till Tuesday."

Marge's whole demeanor changed. Her face was filled with joy. "Why certainly, Mister McAllister. Certainly. That would be perfect. I can meet you both tomorrow morning at the inn and we can go for breakfast there. The food is excellent and we can talk about the house if you're still interested." She handed Shawn the set of keys. "Take your time and see you tomorrow morning. Please, be careful as no one has been in the house for some time and I'm sure there is dust everywhere. Oh, how does nine tomorrow morning sound?"

"Nine tomorrow morning. That's great. That we can do. No problem. And you're right. We ate dinner there last night and the food is excellent." Shawn took the keys from her hand. "And by the way, draw up the papers. I can write an earnest check, can't I? I mean, if we're still interested in buying the house?"

"Certainly! Certainly, Mister McAllister! I will do that. Of course." Marge was very pleased at the prospect of actually selling the house. "Are there any questions you might have as I do have a few minutes?"

"Do you know when the house was constructed?" Shawn looked up at the façade.

"Built just before the turn of the century. Eighteen ninety-six actually. The original house plans are in the courthouse archives. Jeremiah Raines was a financier from New York City. I understand after he died, I think he was around eighty-five or six in about nineteen forty-eight, it sat vacant forever. His heirs never lived in it. Right after he died, they came here and shipped all the furniture and household things to New York to be sold. A few things they knew no one would want are still in the basement. They've kept the house in the family these past fifty-nine years and used to come by around once a year to check on it. They placed it on the market many years ago with no success in selling it, so they took it off the market for over a decade. They decided to try again and put it back on the market three years ago. I thought the price way too low, it being near the ocean and all but when I saw it and realized how much work it was going to take, not to mention they wanted it to sell quickly, I just let it be. I haven't been able to get much more information on the house. Actually, everyone who has come out to see it just drove off after looking at it for five minutes. That's why I thought you would do the same thing."

"Not a problem. We can take it from here. If we have any more questions, we'll talk with you tomorrow about them." Shawn extended his hand, shaking Marge's.

"Don't worry. We'll be careful and take our time." Ethan extended his hand, doing the same.

Marge smiled and headed for her car. "See you tomorrow morning." She was down the drive and out of sight in an instant.

"Well, let's go see it." Ethan headed up the walk to the front door. "I have to admit, I'm shocked at your enthusiasm."

Entering, they came into a large foyer. There was a large arched opening on the left to a huge dining room on the north side of the house. To the right was a large door, the entrance to a front room. Straight ahead was another large arched opening to an enormous great room. There was a huge fireplace on the north end of the room and a wide spiral staircase on the south end. The east wall was floor-to-ceiling French windows, opening onto a broad terrace at the rear of the house, overlooking the back lawns. The ceiling in the great room was at the same level as the second-story ceilings. They walked through the room to the windows.

"WOW! What a fantastic space." Ethan spoke out. "I could put the piano over there in the curve of the staircase. You could set up your drawing tables in front of the windows." He looked at Shawn. "I'll probably have to have the strings replaced with plated ones since we're so close to the ocean. The regular strings will most likely rust even with the house closed up."

"It IS an incredible space." Shawn agreed. He put his left hand up to his beard and stroked it as he looked around.

They unlocked one of the French windows, opened it and walked out onto the wide flagstone terrace. They could hear the roar of the ocean beneath the cliff at the far edge of the overgrown lawn. A view of the eastern horizon was unobstructed since the trees and large shrubs had been placed on the far northern and southern edges of the lawn.

"We could even put a nice swimming pool out here just off the terrace." Shawn thought of an improvement.

"What a great idea." Ethan clapped his hands. "And we can ice skate on it in the winter."

Shawn looked at Ethan and just shook his head. "But remember, we could build a nice glass solarium around it along with the terrace. That would make it usable all year round."

Ethan snickered. "Yeah. Sure. And it would cost a king's ransom to heat it in the winter."

They re-entered the house and walked the first floor to see the dining room, the kitchen and a small apartment behind the kitchen, obviously, quarters for a maid or live-in housekeeper. Also, close to the kitchen was a spacious half bath. These were all the rooms in the north end of the house. Shawn suggested that the bathroom had to have been added sometime in a very early 1940s remodel of the kitchen. It was the look of the fixtures and tile that gave the date away.

The door to the right of the front door went to a very large front room whose large western window looked out onto the parking area, front lawns and down the drive.

In the great room and on the same wall as the spiral staircase was another door, leading to a short hallway to two very large rooms at the south end of the house. These could be used for future bedrooms if necessary. Maybe one could be a library. At the top of the stairs was a balcony that went completely around the south and west side of the great room. Entrances to four bedrooms and one bathroom came off of it. These rooms were above the dining room, the front room and above the two rooms at the south end of the house. The larger front bedroom had its own bathroom located over the western part of the front foyer and would be used as part of the master suite.

This bedroom also incorporated the lower part of the tower they saw from outside as did the front room below it. The main bathroom was over the eastern half of the entry hall downstairs.

Another staircase, off the upstairs balcony, led to the attic. There was a very large area in the attic that could be developed into additional rooms under the steep Mansard roofs. The room in the lower part of the tower could be another wonderful space if they wanted to develop it. There was even a small, narrow stair, leading up to the small room in the top of the tower.

"Well, all that's left now is the basement." Shawn opened the door off the kitchen and started down the steps.

The basement had the kitchen entrance as well as one from the outside on the north side of the house. The whole foundation was of stone and masonry. The floor was flagstone. It was cool and dark since there were no exterior windows. This was very curious to Shawn. He couldn't imagine why anyone would design a basement area with no windows on the perimeter. Since there was no electricity turned on to the house, they used their cell phones to make enough light, so they could see a little. It wasn't easy and they had to be careful. They knew they wouldn't venture very far.

"What a terrific wine cellar this would make." Ethan imagined rows of shelves, containing numerous bottles of wine.

Shawn had been looking closely at the structural integrity of the house. "You know, this place is built like a damn fortress. It's solid as a rock. And believe me, it's really in great shape. I haven't noticed any creaking of floors or any distortions in the framework. And this foundation looks like it would hold up the Empire State Building."

They just looked around right at the bottom of the stairs from the kitchen. They didn't want to go farther into the darkness. Finishing their quick look at the basement, they headed back to the main floor.

Arriving in the kitchen, Shawn spoke again. "You know, we could have this place fixed up in no time at all."

Ethan spoke to Shawn as they walked back to the great room. "Are you serious? I was so afraid you might think it a 'white elephant'. It has a lot of space. Maybe too much for us."

"Yes, but it's laid out just great. A lot of space but not all chopped up. I love the twelve-foot ceilings in the downstairs and nine upstairs. I really like it. The cost for a house like this in the city would be absolutely prohibitive. Not to mention no ocean there." Shawn looked around the great room. Then, after a slight pause, he blurted out. "And for… EIGHTY THOUSAND DOLLARS!!" His voice resounded through the huge space of the empty room. He paused with a big Cheshire Cat grin on his face. "It's a no-brainer! I had to catch myself with Marge. I almost yelled out 'are you shitting me' when she said the price. I can't imagine why no one else hasn't seen its potential and snapped it up."

Ethan looked hard at Shawn. "Ah. Maybe it's haunted with murderous ghosts."

Shawn looked at Ethan. After a few moments of silence, they both roared with laughter.

Shawn looked at Ethan and smiled. "Welcome to our new home." He grabbed Ethan and hugged him tightly to keep him from jumping up and down with excitement.

They drove to the inn in town and discussed the things they could do to the house as they ate dinner. Both were excited over the thought of moving.

The next morning, Marge arrived at nine. She brought all the paperwork just as Shawn had requested. In her mind, she was hopeful but just knew they would hand over the keys with a 'thanks, but no thanks'. She was totally taken aback when they told her they wanted the house.

After breakfast, they went over the paperwork. Marge indicated the down payment would be much lower than normal due to the circumstances of the buy. The owners weren't looking for a large amount in the beginning and they didn't have to have the balance for up to a year if necessary.

"Well, what can I say? Between Ethan and me, we have the down payment in our savings and can write an earnest check for the down payment with no problem." Shawn spoke with happiness in his voice.

"I'm so glad you're coming here. It's not a big town but you did drive through Portland, coming up here. If you really need to go do major shopping, you can go there or over to Bangor. If you need any further assistance with things, let me know. I can steer you in the right direction." Marge nodded. "Wait till everyone finds out you've bought the old Raines House. And when they find out what nice folks you are."

All papers signed, they said goodbye to Marge and they headed for some sun and relaxation by the pool of the inn. Both were very excited about their new acquisition.

There was no need to revisit the house as they had seen all they needed the previous day. They'd start the ball rolling when they got back to the city.

———❖———

On the way home, they continued their conversation about all the things that could be done to improve the house and bring it up to date. Shawn would get hold of the house plans from the archives. He wondered if the house was on any historic registry. Original plans would help in finding what they could do in making repairs or changes without compromising the structure. They could hardly wait to get moved in.

Shawn was right. Because of their professional standing and reputations, getting a loan was not difficult at all, especially when it was heard how much it was. With Shawn's and Ethan's credit, they could borrow it as a signature loan. Getting out of their lease on their apartment in the city was no problem as there were folks standing in line to rent it.

Shawn's trips to the city would be minimal. He had discussed it already with his bosses. They were well aware Shawn was going to relocate. But this wasn't a problem. Everything could be done on the computer and phone. Should a conference be necessary with a client, Shawn could arrange it in advance and come into the city and stay at the apartment used by the firm.

Ethan's agent was always accessible by phone, regarding concert engagements. Everything he really needed would be right in the house.

They were now determined to get moved by the 1st of June. It would actually be easy as they'd been preparing to do it for some time. They were so excited as they were finally on their way to their dream. A home by the sea. They were looking forward to a bright, happy and fun future.

Little did they know they were about to open Pandora's Box.

CHAPTER III

It happened as they'd hoped. Everything from their apartment was moved by Friday, the 1st of June. It really took no time at all. Ethan thought their things got rather lost in the space of the huge house. The movers kept giving strange looks as they brought things in, wondering if it was haunted. They thought Shawn and Ethan were crazy for moving to such a run-down dwelling.

It would be almost three weeks before Shawn could set aside the time to do the research on the old house. Fortunately enough, there actually were drawings in the old courthouse. He took them to a printer and had large copies made. He also found out the house was not on any historic registry.

It was warm outside, being the fourth full week in June when they finally got to get into the basement. They were checking things out as to possible renovations for a wine cellar as a starter. Shawn wanted to put an exercise workout room down there as well.

Looking closely at the space, Shawn realized it didn't seem right. "Something's wrong here. This area should be much larger."

"What?" Ethan questioned. "What do you mean?"

"I know how large the first story is and this area down here isn't the same size. It's smaller. Much smaller. Where are those plans? Just a second." Shawn ran upstairs, grabbed the set of plans he had sitting next to his drawing board table and returned to the basement, placing them on a small table there. He looked hard at the plans of the basement. He pointed. "Look! See what I mean? This area doesn't match up with the drawings. This space should be much larger." He looked at the far southern wall. "Interesting. There has to be a rather large area walled off from the rest of the basement. It has to take up at least the southern area of the basement. Under the two big southern rooms upstairs." Upon closer inspection of the construction, he could see the brickwork of the wall was not part of the original construction. It was definitely hiding a space beyond.

"Oh, yeah! This is rather exciting." Ethan clapped his hands together. "Maybe there's a hidden treasure."

"Yeah. Sure. Believe it." Shawn spoke sarcastically. "And I'm the queen of England."

"No way. You're much too butch and handsome to be the queen." Ethan started to giggle.

Shawn just shook his head.

"I wonder why it was sealed off? I have to admit, I'd love to know what's on the other side." Ethan looked hard at the wall.

"Well, we could chisel out several of the bricks, get a flashlight and see if we can see anything beyond. But there won't be time to explore for a while. I have a major project coming up that's going to take several weeks to complete. We can do it after I get finished with it. In the meantime, why don't you go into town and see if you can find any information on the original owner and family? It could possibly shed some light on everything."

"That's a great idea." Ethan agreed. "I can go in tomorrow. And since you'll be busy till…" Ethan stared off into space calculating in his head. "Till probably the third or fourth week in July, I can take my time."

Over the next several days, Ethan spent hours in the courthouse archives, doing research on the Raines family who owned the house. The original owner was Jeremiah, a financier from New York, who came to the area in the early 1890s. He was living on money he continuously received from investments and money made by the family businesses. Money never seemed to be an obstacle. He was thirty-three when the house was finished in 1896 and married for less than a year.

He was one of four sons of the very wealthy Raines family from old Boston and New York back when New York was called New Amsterdam. They made their money in law and finance. The law side of the family lived in Boston and the finance side lived in New York.

What was very strange is that after several years, in 1899, Jeremiah's wife and two children disappeared. It was right before the turn of the century. He told everyone they'd all gone to Paris and would stay, so the two children could be educated there. His wife had relatives there. This was never questioned.

Living alone for so long, he turned into a virtual recluse. There was never any explanation why none of the family ever returned, not even on holidays. Then, there were the stories of strange things happening at the house by local kids but everyone considered them only stories. Over time, this was the house everyone referred to as the 'haunted house' in Halloween stories.

While researching the Raines family, Ethan also came across several intriguing stories of unsolved disappearances in the area and surrounding towns in the early 1900s. They were so interesting and strange, these stories began to take over his interest more so than the history of Jeremiah and his family. His curiosity was so great, he followed up on this information with the local police department.

Of course, records over a hundred years old weren't easy to locate. But after some two weeks of digging in the police archives down in the courthouse basement, he found out that for many years people went missing and were never found. The police at the time were totally dumbfounded. They even brought in state investigators to get involved with no results. The disappearances continued into the late 1940s then stopped.

E. THORNTON GOODE, JR.

It was thought some of the missing had just picked up and left the area. The younger ones were thought to be runaways, looking to go to the city. There also were the whispered stories. These could have been killings or murders but police could never find any signs of this. Bodies of all who were missing were never found.

Ethan was in the archives every day, reading old police reports. He thought the two weeks had been time well spent, very rewarding and informative. It was now the third week of July and he was back in the library again. Ethan found more articles on the Raines family and Jeremiah. The final headline and story in the paper indicated the prominent local man died while on a trip to Paris in August of 1948. His body had been returned home and interred in the family mausoleum in New York. Everyone thought it very strange his wife or children never came for the funeral. This information was confirmed while talking on the phone with the director of the historical society in New York.

One evening while discussing with Shawn all the things Ethan had discovered, Shawn made an off-hand comment. "I think it's strange the disappearances ended around the same time Jeremiah died. Just for grins. When did they start?"

Ethan thought this an intriguing comment. "I don't know. Just a second. Let me go through these papers and see if I can find a date." He got out his paperwork and shuffled through them. "Yeah. Here it is. Mary English. She was eighteen and lived in Trenton. I think it's about twenty miles from here. Looks like she was the first to go missing. She disappeared one night without a trace. It was in November of eighteen ninety-nine."

"Isn't that three years after the house was completed and not long after is family went to Paris?" Shawn was trying to put two and two together.

Ethan looked at his paperwork. "Yes. You're right."

"Do you think there could be some connection?" Shawn gave a big grin to make Ethan wonder and then flexed his eyebrows.

―――――⟫◆⟪―――――

For the next several days, Shawn worked on his project which had taken longer than expected and Ethan worked on his composition. The relaxed atmosphere of their new house was making it easy to do things they wanted to get done. They were finally settling in and feeling more at home every day. It was midweek. The fourth week in July.

The wall in the basement would periodically come into their conversation, questioning why it was built and what might be behind it. Shawn needed a break. He and Ethan filled their coffee cups and headed to the basement.

Shawn stood back and really began to examine the construction of the wall. Suddenly, he spoke out with surprise. "Damn! How is it I haven't seen THAT before?"

"What?" Ethan looked at the wall.

"Look here." Shawn walked over to some ten feet from the west end of the wall and started running his finger along an irregular mortar joint. "See. This whole area is filled in. Looks like there used to be a small door or opening here. Yeah. This will make it so much easier to get to the space beyond. We won't have to tear down the whole wall." Shawn looked closely at the construction. "I have to admit, it looks like whoever sealed in the doorway was making a concerted effort to hide it, trying to blend it in with the surrounding brickwork. I wonder why? Hmmm."

"Maybe there IS a treasure behind it." Ethan became very excited.

"Yeah. Sure. Don't hold your breath. You'd look like hell blue." Shawn was sarcastic. "We just might have to check into this sooner than we thought. I think we can start tomorrow."

Just as they got back upstairs, Shawn's cell phone rang. It was his office, regarding a major client who wanted to discuss an upcoming project. This meant that Shawn was going to have to go out of the country for a couple of weeks to meet and go over it. He was going to have to leave the very next morning.

"Ethan, I'm so sorry. Business calls and business is business."

"Not to worry. I can work on my composition and do a little more research. The wall isn't going anywhere. That's for sure."

They both gave a 'thumbs-up'.

CHAPTER IV

During the weeks Shawn was to be gone, Ethan was determined to find out more about Jeremiah but everything he'd found so far was just about early social events before and right after he was married. Then, stories dwindled to nothing, especially after the wife and children moved to Paris in early 1899. Ethan wondered if there were any folks in the area who knew anything about Jeremiah. Anyone still alive. After all, it was 2007 and Jeremiah had been dead fifty-nine years. Possibly, Marge would know the ones who had lived in the area the longest. Anyone knowing Jeremiah and still living would have been children before he died.

Marge told him she knew several who had lived in the area all their lives and might be able to shed some light on his questions. She'd contact several of them to see if they wouldn't mind sharing information.

Finally, Marge called Ethan and told him there were many who were interested in telling him stories. Especially, when they found out, he was now living in the Raines House. She said they probably had more questions of him than he had of them. Ethan was not quite sure how to take that, so he just shrugged it off. She would set up several meetings if he wanted. He was ecstatic.

Ethan's concerts weren't lined up yet as he'd told his agent to put things on hold because of the move and getting settled. He also had to really sit down and practice the pieces he wanted to perform for his next set of concerts. Still, there was time to interview those Marge had lined up for him.

⟶⟶➤◆◄⟵⟵

It was Tuesday, the 31st of July and first on the list to visit was Emma Jones. She was seventy-four and would have been around fifteen when Jeremiah died. She lived on the edge of town in a two-story, wood-framed house.

When he arrived, it was obvious he was expected. Emma had hot tea prepared and was a very friendly and open person. They sat in her front room decorated with many pieces of antique furniture.

"Missus Jones. You have such lovely antiques."

"Oh. This old stuff? It's been in the family forever." She slapped her knee. "Oh, honey, call me Em. Everybody does."

Ethan smiled. "Em, thank you so much for the tea. I've been looking forward to chatting with you ever since Marge said you didn't mind sharing what you knew about Jeremiah Raines."

"Honey, you seem to be a very nice young man. I understand you're a pianist. A concert pianist. I'd love to hear you play sometime. I love Chopin."

"Well, you'll have to come for a visit sometime. And you can meet Shawn, too."

"He's an architect and I hear he's very good-looking." She grinned. "I may be older but I can still appreciate a handsome man. And honey, you're a cutie, too."

They both began to chuckle.

Ethan blushed slightly at the compliment. He was rather shocked she already knew something about him and Shawn. Gossip must fly through the area like wildfire. This being the case, everyone must know everyone's business whether they want it known or not. Emma just might be able to recall something from the time Jeremiah was around.

After a while of friendly conversation, Ethan started with his questioning. "Yes, Shawn and I are very interested in the history of the house and about Jeremiah. I understand he lived there alone for many years. Why did his family never return from Europe?"

Emma looked out into space as if pulling memory from the air. She sat back in her chair. "I can remember when I was very young. My parents talking about stories going around about Jeremiah. Some were saying they saw him at nights, walking the streets, staying in the shadows. And they kept recalling very early stories of him being reclusive ever since his family went away. And strange things. Not sure exactly what they meant. One major story that kept coming up was the time some young kids went out to the house on a dare. They had to go at night and there was some stuff about spending the night out there. They came back, talking about weird things and weird noises. You need to talk with Hank. Hank Morris. He was one of the kids then who supposedly went on those dares."

"Did anyone get specific about the goings-on? Any details?"

"No, not really. But as I said, Hank may be able to shed more light on that."

"Well, I do appreciate you seeing me today. If you get our way, come by and if we're there, we'll have to show you what we're doing with the house." Ethan set his teacup down.

"I hope you might play something, too." She set her cup down and stood up.

Ethan stood and they headed for the door. "Again, thank you so much for seeing me today. And thank you so much for the tea."

"Honey, now you come back and visit me sometime, too."

<hr/>

Ethan got in the car and headed to see the next one on the list, Martha Washington. He chuckled at the name. "I'll bet she's been ribbed all her life about it. I swear, I won't make the same mistake."

Martha lived not far from Emma. The thing is that nobody lived far from the others in town. It was only those few larger homes out along the cliffs that were rather isolated and out of the way.

The visit with Martha was similar to the one with Emma. More tea and similar stories. She, too, mentioned Hank and indicated he needed to talk with him to get the real low down. As he left, he was pleased he'd kept his promise, not to make fun of the name.

He stopped by to see Marge at her office to ask about setting an appointment with Hank. She said she would see about doing that. Ethan indicated there was no major rush as he'd called several others to talk to within the next few days.

During the next interviews, he heard the same kind of stories. There definitely seemed to be strange things happening out at the house but nothing conclusive.

Something very interesting was everyone he talked with pointed out Hank as the one he really needed to see. He discovered, Hank was the oldest of all the folks he was to interview.

Why was Jeremiah's the one picked out as being the 'Halloween House'? With virtually no other homes close by out there along the cliffs and Jeremiah being a single recluse in that big house, that definitely could fuel the fire of being different. "I have a feeling Hank may have the key or at least may point toward the right door." Ethan grinned. "Yeah. I'll really drill him. No hemming and hawing. Find out everything I can. Have to admit, the mysteriousness is making this house seem a major focus of interest and strangeness. I think it'll give some character to its history."

It was Monday, August 13th, when Ethan went to see Hank who lived in a small house on the west side of town. The house and yard were well-kept and surrounded by a white picket fence. It was Norman Rockwell Americana in real life. He opened the gate and started up the walk.

In an instant, he heard the front door. Looking up, he saw a tall, handsome man with a mass of white hair and a large, well-groomed mustache. He looked to be about six-three and could have been a dead ringer for Sam Elliott's older brother. Even in his bib overalls and flannel shirt, you could see he had a muscular build. He looked like he should be going out to get on a tractor. Ethan thought him very attractive even realizing his probable age. Everyone said he was the oldest of those Ethan was to interview but he didn't look it. He wasn't the decrepit old man he expected to see. Emma was seventy-four but Hank looked a lot younger.

"Wondered when you would get to me." Hank spoke with a deep masculine voice. "You must be the piano player everyone's been talking about. Asking a lot of questions about… Jeremiah Raines." A huge Cheshire Cat grin filled his face.

Ethan walked up to the porch. "Yep. That's right. Ethan. Ethan Trendeau. Piano player." He made a gesture with both arms and hands as if playing the keys on a piano.

They both broke out with laughter.

"Hank Morris." He shook Ethan's hand. "Well, come on in, you young whippersnapper and have a seat. How'd you like a shot?" They entered a small living room, appointed with cozy furniture.

"Usually not this early but what the heck. As Alan Jackson and Jimmy Buffett sing it, 'It's five o'clock somewhere.'" He was rather amused as it sure was a far cry from the tea that he'd had with the ladies.

"You've got that right. I've got some cola if you want it that way."

"Cool. That would be great. Thank you." Ethan sat down as Hank went to the kitchen and fixed a glass of iced bourbon and cola. He called out. "Hank, with that voice, you should be doing commercials on TV. Geez!"

Hank heard the comment and responded. "I appreciate the compliment. Thank you." Coming back to the living room, he carried a large wooden tray with Ethan's bourbon and cola as well as the whole bottle and Hank's glass containing only ice. He set it on the coffee table and sat down across from Ethan. He picked up the glass and handed it to Ethan. "Hope it's not too strong."

Ethan accepted and sipped. He was pleasantly surprised at the drink. It was refreshing and smooth. "Thank you. It tastes really good."

"I only drink the good stuff. I owe it to myself at my age. Don't like to make them too strong this early. Like to give a good impression to new neighbors." He poured some into the glass containing just ice and took a sip. "So. What do you want to know? I'm sure you have a million questions, having moved into the…" He paused a moment and looked right at Ethan with a huge grin on his face and spoke quietly. "The 'haunted house'." He flexed his eyebrows several times.

Ethan looked directly at Hank and shook his head. "Okay. Have to tell you. When we first saw the house, I jokingly made a comment about it being haunted. Yes, long before any research or talking with locals about it. Now, what can you tell me and why do folks think it's haunted? Almost everyone told me you're the one who really knows the most about the place and the strangeness of Jeremiah Raines." He paused for a moment. "I hope you don't mind me saying but because of the timeline with all this history, I thought you had to be in your eighties. But Hank, you look like you're maybe around sixty-one or two. But that would make you younger than Emma Jones. How can that be?"

Hank beamed. "Well, thank you, young man. Guess it's my genes. Both my parents never looked their age, either. But I'm not sixty-one or two. I'll be eighty-three later this year."

"Really!? You're shitting me!?" He paused for a moment. "Sorry. It's just that I'm truly surprised. Damn! You look GREAT!" Ethan was astounded. "Well, here's to good genes." He raised his glass.

Hank smiled. "Thank you, Ethan. That's mighty kind of you." He raised his glass as well.

"Well, back on subject. I'm very interested in anything you can tell me about the house and Jeremiah."

Hank scratched his right cheek with his right hand then pulled at the right side of his large white mustache. "Let me see. I was. Hmmm. Yep. I was twenty-four when Jeremiah died. Now. Not sure when it was but I was real young. Maybe about eight. There were four of us. Johnny, Mark, Billy and me. One of the big bullies at school dared us to go spend the night out there. Being who we were, we weren't going to chicken out. We were going to show him. You bet. I can remember it just like it was yesterday."

"What were you going to do to prove you'd been there and spent the night?" Ethan was curious.

"Proving we were there was no problem. We had to put a certain handkerchief on the front railing. But no one could think of a way to prove we'd actually spent the night. We said we would and so we did. Kids back then weren't like the kids today. The little bastards today lie through their teeth about everything. Back then, your word was as good as gold and everyone knew it. No matter who you were."

"Okay, we did tell a fib to our parents that we were spending the night at each other's places, so no one would be the wiser. Fibbing is something we hardly ever did. Since it was a Friday night, there was no bother about school the next day. You should have seen us, trying to act cool but scared shitless as we went over there on our bikes. Johnny was the leader at first but the closer we got the farther behind he got. By the time we got there, the sun was going down, so we hid the bikes in the bushes down at the gate. As it got dark, we made our way up to the house."

"We were there for about an hour, feeling better and wondering what all the fuss was about. Then, all of a sudden, up the drive came Jeremiah in his truck. Scared the shit out of us. We were so quiet. Saw him get out of the truck, go to the back and pull down a ramp. Soon, he rolled down some damn long box on a dolly. Looked like a damn coffin box and he maneuvered it to the walkway. Then, something happened which made us all about shit in our pants." Hank looked up in the air and started snickering. "Yeah. He started rolling it around the north side of the house. Where we were." He slapped his leg. "You have never seen four kids more quiet in the bushes than we were."

"Old Jeremiah rolled the box along the walkway to the double doors, going down into the basement on that side of the house."

"Really?" Ethan was caught up in the story.

"We waited what seemed like forever, being quiet but didn't see him come out of the basement. Have to say, I got real curious what might be in the basement. Hey! I was a kid and thought there could be treasure down there or something." He looked over and saw Ethan's almost empty glass. "Can I fix you another? Not a problem."

"Oh, hell. Why not." Ethan handed his glass to Hank.

Hank went to the kitchen and put a little more ice and cola in Ethan's glass. He also got a spoon then came back and poured some bourbon in the drink. He stirred it a few times and handed it to Ethan. Then, Hank sat back in his chair after refreshing his own glass and continued his tale.

"We did spend the night out there and left as the sun was coming up. Mark put the handkerchief on the front railing as we scurried out of there and home. Never heard anything in the house all night long."

"Geez. Then, what's all the hullabaloo about?" Ethan was disappointed.

"Well, hold on, sonny. I'm not finished yet." Hank spoke in a scolding tone.

Ethan's eyes lit up with glee, hearing there was more.

"As I said, my curiosity got to me. So." His voice then spoke in a more hushed tone. "One night on my own, I went out there again. I just had to see if I could get in the basement. Have to tell you. I was so shocked when I got out there and the doors to the basement weren't locked. I thought it a real stroke of luck. Man, was I wrong."

"Did you get in?"

"Yep, I got in and got more than I bargained for. I closed the doors behind me and slowly made my way through the dark. Damn that basement was dark. You know there are no damn windows in the thing. And when it's night out, there's NO light in that place." He looked at Ethan with a questioning stare. "What the hell's wrong with me? Of course, you know. You live there." He slapped his left cheek with his left hand. "Did you all find anything weird in the basement?"

"Weird? No. The basement has a bunch of junk stuff in it but nothing weird."

"Just wondered. Kind of thought you might see something beyond that little door on that far south wall."

"Little door?"

"Hell, I'm getting ahead of myself. Where was I?"

"You got in the basement and closed the doors."

"Oh. Yeah. So, I was trying to get used to no light and trying not to trip over stuff. Suddenly, the lights came on. I almost yelled out loud, it scared the immortal shit out of me. I knew I had to hide. He had to be coming. You have never seen anyone searching for a place to hide so fast in your life. I saw an old armoire up against the wall. I ran over and got as far behind it as I could." He looked down at himself. "I was much smaller then. Remember. I was eight." He grinned.

Ethan gave a big smile and nodded.

"I was looking through all the stuff down there and could see Jeremiah come down the steps from the first floor, cross the room and he went to the little door. He unlocked the little door, went in and closed the door behind him. He was in there for hours. I couldn't move. I was so afraid if I tried, I would knock something over and get caught."

"What was he doing? And I still have no idea what little door you're talking about." Ethan shook his head in question. "Maybe it's where Shawn said there looked like there had been a door but was now bricked in. Maybe."

"Have no idea what he was doing in there but did hear some strange talking, yelling and I know this might sound odd but there was a chanting thing, too. Almost sounded like I was in church but very different. Now, this may sound really weird but it sounded like there was more than one person in there."

"What?"

"Yeah. Never could figure that out since he was the only one I saw go in and come out." Hank shook his head.

"Everyone said his family went to Paris and never returned. Holy crap! Wouldn't it be a bitch if he had them all locked up in there?" Ethan's mind was going crazy with the conjuring of a horror story.

"Damn! I never thought of that! Guess I was too young and they had gone to Europe, so many years earlier. Hell. What if he had gone batty and locked up the whole damn family? No one would have ever known. He lived out there where nobody went unless they had business there. Which was never. Damn. Now, I'm REALLY wondering what was behind that door."

Ethan spoke out. "I have no idea what door you're talking about. There are no doors down in the basement. There's the door from the first-floor kitchen and the double doors, from the outside on the north end of the house but no other doors there. And there's no door in the south wall but Shawn says the wall isn't original to the house and there should be a very large space behind it. He also said it looked like an opening had been sealed up with bricks. Maybe that's where the door was originally."

"Well, I'm not finished yet." Hank continued. "Finally, he came out, locked the little door and went upstairs. Then, the lights went out again. I waited for a while, not sure if he was coming back down before I slowly got out and made my way to the doors to the outside. It seemed to take forever to get to them. I was so careful not to make any noise. Now, you'd think that would have cured my curiosity. Well, hell no. I went out there several times. Each time I got bolder and would see if he was actually in the house before going back into the basement. There were a few times I watched him move one of those big coffin-like boxes down and through the little door. And that same noise came again. That chanting noise. Never got to see beyond the door as it was never unlocked when he wasn't in the room."

"Would you come out sometime and show me the little door you're talking about? You can meet Shawn, too. You can come for dinner and tell Shawn about things you saw. Everyone says I'm a pretty good cook." Ethan breathed on his left fist and rubbed it several times on his chest as a sign of self-accomplishment.

"Why, thanks, Ethan. That would be great. I don't get out much anymore."

"When would be good for you?"

"How about Thursday? Is that all right?"

"Great. Shawn said things have gone well with him and he should be home tomorrow or Wednesday. If that doesn't happen, I'll call you. Write down your number just in case. Now, how does around five sound? I see you drink bourbon."

Hank smiled. "Looking forward to it. See you then." He wrote his phone number on some paper and handed it to Ethan.

They headed for the door and out onto the front porch. Ethan extended his hand. "Thanks, Hank. I appreciate the information. Have to say, it's got me wondering a lot."

Hank shook his hand. "You drive safe."

Ethan headed back home.

CHAPTER V

Thursday, August 16th, finally arrived and Hank was on his way. He arrived about half an hour early and dressed completely unlike 'Farmer Jones'. He was in a suit, tie, boots and cowboy hat. Shawn met him at the door, shaking Hank's hand.

Hank looked Shawn up and down and smiled. "Well, I heard you were a 'looker' but that doesn't even scratch the surface." He flexed his eyebrows a few times.

Shawn responded. "Thanks, Hank for the kind words. Have to say, you look damn good to be your age. Hell yeah!"

They all congregated in the great room. Shawn fixed drinks and they began to sit down when Ethan said he wanted to check on dinner and headed to the kitchen.

Shawn turned to Hank. "Ethan tells me you've been here in this area all your life."

"Yep. Born in the house I'm in right now."

"Did you raise a family there?"

"No. Never married. Saw too many of my friends do it and get dissatisfied. Saw cheating on both sides in a few of them. Always knew that was something I never wanted to do. Really never found someone I wanted to live with, either." He paused for a moment. "Well, that's not quite true." He seemed to be picturing something in a memory. "Of course, it wasn't possible back then." He looked right at Shawn and then in Ethan's direction toward the kitchen. "A lot has changed in all these years."

Shawn found Hank's comment curious but immediately responded. "You have that right." He saw Hank's expression and pondered his earlier comment about him being a 'looker'. He began to wonder if there might be a possible and probable hidden meaning in what Hank had said. But he didn't want to pursue the issue as it was way too personal and they had just met.

Hank looked around the huge room. "Always wanted to see the inside of this place. Had no idea it was this big. When old Jeremiah died, this place got locked up tighter than a damn tomb and the relatives wouldn't let anyone in it."

"Well, come on. I'll give you the ten-cent tour." He and Hank got up and went around the rooms on the first floor. "There's four bedrooms upstairs and two baths. I think the powder room down here was added after the fact, taking part of the original kitchen. All of them need severe remodeling." They returned to the great room.

"You have a great view here of the ocean. Bet this place is a bitch to heat in the winter with all this glass." Hank surveyed the wall of French windows.

"I have a feeling we're going to find that out real soon." Shawn agreed. "Another two weeks and it's the start of September."

"So, why did you all come way out here and buy this place if you don't mind me asking?"

"To be honest, we were both tired of the traffic and noise in the city. Wanted to be somewhere with peace and quiet, yet close enough to the city, so I could get back and forth without much effort. I do admit it's a bit farther than I thought but with our schedules as flexible as they are, it isn't a big problem. Ethan rarely has to go see his agent. They do most of their business on the phone. This place just seemed great for us. I have all my drawing boards and stuff over there and Ethan has his piano over there. We can work on our own things and yet be right here, together."

"I think that's great. Technology sure has changed the way folks do things today. And it keeps getting better and better every day." Hank nodded.

"We both like the ocean and the price was right. Yes, it needs some work but most of it's really cosmetic."

Ethan came in from the kitchen. "Okay, gentlemen. Dinner is served. Grab your plates and get what you want from the buffet in the dining room then go sit down at the table."

During dinner, Hank told some of his history as did Shawn and Ethan telling theirs. It became immediately obvious Hank was not some country bumpkin. He was quite well-educated and quite knowledgeable on many subjects. He knew carpentry and plumbing. He also knew others in town who could be of service in the remodeling of the house. Shawn was so glad to hear that. Not only did the baths need redoing but so did the kitchen. Ethan agreed.

Dinner finally over, they went back into the great room and continued their discussion of Jeremiah. Finally, Ethan shouted out. "Okay! Okay! I can't wait any longer. The suspense is killing me. Hank, would you mind coming with us downstairs and showing us where the 'little door' is located?"

Everyone stood up, responding to Ethan's comment and they headed to the basement.

It took Hank just a short time to get oriented. "It's been a long time since I was in here and I never came down the steps from the kitchen." He turned and looked around. "Oh. There are the doors to the outside." He walked over to the doors and began to walk as if retracing a distant memory. "The armoire was right over here." He walked over and stood up against the stone foundation wall. He looked in the direction of the wall in question. "The door was right over there." He pointed toward the wall Shawn knew was hiding some space beyond. "But now, there is no door."

They all walked over to the place where Hank said there had been a door. Shawn looked closely. He placed his finger in the mortar joint he had indicated weeks earlier. "Interesting. I wondered if this had been an old doorway, bricked in."

"I'm dying to know what's on the other side." Ethan immediately chimed in.

"Maybe I can go into town tomorrow and get some tools and see about taking out those bricks." Shawn kept staring at the wall.

"I have plenty of tools at the house. I could come out tomorrow and help." Hank added.

"That would be terrific. And you can let me know how much it will be." Shawn commented.

"How much it will be?" Hank looked puzzled.

"Yes. For your work."

"I swear. You city folks just don't get it. You think everything has a price tag." He slapped his leg and shook his head. "Here you have met me and we have started to become friends. And you invite me here to dinner."

"I'm sorry, Hank. I never like taking advantage of someone's expertise. I've known people who know others with certain abilities and they are constantly using them. I find that appalling and despicable." Shawn responded.

"Well, I do see what you mean and I'll bet it does happen a lot in the city. But we out here tend to not mind helping where the help is needed. Now, if you want me to build some cabinets for you or help with your remodeling, that's a different story." Hank gave a big grin.

Shawn nodded and gave a 'thumbs-up'. "Got it."

"Actually, I want to know what's behind the damn wall, too." Hank stared right at the spot where the door used to be.

"Tomorrow it is. Whenever it's easy for you." Ethan insisted.

"How about you come out for breakfast and then we can get started?" Shawn suggested.

"I would like that. See you tomorrow morning around eight-thirty."

They left the basement and led Hank to the front door, watching him get in his truck and go down the drive. Friday was going to be a very interesting day. They all knew it.

CHAPTER VI

It was just after eight when Ethan saw Hank, coming up the drive in his truck and parking out in the front. He went in and told Shawn who went out to greet him. Ethan went in and got the sausage and eggs going for breakfast.

"Can I help you carry anything in!?" Shawn yelled out.

"Sure! I know a strapping young man like you would have no problem carrying some of this stuff." Hank called back as he walked to the rear of the truck. He started pulling out two toolboxes and a large hammer and chisel.

"We can carry it all down and then have breakfast." Shawn picked up the largest of the toolboxes, the hammer and they headed for the basement. Hank grabbed the other toolbox, the chisel and followed.

As they passed through the kitchen, Hank called out to Ethan. "Morning, young man! Smells great!"

"Hey, Hank! Good morning to you as well. It's almost ready."

They went into the basement and put everything within proximity of where the bricked-up doorway was located in the wall then came back up to the kitchen. Ethan had the kitchen table set up for them to eat.

"Have to say, Ethan really is a damn good cook." Hank finished his last bite. "How do you keep in such good shape with his cooking?" He looked right at Shawn.

"I do have to watch it. Working out helps, too. Thinking about putting in a workout room in the basement."

Ethan gathered up the dishes and put them in the kitchen sink. "Is it time?" A big Cheshire Cat grin filled his face.

"Yep. Let's go see what's behind the wall." Hank gave a 'thumbs-up'.

Although there was some excitement about what they were about to do, there was significant apprehension as well as they headed to the basement.

——————>◆<——————

Assembled in the basement, Shawn and Hank looked closely at the area where Hank indicated the door used to be. They both agreed, they would proceed with the removal of those bricks to prevent damage to the rest of the wall.

"I just know something bizarre has to be there." Ethan commented. "Otherwise, why would it be bricked up?"

"Have a feeling you could be right." Hank added. "Never knew what was in those big wooden boxes he dragged in there."

It took about thirty minutes for the initial slow chipping away, so as not to damage the surrounding wall. But finally, the mortar came loose. Hank slowly pulled out the first brick right at about eye level. Carefully, he hit the adjacent brick with his hammer and it popped loose.

Suddenly, there was a strange smell, issuing from the hole. Shawn looked at Ethan. "Is this what it's like when they open some tomb in Egypt?" His face was filled with a questioning expression.

"Damn! We forgot the flashlight. Just a sec." Ethan immediately ran up to the kitchen pantry to get the large flashlight and quickly returned. He clicked it a few times to make sure it was working.

Hank removed four more bricks to make sure the hole was big enough to see through with the light. He stared right at Shawn and Ethan. "Okay. Who wants to be first?"

"You've done all the work and you know more than we do, so you go first. And I think you have waited way longer than we have for this." Shawn insisted, handing the light to Hank.

Hank took the flashlight and directed it through the opening and looked into the space beyond. "HOLY SHIT! HOLY SHIT!" He moved the light around. Oh, my God! Holy shit!" Hank stood back with a look of shock and horror on his face.

"What!? WHAT!?" Shawn and Ethan spoke in unison.

"Holy shit! Here! Look!" Hank handed the light to Shawn.

Shawn looked in. "HOLY SHIT! DAMN! HOLY SHIT!"

"WHAT!?" Ethan yelled out. "WHAT!?" He put his head close to Shawn's, so he, too, could peer through the hole. "HOLY SHIT!" He looked at Shawn and then at Hank. "HOLY SHIT!"

Hank picked up the hammer. He and Shawn went at the brickwork like gangbusters to remove much of the masonry that filled the sealed doorway. They pulled the bricks and chunks of mortar out into the room where they were standing. Finally, all the bricks that had filled the sealed doorway had been removed and they all slowly walked through the opening and into the space beyond.

Once inside, they were extremely careful not to disturb their find. Shawn always thought the hidden room was going to be pretty big from what he could see on the original house plans. He now realized he was correct. It was virtually the entire area beneath the two southern bedrooms of the house. "I don't believe it! I just don't believe it!" They all stood there, not moving, trying to comprehend everything they saw in the slowly shifting beam of the flashlight.

The room was very large. The space was only interrupted periodically by structural columns and stone arches, supporting the structure above. The far wall of the room was the southernmost stone foundation wall of the house. Hank moved the light throughout the huge room, exposing the frightening contents.

In the middle of the room was a large monolith of stone, looking very much like some church altar. A set of tall candlestick holders stood on the ends of the stone surface. In the center of the stone was a huge, thick book, open to the middle. On the walls and ceiling, were drawings and markings that looked like those that one would associate with witchcraft and the occult.

On the floor, along the walls and in the far reaches of the room, were piles and piles of human bones and old apparel. One of the wooden boxes Hank had described was sitting not far from the altar. On the floor, in front of the altar were metal chains and shackles bolted to the floor.

"My God! I had no idea. Damn. I was probably here several times while some crazy shit was going on in this damn place." Hank spoke softly, attempting not to disturb the atmosphere.

"We have to tell somebody." Ethan spoke out. "Somebody needs to find out what this is all about."

"We need to call Jake. He's the local sheriff. He'll know what to do." Hank advised. "And he's good people."

They carefully left the room and went upstairs.

Hank spoke out. "Let me talk with Jake. He knows me." Hank took out his cell phone and called. "Hey, Harriet. Yeah. It's Hank. How are you? Good. I'm doing fine. Is Jake in? Let me speak to him, please."

There was a moment of silence then Hank spoke again. "Jake. Hank here. Yeah. We do need to have a drink sometime. It's been a while. Too long. Hey. Listen. I'm out at the old Raines place. They're really nice kids. Wait till you meet them. Listen. I need you to come out here. Like, right now. Seriously. Right now. You need to see this. I think you just might have to call in some special investigators, too. You'll see. This is some crazy shit here. Okay. See you shortly. Okay. Sounds good. Bye." He turned to Shawn and Ethan. "Jake'll be here shortly."

"How about some coffee while we wait?" Ethan asked. "It's still hot."

"Think I could use something stronger than coffee. But I think we need to be extremely sober for this one." Hank was still shaken by what he had seen.

They all nodded in agreement and fixed their cups of coffee.

From the front porch, they saw the police car, coming up the drive and park at the walk near Hank's truck. Out stepped a man in his well-pressed uniform. Jake looked to be in his fifties but they found out later, he was actually in his mid-to-late seventies. He was average height, around five-nine and had a great build. His dark wavy hair and full mustache looked terrific on the man in uniform. Ethan could tell it was colored but with his square jawline made him look so much younger. Ethan just smiled and chuckled to himself. "Damn. How I love men in uniform."

"Hey, Jake." Hank went down to shake his hand and a quick 'man hug'. Ethan and Shawn followed. "Shawn McAllister and Ethan Trendeau. This is Jake Banister. He's the sheriff here and a super nice guy." They all shook hands.

"Nice to meet you, fellas. Heard some nice things about you. Been meaning to come out and welcome you to the neighborhood but just didn't get here yet. Sorry about that." Jake gave a big apologetic smile. "So, what have we got here? Hope it's not too bad. I mean you being new here and all."

Hank started to explain. "You're not going to believe it. Hate to say it but those weird-ass stories about Jeremiah were probably not only true but much, much worse. Wait till you see."

They headed into the house and to the basement. Shawn gave Jake the flashlight and pointed at the now open doorway in the wall.

Jake slowly walked through. "HOLY SHIT! HOLY SHIT!"

"Yeah! That's what we said!" Hank yelled back."

"I wouldn't believe this if I weren't seeing it with my own eyes! Damn! What is this all about?" Jake called out from the room.

"We'd like to know the same thing." Hank responded.

Within a few moments, Jake emerged shaking his head in disbelief. "Yep. You're right. We need someone here with some expertise in crazy shit." He turned again, looking into the opening. "I'll call the state but I'll bet they are going to have to call in some REAL special folks for this one. Just leave this damn thing be until they can come and check it out."

Hank spoke up. "I know of this guy in Boston who's supposed to be incredibly good at this kind of craziness. Name's Peter something or other. I'll tell you about him later. Might want to have one of your guys call him."

"That sounds good. Let's talk later." Jake wanted any input he could get.

Ethan looked at Jake. "Would you like some coffee? I just made a new pot."

"Sounds good to me. Let me run out and call Harriet on the horn and have her start the works in getting the right folks here. State has an office in Bangor. Even though it's Friday, they'll probably be here in a few hours when they hear how strange this is. Hell yeah. With Harriet calling, I can guarantee it'll be all over town before you can blink an eye even when I tell her to keep a lid on it."

"Wait till the media gets hold of it. This place is going to be a circus." Hank shook his head.

"I'll have Jerry and Buddy come out here to keep things civil if it starts."

Hank looked at Shawn. "That's a good thing. They're Jake's deputies. They're good guys and can stand their ground when needed. They'll keep everything under control here. Don't worry."

"Geez. This thing won't stay local. Damn. I'll bet we're going to be all over the national news, too. We better let folks know before they see it on the damn news." Ethan shook his head. "I'm calling my agent right now. Shawn, you better call the office and let them know. I can only imagine how it's going to affect your job. Geez."

"Yeah. And you'll be known as the 'Haunted House Piano Player'." Shawn was trying to bring a bit of levity to the situation after all they had seen but no one was amused.

Ethan heard what Shawn had said, realizing he was trying to lift the veil of horror they all had seen. He wanted to add to that. "Maybe when I perform, I should wear a damn black cape and put fangs in my mouth. Crap. I can see it now."

The mental image of Ethan, sitting at an ebony grand, wearing such an outfit, did make them all chuckle a bit.

Shawn knew this event would explode and knew the right people needed to be forewarned. "You're right. We better contact everyone who needs to know."

Jake went out to his car to make his call while Shawn and Hank went for more coffee and sat in the great room. Ethan couldn't get over the macabre nature of it all and with his curiosity just had to take one more look before the place was overrun by police.

He ran down with the flashlight and entered the room again. It just amazed him as to the horror of the whole thing. After a few moments of looking around the interior of the room, he turned to leave when he saw a small niche in the wall beside the entry. A small wooden box was in the niche. "What is this?" He picked up the box and opened it. Inside was a set of incredible gold rings. "Damn. These are beautiful. Why the hell are they down here?" He reached in a touched the rings.

At that moment, something happened. A strange feeling seemed to surge from his hand and through his entire body. Instantly, he became obsessively possessive of the box and its contents. He felt like Gollum with his desire for his 'Precious'. He suddenly knew the rings were his and no one could have them. And he knew he could tell no one about them. He stuffed the box into his pocket and headed back upstairs.

Ethan returned to the great room. Shawn looked at him come into the room. "Well." He looked closely at Ethan. "What have you been up to? You look like you just swallowed the canary. What is wrong?"

"Nothing! Nothing." Ethan tried to pass off the strange feeling inside him and look normal. But he could feel the guilt, welling up inside him for lying as he had never lied to Shawn ever before. It didn't matter. He knew he could say nothing about his find. No one could know. They were his now. Finally, the strange sensation inside himself eased and faded away. He changed the subject. "Does anyone need more coffee? I need a cup."

<hr />

The state investigators and police invaded and were there through the entire weekend and the whole next week. Photographs were taken of every square inch of the room before and during the removal of the bones, clothing and other contents. They were taken to be examined to see if they could shed light on who they all were.

Jake was happy since he didn't have the resources for such a project. He did take the big book from the altar to the station and placed it in security. He also had talked with Hank about the man in Boston. From what Hank told him, the guy was extremely knowledgeable of the occult. He had Jerry call him and find out if he could come and help with the situation. Unfortunately, he was leaving the next day to go out of the country and would not be back for several months.

Hank was correct about the media. By the first of September, word regarding the discovery spread like locusts on a wheat field or some devastating plague. And not just locally but across the nation. Local, national TV stations and syndicates had cameras and reporters everywhere. Jerry and Buddy were extremely efficient at keeping everything civil and orderly. Shawn and Ethan were quite pleased with how orderly it all stayed. Jake would stop by almost three times a day to make sure Ethan and Shawn's house was not trashed. No TV cameras were allowed into the room as investigators wanted it kept as much in its original state as possible until they completely finished all they wanted to accomplish.

A specialist in the occult and anthropology came in to examine the drawings. Jake told Shawn about the one in Boston who was unavailable. The one who did come was the second recommendation.

One thing that didn't seem to fit with everything else in the room was the empty little niche in the wall near the doorway. Why was it empty? What was supposed to be in it? Anyone could look at it and would know it had to have some function. But no one could understand its purpose or any connection with the horror of the room. When it was mentioned, Ethan couldn't bring himself to disclose what he knew the power of the rings on him was so strong. The rings were his and no one was going to take them from him.

Of course, when reporters dug into the history of the house, they began to search high and low for relatives of Jeremiah. When found, most were so far removed, none seemed to know anything about him. Their only connection was the inheritance of the property. This being the case, interviews with them quickly came to a halt and focus returned to the house and the time period when Jeremiah was alive. In-depth reviews began on past reports of disappearances in and around the area all the way back to the times of the building of the house. Of course, the information Ethan had already discovered in his research helped considerably.

One rather gruesome find was the remains of what they believed to be that of Jeremiah's wife and children. Clothing with the embroidered initials and names were discovered in the piles of garments. This explained why no one ever saw them leave for Paris and why they never returned.

With close examination of the altar, it was discovered to have a movable stone panel in the back. In the space behind the panel, were found several large books. These turned out to be journals kept by Jeremiah. When read, they were frightening from the very beginning as they were about the rituals conducted and their questionable purpose. Everything started long before Jeremiah married or even before the house was built. And there was mention of a large book. It had to be the one that was on the altar when the room was opened. It had been taken to the local police department as evidence and locked away.

⟶⟫◆⟨⟵

The journals began with a trip Jeremiah took to France when he was in his late twenties. It was this trip that led him to a book among a huge collection of old volumes in an old antique shop. The owner of the shop indicated many of the things in the shop had been there since before he became the proprietor. The shop had belonged to an old uncle who died and left it to him. He was trying to sell everything off as he wasn't interested in maintaining the shop.

Before discovering 'the book', Jeremiah went through several of the volumes piled in a corner of the shop. They were oversized books and many looked valuable. When he came across 'the book', he opened it and saw the fine handwritten texts and colored drawings obviously hand-painted. What was very intriguing is the bindings seemed to be made of some sort of skin. Hearing the price being asked for them, he realized it was impossibly low compared to what he knew he could probably ask for it and the other books. He immediately snatched them up.

Unable to read Latin, he sought out a local priest to ask him to decipher what was in the pages. The priest was more than willing to help but when he opened it and started reading, he immediately closed it and looked at Jeremiah, telling him to burn the book with haste as the book contained only evil. Then, he handed it back to him and walked away, not saying another word.

This just piqued Jeremiah's curiosity as he couldn't believe the contents of the book could be that bad. He knew he was going to have to seek help from other sources. He placed a very large ad in the Paris paper that couldn't be missed and waited for results.

It didn't take long. After several days, waiting at his hotel, one afternoon the bellboy came to his door to inform him of a visitor, regarding his ad. He gave the boy a big gratuity and told him to tell the person to come up to his rooms.

Shortly, there was a knock at the door. Opening it, Jeremiah saw a short, old man standing there. His dress was nothing special. He looked down at the old man.

The old man looked up and gave a weird grin. "I know I can help you. And to let you know I know what I'm talking about, let me describe the book to you." With his hands, he indicated the physical size of the book. "The text is in Latin and Greek with many painted drawings and symbols." He gave a huge grin.

"That's correct. Come in and sit down. I'll go get it." Jeremiah went into the bedroom of the suite and brought out the book, placing it on the table between him and the old man.

The old man's eyes lit up and opened wide. A look came over his face like that of a starving man who had just been placed in front of a piled-high banquet table. He reached toward the book.

"No! No! Not so quick. I'll let you see it in a minute. First, I want to know how much money you want to help me with explaining and translating the pages."

"One thousand francs! And five thousand francs for this set of gold rings I have here in this small box." The old man grinned and showed the box to Jeremiah.

"One thousand francs? Five thousand francs? You must be kidding. What I paid for the book is a pittance of what you want." He paused for a moment. "And what do I want with a set of gold rings?"

"When I tell you all you need to know about the book and the rings, you'll agree the price is small."

"Really?"

"You have no idea what you have here. This book is worth more than its weight, not in gold but in diamonds. It holds secrets that can only be imagined. In the circles I have traveled, this book was talked about many times. Most wondered if it truly existed. When someone told me about your ad, I wondered if the book you wanted to be translated could possibly be… 'the one'. I had to find out. And lo and behold, here it is. Also, what no one has known is that I have the set of rings. Its companions."

"I can't imagine any book, being worth so much. What makes this one so special? And how is it you have a set of rings you say are connected to the book? How did you get hold of them? If they belong together, how did they get separated?" Jeremiah kept up his interrogation.

The old man looked greedily at the book, sitting on the table. "I know when I tell you, you're not going to believe me. But every word I tell you is true. When did you want to start?"

Jeremiah insisted. "Let's go down and have some tea first. Afterward, if you think there's enough time, we can start today."

"When it comes to that book and these rings, there's plenty of time. They know no time. Night or day makes no difference to them."

"Very good. Then, we shall begin when we get back from tea."

⟫◆⟪

Before they returned to the room, Jeremiah left the old man at the table and went to the front desk. He called for the manager to explain that the old man was a relative he'd not seen in many years. If there was an additional charge to have him stay in his rooms that would not be a problem. He also explained that since they didn't want to be disturbed he asked them, starting at six that evening and continuing at six the next morning, to leave a cart of food and drink for two at the door of his rooms. They were just to leave the cart and take away the older one. This was to continue until they were instructed differently. It was also not necessary to come and clean the room. This could be done when his relative left. He was sure this would last for maybe a week if that. The manager thought it rather a strange request but he had no problem following Jeremiah's instructions.

Jeremiah had a feeling the telling of the book and rings wasn't going to be some short stroll in the park and didn't want to stop and interrupt any part of the learning. Completing his discussion with the hotel manager, he returned to the table in the hotel dining room. He and the old man headed up to Jeremiah's rooms.

Entering the room and sitting down, the old man started with the explanation of the book and how it was divided into sections. Each for a different purpose. Before going into detail, he read the titles of the different sections, so Jeremiah would get an overall perspective of the book.

Each section was specific for whoever had possession of the rings and the path to be taken. There was a path for someone who was possibly up in age and single. A section was devoted to someone already married. Then, there was a section for a young person who was just starting out in life. All were devoted to bringing the one who had the rings to the highest level of his profession with wealth and recognition. While wearing the rings, that person would produce the most amazing thing related to his profession. The wearer was to reach a final goal at which time he would then return to the place where he had found the rings to receive his final major reward. It was not necessary for him to have the rings at that time. What was interesting is that the final reward was never explained in the book.

He explained the rings were in existence long before the book but the book became the integral companion of the rings in Italy back in the 15th century. It was a wealthy merchant who joined them. He was very much into the Black Arts of the Occult and had the book made and written to include all the black spells, incantations and information. It was written in the very beginning of the book that the merchant had joined with a demon he had conjured up when performing a satanic ritual including the rings. This demon was named Balzar. Balzar instructed him to write down the different paths, so that whoever found the rings could get the most benefit from them.

So, for the first time, the powers of the rings would give a direction to the wearer. The rituals along with the power of the rings were formidable. He was the first to realize the power of both, together. He also made it clear in the book that every time the wearer of the rings accomplished something amazing in his profession while wearing the rings, that person would get closer to his final reward. What the final goal and great reward would be was never given or explained. The assumption was that it would be very beneficial to the one wearing the rings by creating something new and original in his profession and to receive incredible recognition and vast wealth.

The merchant did something no one had ever done before. He brought in several who became apprentices to him. He would explain the power of the book and also the power of the rings. But what became very clear was the fantastic power of the book and the rings working together. He knew this would ensure the continuation of the two together after he reached his final goal and collected his last big reward.

The old man rubbed his hands together and gave a sinister grin. "How they work together will become evident as I explain the entire story. So, let the learning sessions begin."

Neither had any idea the passing of time. They would sleep when they were tired and take periodic rest breaks before continuing the lessons from the book as well as the history of the rings discovered by the old man.

Soon, it became evident almost a week had passed but things Jeremiah was learning from the book were extraordinary. The rituals it described were unbelievably gruesome and abominable but what they promised in return was unmistakable. He contemplated his ability to follow through with such deeds.

The old man just grinned and snickered. "If you wear the rings, nothing is impossible. You'll do it. And the more you do, the easier it will get, especially when you reap the rewards."

Jeremiah stared at the old man. "But how do you know? You tell me you have never worn the rings much less touched them."

"Trust me." The old man shook his head. "What I have told you of their history is from my research." He peered off into space as if remembering very old memories. "The rings are powerful and that is the reason I have never touched them or put them on. I could tell that the instant I did, I would have no control. This I know from what has been passed down through the ages by those familiar with the book and the rings."

Finally, the in-depth session was finished. It was early morning. Jeremiah left a note on the door to stop deliveries of food. Both he and the old man were exhausted. He knew they both needed a very good rest. He told the old man to go sleep in his bed. He'd rest on the settee for a few hours. Then, the old man could go.

It was mid-afternoon when Jeremiah got up and sneaked into the bedroom. He wanted the rings and knew the old man wanted the book. Whoever had them both together could wield significant power. He knew he had to eliminate the old man.

Grabbing a pillow, he rammed it over the head of the sleeping old man. "I know you want the book! You old bastard! And you're not going to get it! I know you came with the intention of stealing it and getting away! But now, it is I who will have the power. Not you! So! Die! Die! Die!"

The old man struggled and screamed out into the pillow but the sound was significantly muffled by the pillow. His arms flailed and reached to try and strangle Jeremiah. But, it was useless. Jeremiah was a lot younger and stronger. The old man kept thrashing around, trying to attack Jeremiah and get the pillow off his head. Soon, it all slowed until the old man stopped moving on the bed. It was over. The old man was dead.

Jeremiah placed the old man in the bathtub and filled it with water. After a while, he ran down to the front desk with an alarming tale. His relative had gone to take a bath, slipped and drowned before he knew it. The police were called. But due to the reputation of the hotel, things were kept quiet, so as not to cause concern for any of the influential guests who stayed there. The body of the old man was taken out the back delivery door of the hotel. He told the police since the old man had no other relatives, he would like to pay for his funeral and interment. Jeremiah was pleased no fuss was caused by the incident and that it was written off as an accident.

With all his newly gained knowledge, he was ready to go home and start the process. He wanted to go slow. He wanted to make sure every step would bring him closer and closer to his final goal of wealth, influence and power. It was something that would take time but he knew time was on his side. All he had to do was follow the instructions in the book for it all to unfold.

He packed everything in his shipping trunks. Everything but the book and the rings. They would stay with him. He wrapped the book in some butcher paper from the hotel kitchen. It was time to arrange passage home. He had no problem getting a suite on the next ship back to New York. He'd check out of the hotel the day the ship was to depart.

CHAPTER VII

When Jeremiah returned home, he began his quest. It was all part of the process laid out in the book and explained by the old man he killed in Paris. He would be taking the path described in the book designated for a young, single person. That way he would be able to reach the highest reward possible.

The first step was to build a house and make an area in the house for an altar. This room should be on the lowest level of the house. He knew he would have a basement, so a room there would be perfect. The second step was to marry and have at least two children. He knew he didn't care about who his wife was. She was a means to an end. It would be the same for the children.

This was also the time he began writing his journals, starting with the discovery of 'the book' at the antique shop in Paris. He wanted to write down everything from the beginning, so the story of the rings and how they became joined to the book could be told.

To build a house, meant, he needed to acquire some property. Finally, after a few years of searching, he found just what he was looking for. He lined up the contractor and began the house.

As the basement was being completed, several large pieces of stone were delivered from a local stone quarry and placed in the front yard area. These were to construct a stone altar. Several were so heavy, he hired several laborers he found from the streets in town to help him hoist the pieces down into the basement. He had to use rolling winches and rope to lift and put them in place then put the pieces together to form the altar. The workers could not imagine why such a thing would be needed in a basement but none of them questioned it since they were being paid very well.

Finally, the entire house was finished in 1896. Jeremiah was thirty-three years old.

The house was secondary to the real purpose. A wall from east to west would create a large room at the south end of the basement. This wall would not be shown on the original construction plans. Jeremiah would do the building of the wall and install a little door. With the bricks delivered, it was time to build the wall to define the large room where the altar was located. Once finished and the door installed, he immediately placed the book in the center of the altar. The box containing the set of rings was placed in the little niche at the doorway.

It didn't take long to find someone suitable for a wife. With his wealth and position in society, there were many to choose from. They married just as the house was beginning construction. They would live in town until the house was completed. Within two years of marrying, he had two children. Everything was going as planned.

Soon, it would be time for the consecration of the altar to begin. This would start with the first sacrifice. But all in good time. He was following the steps as described in the book.

<hr>

Since no one started living in the house until everything was complete, it was obvious to anyone going into the basement there was a space or room behind the wall as the little door had to lead to somewhere. But no one ever went there. Jeremiah was the only one who ventured into the basement. The little door was always kept locked with him having the only key. His wife hated the basement and never went down there. Even though still small, he just had to think about the children, sneaking down there or someone going to get something from storage. But it was of no consequence. Less than three years after moving into the house, it was told that his wife and children went to Paris in early 1899 as his wife supposedly had relatives there and wanted the children to be educated there.

For Jeremiah, it was a hallmark moment. He was taking one of the biggest steps in his initiation. It would bring him higher on the ladder to his Nirvana. It was described in great detail in the journals. The first sacrifices took place to consecrate the altar. Later in 1899, he made a night trip to Trenton. This would be the beginning of his next steps to reach his reward.

As the details of the journals became evident, they answered so many questions, regarding all the bones and clothing in the room. It described the sacrifices, using those Jeremiah sought out and where all the missing individuals went over the years. The satanic worship and sacrifices were gruesome and beyond comprehension. But from the writings, it brought him nearer and nearer to his final major reward. Of course, no one would ever know if he achieved it. The journals ended with his last sacrifice and his great need to return to Paris, so he could collect that reward.

The last passages in the journals indicated why the little door would be removed and the opening bricked up. He must have accomplished all he needed to do and his trip to Paris would finalize his quest. His final words written down were 'I have almost reached the end… now, to Paris, where I first got the rings and where I will be met by one of Satan's legions and reap my reward'. The room, the book and the rings were no longer necessary for him.

After reading the last lines of his journal, no one could understand why it was that Jeremiah died not long after arriving in Paris. Did he get his reward before dying? Whatever the case, his body was returned home for burial.

After being read by the person hired with knowledge of the occult and anthropology, he explained the whole story to every one of import. Then, the journals were taken to the local police department and placed with the book from the altar in the evidence locker. The question now was where were the rings? It was only conjecture but the thought was the little niche by the door was where Jeremiah kept the rings. It would have been a perfect place for them, so no one could get to them except Jeremiah. But the rings couldn't be found. Could it be possible he'd taken them with him when he made his last trip to Paris, even though he indicated in the journal that he no longer had need of them? Maybe the hold they had on him was too strong to break. Strangely, they weren't among his possessions at his death, either. Where had they gone? Everyone was stumped.

Of course, with the end of September and the beginning of October, the story of the discovery in the Raines House grew even more prominent with the approach of Halloween. The news media just wouldn't let it go. Ethan's and Shawn's names were all over seemingly every news report. It was even going international. They couldn't decide how all this was going to affect their careers. Ethan and Shawn seemed to be the center of attention.

Shawn's clients always gave him a strange look when they realized who he was. Even after finding this out, there was a sympathy that he'd been pulled into a situation, not of his making. Many thought it fantastic that they were working with 'the architect who lives in the haunted house' in Maine.

Ethan couldn't shake the title of the 'Haunted House Pianist' every time he was mentioned in the news. He jokingly considered adding to his repertoire *The Funeral March* from Chopin's *Sonata No. 2*. It seemed a great way to end a concert. "Yeah. Play that at the end of every concert. Wonder what my agent would think about that?"

Shawn couldn't resist and started laughing. "Hey! You said it, not me! Sorry."

It took time but finally, the horror story, running through the media, passed into history. It was heading toward Thanksgiving. Slowly, things began to return to normal in the area but for Ethan and Shawn, they still had to contend with investigators and those attached to the situation.

In the beginning, forensics began organizing the bones in groups, trying to find out how many victims there were. The number of skulls did help a lot. Many bones were so old, they knew it would be virtually impossible to identify them all. Even with Jeremiah's journals and police records of missing persons, going back decades, it might not be possible to identify and attach names to all the bones. All they could do was try.

Shawn and Ethan just immersed themselves in their work for the time being. Shawn went into the city for long periods and Ethan worked diligently on his compositions. Ethan would join Shawn in the city when he needed a break from practicing just to get away. They knew Jake and his deputies would watch their place.

Finally, Ethan's agent called to let him know he'd arranged a charity concert for him to play. It was going to be just before Christmas and in San Francisco. This gave Ethan three weeks to get ready.

Ethan's agent commented. "Now, if you don't want to do it, I can cancel it."

"No, Bob. I'll do it. I need to get back in the groove again." Ethan knew it was important. This would be his first concert since all the uproar began. He wondered if people would look at him funny. The image of himself on the piano bench with a black cape and vampire teeth popped into his head. Shaking his head, he couldn't help but giggle.

Over the time from the opening of the room, Shawn seemed to notice a slow change in Ethan's demeanor. At times, he seemed to be getting a little more aggressive than usual.

One morning they came down to have breakfast when Shawn questioned. "Okay. What was that all about last night?"

Ethan had started cooking. "What?"

"Just curious. Things have gotten more, shall we say, interesting. That's a good way of putting it. It started about two weeks ago. Thought it was just an isolated thing but it's been getting more and more aggressive. Then, last night I wake up in the middle of the night with my hands tied to the bed and you grabbing hold of me like a damn vice. Made me yell out. Damn. Have to admit, it was fun in a strange way. Seems you're turning into a cute tiger cub." A big grin filled his face.

"What are you talking about? I did no such thing." Ethan looked at Shawn with an unknowing expression.

"And those rings you had on." He looked at Ethan's hands. The rings were not there. "You had on some unusual rings. And they got hotter than hell. I could feel them when you touched me. They aren't the rings everyone is looking for, are they?"

Ethan realized he didn't remember. And he didn't remember taking them off. He had to quickly think of something. It was now obvious that the rings had taken a strange hold of him. He wanted to confess that the rings he had on were the ones he found in the nitch in the basement room but the power of the rings would not allow him to tell the truth. The words coming out of his mouth would be a lie.

He started to chuckle as if nothing had happened. "I forgot to tell you. Bought them while you were on one of your trips. They're nothing special. Don't really like them. That's why I don't wear them all the time. I'm thinking about returning them to the jeweler in Portland. Now. Okay. How many eggs do you want? Or would you like an omelet?"

"Oh, terrific. An omelet would be great." Shawn sipped his coffee and let the previous conversation go for another time.

Ethan realized every time he put the rings on, he lost all knowledge of the time and memory. He couldn't explain it. It made him feel so guilty because he had never lied to Shawn before and he ached inside for the major lie he had just told. It was becoming evident that the rings had a very strong hold on him even when he wasn't wearing them.

He had examined them closely from time to time. They were exactly alike. The bands were designed like twisted thick rope and the main ornament on each was a detailed ram's skull with coiled horns. The coiled horns and their position close to the skull reminded him of the hairstyle Carrie Fisher wore as Princess Leia in the 'Star Wars' movies. There were strange markings engraved on the insides of the bands.

The few times he'd put the rings on, several hours passed that he couldn't account for. This was rather scary but for some reason, it didn't seem to bother him. Maybe some alter ego was taking over like it did Sally Field in the movie, 'Sybil'. He knew if he gave up the rings, these episodes would most likely stop but he couldn't. They were his. Each day that passed he became more and more addicted to them. But he didn't care. He couldn't help himself. He liked them.

This is what must have been happening, regarding the times Shawn was referring to. He had no recollection of tying Shawn to the bed. But when told about it, he realized this was totally out of his normal character.

———✦———

The three weeks of practice seemed effortless, especially when Ethan would wear the rings. Shawn had told him he was plowing through the repertoire like it was nothing. And he was playing the pieces with interpretations Shawn had never heard before. Ethan realized he kept losing the time periods he would practice. He knew he did them but had no recollection of them.

Shawn continued to comment, telling him how vibrant his playing sounded. Shawn never mentioned the rings again even though it was impossible to miss them, one on each hand and as large as they were. He always saw how confused Ethan looked when the subject was brought up. In order not to create conflict, he just decided to drop the subject for now. Maybe sometime down the road, it might become possible to talk about them.

———✦———

Ethan left two days early for San Francisco, so he could see the location of the concert and get prepared. The whole time he hoped all would go well since he knew he wouldn't remember his playing while the rings were on his hands but there was no way he would play without wearing them. The rings seemed to take hold and force him into wearing them.

The local media did refer to him as the 'Haunted House Pianist' but it was rather tongue in cheek. The audience even laughed out loud when he was introduced and he came to the stage making 'Wooooooo' sounds, wiggling his finger up in the air.

Ethan played the program flawlessly. Everyone couldn't believe the dynamic levels and interpretations. It was like they were hearing the pieces for the first time.

Strangely, Ethan vaguely remembered putting the rings on before leaving the hotel but he didn't remember leaving for the concert. The next thing he remembered was standing in front of the dresser where he kept his things. It was the next morning. He looked down at his hands. The rings were not on his fingers. Opening the top drawer, he could see them in the small open box. He was exhausted but he had to get things together to leave. His flight would be taking off in a few hours. He'd be able to rest on the plane.

Only just a few days to go and it would be Christmas. He wasn't sure if they'd put up a tree this year with all that had been taking place. When he got home that night, it was late but Shawn was there to pick him up at the airport in Portland.

"Well, how did it go? I'm sure you were great." Shawn spoke with happiness in his voice as Ethan got in the car.

"I think it was pretty good." Ethan didn't remember the first note.

"I'm sure you're tired. Why don't you rest while I drive home? I'll wake you when we get there."

"Thanks. I really am tired." Ethan curled up against the door of the car.

CHAPTER VIII

When Ethan awoke the next morning and went downstairs, Shawn was already up and standing next to a small Christmas tree. "Sorry, it's so small. It's dwarfed by the room. But we'll have a big one next year."

As they headed into the kitchen, Ethan called back to Shawn. "Let's get some coffee and I'll help you decorate it."

Just then, Ethan's cell phone rang. It was sitting on the coffee table in the great room. He quickly returned, picked it up and answered it. "Hello? Hey, Bob and a Merry Christmas. What's up? Really? You're kidding. Well, we just might have to get a paper and read it." There was a pause, as Ethan listened. "I can't believe they were that kind. Did they make any reference to the 'Haunted House Pianist' anywhere? They did? At the end. But they were extremely complimentary? Wow! I'll tell Shawn. He's here wide-eyed. Yes. Listen. Thanks for calling. Maybe I'll play as well in January there in the city. Yes, it's going to be a terrific program as you well know. Thanks, Bob, and Merry Christmas to you and yours. Thanks. Bye." Ethan put his phone back on the coffee table.

"Well???" Shawn stared at Ethan. "What was that all about? Obviously, it was about your concert. Good news?"

"Bob said the write-up in the music section of the paper was fantastic. Not only in the San Francisco paper but the one in New York, too. He read bits and pieces to me. They said they'd never heard such playing. They were truly amazed. Maybe this will be a step up in my career." He gave a 'thumbs-up'.

But it was rather frightening to him because he didn't remember any of it. He turned away from Shawn as he didn't want him to see the concerned look on his face.

"Wow! That's great! Come over here."

Ethan walked over to Shawn who wrapped his arms around him and gave him a big hug. "What a great Christmas present. And you deserve it. I've heard some of your practices lately and I have to admit, your playing is truly remarkable. It has surprised me, too. Are you doing something different? Whatever it is, keep it up. If things are that good, I hope you have a good encore to play."

"Yep. The Mussorgsky. The *Great Gate of Kiev* from *Pictures at an Exhibition*."

"Oh yeah! That's a great bravura piece to end with. I love it."

It was scary. Ethan realized more and more, it had to do with the rings. Something was totally altering what happened to him when he put them on. Another force took over when they were on his fingers. But if it made his playing that much better, why not? Maybe he could find a way to control the total blackouts he was experiencing at those times. Only time would tell.

It was the day after Christmas and the police in San Francisco were starting the investigation of a gruesome murder. Family members had expected their son in for Christmas dinner. When he didn't show up and he didn't answer his phone, they went over to his apartment and discovered the horrible scene.

The local TV media had a field day with the murder. Police indicated the man had been dead for several days and his body had been mutilated in the most horrific manner. Descriptions were coming out. It looked like he was attacked by a pack of wild animals. No one could understand why since he was a quiet man and seemed to have no enemies. He worked for a local business as a salesperson and was liked by all the customers and employees of the establishment.

The police narrowed down the day they thought he had been murdered but no one could establish his comings and goings around that day or the previous ones. His last day at work had been two days prior to that date.

Even his neighbors had no idea as they didn't remember seeing him or hearing anything out of the usual. This gave the idea to the police that he must have known his killer since there was no sign of forced entry. The thought of multiple killers was dismissed. A group would have been obvious and no one made mention of any unusual group. Somehow, the killer must have made his move on him before he could make any outstanding sounds.

All of his friends were interviewed and taken off the list of possible suspects. It made no sense to anyone why he should be dead, especially in such a gruesome manner.

There were several important pieces of the puzzle never released to the public that might help catch the perpetrator down the road. The case though sensational grew cold after a few weeks and went out of the limelight. Other cases took its place.

The New Year came and it was almost time for Ethan's next concert. It would be the first of his 2008 season and would start in New York. Shawn said he would drive him into Boston, so he could take the train. He could stay at Shawn's company's apartment for the few days he was there. This had been cleared with Shawn's boss. Shawn would have attended but had to fly to Florida for the day of the concert to consult with a new client.

Ethan was booked to play fifteen concerts this year. Twelve were solo and three were with the local orchestras. His solos would consist of several popular classical pieces but would also include his most recently finished composition. Although exhausting, he liked to play at least two and a half hours' worth of music. With the price of tickets, he thought his public deserved to get their money's worth.

Chopin, Liszt, Debussy and Rachmaninoff were among his most favorite composers. To him, their music wasn't only filled with dynamics and expression but they were the kind people could hum and always liked. He shied away from many composers, thinking most of their music being too academic for the average listener. Ethan always said he liked to play 'pretty stuff'. The work he'd be playing with the orchestras this time would be the *Rhapsody on a Theme of Paganini* by Rachmaninoff. He knew everyone loved the *Eighteenth Variation*.

This first concert would be at Carnegie Hall. It was a place he'd played before and liked. He liked the piano there. It was a bright and full-sounding instrument.

During the drive into Boston, there was some small chatter about Shawn's new client and Ethan's concert. Ethan would have two days to practice on the piano in the concert hall before the actual concert. It would be strictly a formality as he had all the pieces well under his fingers.

Over the four-plus months, since Ethan first found the rings and put them on, the initial overwhelming power surge had finally passed while he had the rings off. He accepted he would only wear them when he was to perform or practicing. This would prevent any strangeness at other times. After all, they seemed to be providing the best results, during a performance.

Ethan was taking a short rest the day of the concert when his cell phone rang. "Hello? Oh! Hey, Bob. You're coming tonight? Great. No. Don't worry. I'm taking a taxi. Sure. See you tonight. What? It sold out? Standing room only? You're kidding! Wow! Okay. Tonight. Bye."

Ethan began to get ready and dress. He looked in the mirror and smiled. He went to his bag and pulled out the small box and opened it. There they were. He went over to the mirror again and looked in it. He put on the rings.

Suddenly, he looked in the mirror again. He shook his head. He was standing there in casual clothes. "What the hell?" He looked over to the bed. There were the formal clothes he was wearing to the concert. Beside them was a program of the concert. He looked over at the clock by the bed. "It's one-thirty. But it's bright sunshine out."

It had happened again. The concert was over and it was the next afternoon. He looked at his hands. The rings were gone. He checked the box. They were there. It was exactly what happened in December.

"Holy shit." He whispered. "Damn. I don't remember a damn thing. Hope the concert went all right. Hope I didn't kill anyone." He began to giggle but his fears were rather upsetting.

Suddenly, his cell phone rang. It was sitting on the coffee table. "Hello? Bob. Hey. What? Incredible? Really? Dinner? Okay. We can talk then. Yes. I left quickly after the reception. It was exhausting. I'm resting still. Okay. See you tonight. Six? That's cool. Come up and we can go somewhere. Okay. See you then. Later."

He didn't feel tired but he thought he should lie down for a while. He set the clock for five. He got in the bed and fell immediately to sleep.

It seemed like no time had passed when the alarm went off. Ethan got up, took a shower and dressed. While waiting for Bob to arrive, he turned on the TV. The local news was on. The sports information was chattering and then they were about to wrap it up before the national news was to come on. The last report was regarding some late-night murder the night before.

"I'm so glad Shawn and I are out there in the country. All the violence and crime here in the city. I swear." Ethan shook his head.

At that, there was a knock at the door. Ethan got up, turned off the TV, headed to the door and opened it. "Hey, Bob. Ready?"

Even with the length of time he and Shawn had lived in the city, Ethan had cooked and they didn't go out that often. Occasionally,

Shawn had to entertain a client but that was every blue moon. Bob, being an agent for several clients and meeting with folks to set up tours, did a lot of entertaining. Bob always knew the places to go.

⟫◆⟪

"How are you tonight, Mister Baker?" The host was cordial as he showed them to a secluded corner table. "Your waiter will be with you shortly. Good to see you again." He smiled, bowed slightly and left the table.

Shortly, a young man approached the table and smiled. "Mister Baker. Good evening to you, sir. And how are you doing?"

"I'm fine, Franklin. Thanks for asking. And a Happy Belated New Year."

"Thank you, Mister Baker. To you as well."

"Franklin, this is my friend, Ethan Trendeau."

"Yes, I know. I recognized him." He turned to Ethan. "Mister Trendeau, I was at your concert last night. Amazing. Simply amazing. I thoroughly enjoyed every note." He smiled.

"Thank you, Franklin. Thank you very much." Ethan smiled back.

"May I take your order for drinks? Mister Baker, I know what you want unless you want something else? And what about you, Mister Trendeau?" Finding out the cocktails, he bowed slightly and left the table.

Real conversation began right after the cocktails arrived and orders were taken.

"Well, I knew you played exceedingly well or I'd never have taken you on as a client but that last night. It was remarkable! Unbelievable! What has happened to you? Geez! Your playing was spectacular. The audience went ape-shit at the end. Then, you came back out for your encore. What can I say?! I thought you were going to take out the piano with the *Great Gate* at the end. Holy crap. Fantastic."

"That good? Really? I didn't realize."

"Didn't realize?? The people were going wild. How could you not realize?" He paused for a moment and looked up in the air. "I have to admit, you did keep a rather aloof attitude throughout the whole thing. And at the reception, you were cool as a cucumber. Even with all the doting from your fans. Friendly but aloof. And the write-up today was amazing. Even the critics who showed up after hearing about your charity concert last month were flabbergasted. They're all saying you have a new life in your playing. I have to completely agree."

"Well, I'm glad everyone thinks it went so well. That's a good thing."

"And what happened? All of a sudden, you were gone. You were talking with some young man and when I turned around, you had disappeared. No goodbye, no nothing. But I guess you were tired like you told me on the phone. Hell, I'll bet you burned a shitload of calories the way you went at the keyboard. Wait till you hear the recording. I'll get a copy to you as soon as I can. Shawn is going to be totally surprised at the applause and cheers. I asked the technician to leave them in so Shawn could hear them. Damn. You deserve every one of them, too."

They shared some additional talk about upcoming concerts. Bob thought the program was great, well-balanced and he suggested Ethan play the *Great Gate* as an encore often. It was a smash hit with everyone. He chuckled when he said he thought they were going to have to get a new piano after Ethan had attacked it the way he did with all those big chords at the end.

***

Shawn was waiting at the station when the train pulled in. "I'm so glad it all went well. Things went great for me, too. They want to build a small office complex down there. It should be a snap."

"Well, I'm so sorry you didn't get to hear it. Everyone said it was pretty good. Bob is going to send me a copy of the recording. He said he's going to work on having it turned out as a CD for sale. He's always looking for a way to make a buck. But that's okay. It's also more bucks for us." He gave a big grin.

Shawn agreed. "Hey! You've got that right."

CHAPTER IX

Headlines in the New York City papers and the TV news were about a horrible murder that took place in a rather upscale area. A man, thirty years old, was found mutilated in his apartment. Police couldn't find any point of forced entry, bringing them to believe he somehow knew his killer. Body parts were all over the bedroom. They had to find his wallet to realize who they thought he was. They wouldn't be completely sure until the coroner compared dental records. One of the police said it looked like some wild animal tore him to shreds. This was definitely one for the books.

Although there was a thorough investigation, nothing was found, giving them some lead as to whom or what committed this grizzly murder. Interviews were done with other tenants in the building who saw and heard nothing.

Investigators knew it had happened the night before. The victim's friends had seen him the day before. He was supposed to meet with a few of them for lunch the following day. His phone was never answered. This was something very unusual for the man. Concerned, they came by and asked the manager to check on him. That's when they all discovered the horrendous scene.

It took some time but after several days, the police got the dental records. The remains were who they thought it was. After several weeks, nothing turned up, leading them in a direction. There were several pieces of evidence they kept from the public due to their unusual characteristics. They could be used should some solid lead arise.

<hr/>

After Ethan's concert in January, Bob's phone kept ringing off the hook from music societies and organizations, seeing about booking Ethan for a concert. Ethan's name was racing through the music community like a flood due to his astounding two recent performances. He knew there were thirteen more concerts already lined up during the year and didn't want to overburden Ethan. He knew playing a two-plus hour concert was no easy feat. It was both physically and mentally exhausting. He'd always joke with Ethan that it sure was a lot of notes to remember much less get them in the right place and at the right time. He wouldn't book anything without Ethan's approval.

Ethan was pleased with the response and Shawn was ecstatic at Ethan's fame. He told him he should go for it. "Strike while the iron is hot." But he didn't want him to feel under any great pressure either... only if he wanted to do them.

Ethan called Bob. "I'll tell you what. If you can line them up, so I'm not jumping from pillar to post, back and forth, it would be great. They'd have to be in close proximity and around the same time. I don't want to do one in Miami then to Chicago then back to Orlando. Can that be worked out? Cool. July? I think that would be fine. Great. Lump them together? Yes. Just make sure you give me at least a day before so I can check out the piano. No. That should be fine. I can do that without getting overly tired. Just make sure I have about two weeks where I get to come home. I don't want to forget what Shawn looks like." He chuckled. "Let me know what you set up, so I can get with Shawn and let him know. Yes. He's all for it. He told me to strike while the iron is hot. I think he's right. Okay. Thanks, Bob. Talk with you soon. Bye." He turned to Shawn. "Bob is going to set up additional concerts, starting in July. I can do that."

"For you, it'll be like falling off a log." Shawn clapped his hands. "And I can tell everyone I'm the one who lives with the most famous pianist in the world."

"Yeah. And gets to sleep with, too." Ethan gave a huge grin and flexed his eyebrows several times.

They both slapped their hands together in a high-five.

"I'm taking one of the Chopin pieces out and adding the Granados. It's so beautiful. My piano teacher played it once in a while. I have never heard anyone play it as well as she does and I've heard Rubenstein and several others do it. They can't touch Jeannine. I swear if I can ever play it as well as she does. Wow!" Ethan shook his head.

"I've heard you. The *Maiden and the Nightingale* is a beautiful piece. You play it very well. What's your complaint?"

"But you never heard Jeannine play it. What can I say?" He paused for a moment. "I'm going to check out a few other pieces I can switch out, so the program will be varied somewhat. It'll give a little variety. And I can tell them the changes when I walk out on stage. I don't think anyone will mind. Have to find a few good bravura pieces to play as an encore, too. Can't keep playing the *Great Gate of Kiev* forever." He snickered. "There's the solo version of the *Liebestod* by Liszt from Richard Wagner's opera, 'Tristan and Isolde'. I can also do Debussy's *La Cathedral Engloutie* as an encore."

"Oh, yeah. But I do love the *Great Gate*. It gives the piano a major workout."

"Hey. It gives the piano player a workout, too."

"Liszt did several good pieces besides the *Liebestod* to choose from. There's the *Harmonies du Soir* and the *Andante Sostenuto* section from the *Sonata in B Minor*. That one is a real bravura selection. I love it. I have a couple already in the program. Maybe instead of taking out the Chopin, I'll take out some of the Liszt and use them for encores. Yeah, that would be good. Rachmaninoff as well."

"His *Eighteenth Variation* for solo piano would make a great encore." Shawn commented. "I know the purists want it played with the orchestra but I love it as a solo work. It's just as pretty. And don't forget Liszt's *Sixth Hungarian Rhapsody*. Yeah."

"I'll think about that. And hey, if they don't like what I'm playing, they don't have to come."

"Damn." Shawn got a surprised look on his face.

"What?" Ethan scrunched his face.

"You're turning into a damn diva already. Geez!" Shawn shook his head.

They both roared with laughter.

CHAPTER X

Over the next three months, Ethan played his established touring schedule. Four concerts in all. In early February, he played in Chicago. Early March was Houston. Then, New Orleans in late March. He returned to San Francisco for his regular concert in mid-April. His repertoire wasn't the same as his charity concert the previous December. After each and every one, the raves and adulations poured out. Selling tickets was no problem. They were selling out far in advance, knowing he was coming.

The additional concerts Bob had placed in Ethan's schedule, beginning in July were selling out as soon as people found out about them. Bob couldn't believe it. Needless to say, the increase in the bank account was a nice thing, too. Bob had also been setting up several recording sessions. With Ethan's popularity racing to the top, there was no time like the present to cash in on this side of the business. One session had taken place in March between the two concerts that month. Ethan had played enough pieces to make a two-CD set. Those would be hitting the market right after his San Francisco concert. His first CD was already selling like hotcakes.

Shawn was so proud of Ethan, he took a loan to get him an Imperial Grand made by the Bösendorfer Company of Austria. He had it delivered while Ethan was playing the San Francisco Concert.

The day Ethan returned, he walked into the great room to see it where his old piano used to be. "Oh! WOW!!! I don't believe it. One of the things I've always had on my bucket list but knew I'd probably never have. It cost more than twice as much as the damn house did."

"You deserve it. You should have an instrument that's of the highest quality as your playing. The best for the best."

Ethan ran over to Shawn and hugged him tightly and started to cry. "But you shouldn't have. It's too much."

"Hey." He looked into Ethan's face. "As I said. The best for the best." He gave Ethan a big kiss. "You have worked hard for this and you deserve it."

"Okay. But only if you let me pay for at least half. I mean Bob said the money's coming in, hand over fist."

"Yeah. And most of it is going into your retirement fund." Shawn responded.

"You mean, OUR retirement fund." Ethan insisted.

They both cheered and raised fists into the air.

Meanwhile, the police in San Francisco were investigating another murder there. It was just like the one the previous December. Everything about it was the same. Even to the unpublicized evidence. It's how they knew it had to be the same killer.

The police decided it was time to see about getting some extra help. Luckily, the commissioner knew of a close friend who was extremely good at putting crime puzzles together.

Bruce stood at the sink, brushing his teeth. His dark brown hair was constantly falling down over his eyes. "Maybe one day they'll invent a toothpaste that won't stick to a guy's mustache and beard." He finished and wiped his face with a towel. He looked in the mirror and saw some had fallen onto his chest. He shook his head and wiped it with the towel. "As much as I like fur on a man, why couldn't I have been allowed to grow hair on my chest? There's something about a furry chest that just makes a guy more masculine looking." He kept looking in the mirror. "Well, I don't look that bad." He turned to the right and left several times to see himself. "Wait! Am I shrinking?" He stood erect to view his five-foot-eleven, well-built frame. "Maybe not." He thought he looked pretty good for a man of forty-two. He struck a quick muscleman pose, turning again to see himself in the mirror. He had a big grin on his face and he gave a quick chuckle. "Now, off to work!"

———⟫◆⟪———

Bruce stood at a table in the conference room, looking down at several piles of paper and photos. He began to peruse the collection, picking up several photos. He picked up two photos similar in subject matter but from the two different murders. "Is this all?" He spoke softly.

The police sergeant, standing in the room with him, looked at him. "What?"

"Is this all?"

"Yes, sir. These are all the photos."

"Oh. I'm sorry. My bad. No. I mean, murders. Is this all the murders?"

The sergeant looked confused. "Why, yes. There have only been two that are similar to this."

"Okay. I'm sorry. What I meant is are there any more like this? Anywhere else? Anywhere else in the state? The country?"

"Oh, geez. I have no idea. I'm not sure anyone has checked anywhere else."

"Well, do me a favor. Ask someone to send out some inquiries, asking about similar events. I'd like to know if there have been any. Check major cities first. Then, we can go from there. And if there have, I'd like to see what information they've got. Ask them if they would be so kind as to fax and email any information they have to us here."

"Yes, sir. Immediately."

For the next few days, Bruce plunged headlong into the project, looking for connections or possible unseen clues. He was very pleased the local investigators had tied everything together as best as possible and not left any strings hanging.

He started going over the last victim's comings and goings to try and find out when he was most likely murdered. Checking the interviews with those who knew him, the last time anyone remembered seeing him was at a piano concert the night before his remains were found. They had seen him at the reception after the concert. Among the collected items from his apartment was a ticket for the concert found in his wallet. The program was found on the coffee table.

He looked at the information on the program and saw the phone number. Pulling out his cell phone, he called it. "Yes. I'm calling about the piano concert last week. No. I didn't get to attend. Yes. I'm sure it was spectacular. Ethan Trendeau. Yes. I will. But I have a question. I understand there was a reception afterward. Could you tell me when it ended? Around eleven-thirty? Interesting. Why so late? Oh. Sounds like he is really trying to give his audience their money's worth. Yes. I'll have to see about going to one and hearing him play. Thank you. Thank you so much for your help. Goodbye."

At that moment, Sergeant Johnson came into the room. "Glad you asked us to check. There have been two others very similar. Houston and New York. Here's the stuff they faxed over to us." He placed everything in two additional piles on the table.

Bruce looked through the papers and photos from Houston. Then, he went through the information from New York. "Interesting. Very interesting. I need to go over this stuff more closely."

"Would you like some coffee?"

"Thank you, Johnson. I'd love a cup. Cream. No sugar."

Reading through the information from both cities, the interviews made all the victims seem to have regular routines with the things they did. One thing that did stand out the same was they both had gone to a concert the evening before. A piano concert. He looked closer at the faxed copies of the concert tickets and programs from both.

"Damn. This is so weird." He looked up at Sergeant Johnson. "Did you see this?" He held up the pictures of the tickets and the programs and handed them to Johnson. "What do you see there?"

"Pictures of two concert tickets and two programs. Piano concerts." He looked right at Bruce. "Damn! This is something rather strange. Both concerts were played by the same person. Ethan Trendeau."

"Yes. And both of our victims here went to a piano concert played by the same Mister Ethan Trendeau." He held up the bagged tickets and programs from both crime scenes. "Johnson, please get me some information on this Ethan Trendeau. Find out who his agent is. I want to give him a call."

"Certainly." Sergeant Johnson left the room.

Bruce looked at the two tickets and programs from the local murders and the photos from the other two murders. This couldn't be just coincidence. There had to be some connection. "Four concerts and four murders. Yep. There's something very strange here."

It didn't take long for Sergeant Johnson to come in, handing Bruce a piece of paper. "Here's the number you wanted. Mister Robert Baker in New York."

"Thanks. Oh. What time is it?"

"It's just after eleven."

"Great. It's just after two there. Thanks." Bruce picked up his cell phone from the table. "Yes. Hello. I'd like to speak to a Mister Robert Baker, please. Oh. Mister Baker. Oh. Okay. Bob. My name is Bruce Livingston and I'm calling about one of your clients. No. I'm not trying to set up a concert with Mister Trendeau. I'm working in an official capacity here in San Francisco with the police department and needed to find out information as to Mister Trendeau's concerts and schedule. No. No. No trouble. Just putting a puzzle together here and he happened to become one of the coincidental pieces. No need to bother him about it. Yes. I know he played two concerts here. Yes. One last December and one the middle of this month. That's right. I was wondering if you could tell me about any concerts he played prior to the one in December. Going back about a year. Thank you. Okay. One in January of two thousand and seven, two in February and two in March. He didn't play anymore? Oh. He was working on his new program and he was also taking time off to move from the city. Could you tell me where he played those concerts and any he played since then? Okay. Let me write this down. January twenty-third last year in Miami. February second in Saint Louis. February eighth in Chicago. March twelfth in Boston. March twenty-first in Richmond. December nineteenth in San Francisco. January fourteenth this year in New York. February sixth in Chicago. March seventh in Houston. March twentieth in New Orleans. And April eleventh here in San Francisco. That's all. Okay. Thank you. I'll have Sergeant Johnson contact you with the fax number here. And if you wouldn't mind, could you fax me his upcoming schedule for the rest of this year? I'd gratefully appreciate it. No. Don't worry. If we need anything else, I'll get back to you. Thank you again. Yes. Goodbye."

"Johnson. Please, check these police departments and see if there are any murders similar to ours on or around these dates. And please, call Mister Baker, so he has the fax number here. Thanks." He handed him the list he'd written down. "If so, ask them to send us copies of all they have. Thank you. Think I'll go to lunch. I need some rest, too. I'll be back tomorrow." Bruce headed out of the office.

CHAPTER XI

Bruce had been going over all the information that had come in. There seemed to be no bizarre murders in any of the cities where concerts had taken place before the one in December in San Francisco. He wondered about the two played in Chicago and New Orleans. Nothing had been reported there. At least not yet.

He began going over the upcoming concerts. Here it was Sunday, May 4th and surprisingly, one was scheduled that night in Saint Louis. He had an idea. He called in Sergeant Johnson. "Could you do me a favor? Fax some details of the murders we've been working on along with a set of photos over to the Saint Louis Police and ask them if they've had any recent murders that could fit these."

"Right away."

"Let me know what they say as soon as you hear back. I'm going to take an early lunch."

Returning about an hour later, he was told there had been murders in Saint Louis recently but none that fit the description that had been sent to them.

It was Tuesday, May 6th around eleven in the morning, when the phone rang at the San Francisco police department, asking for Bruce Livingston.

Bruce picked up the phone, sitting at the end of the table in the conference room. "Yes. This is Bruce Livingston. Captain Carmichael. Saint Louis. Yes. How are you? Yes. I'm a friend of the commissioner here and he asked me to look into two murders we've had here. Yes. Several police departments consult with me on some of their cases. There was? You say the photos I sent you are virtual duplicates of your murder. Interesting. And the murder took place on the night of the fourth, didn't it? Oh. I had a hunch. And there was no sign of a break-in either, was there? Thought so. No. No crystal ball. But listen. I'd be truly grateful if you could send copies of all the info you have on it. And photos, too. Especially, the ones of the concert ticket and program. No. Seriously. I swear I don't have a crystal ball. Just a good hunch. Yes. Thank you so much, Captain. I will. Goodbye." He hung up the phone and looked at Sergeant Johnson who was sitting across from him at the table. "Yep. Another one in Saint Louis."

He pulled out the concert schedule. "Hmmm. The next one is in Seattle on the twenty-second. That's just over two weeks away. I think it's time for a road trip. Do me another favor. Could you ask someone to book me a flight to Seattle tomorrow and get me a place to stay close to the police department? Thanks."

<hr/>

It was May the 8th and going on nine in the morning when Bruce walked into the Seattle police department and to the main front desk. "Good morning. Good morning. I'd like to speak to your captain, please." He paused slightly. "It's regarding a murder."

The officer at the desk scrunched his eyebrows. "A murder?"

"Yes. My name is Bruce Livingston and I've been working in coordination with the San Francisco police department."

"Just one second." The officer got up and walked down the hall.

After a few minutes, the officer returned accompanied by a young-looking Hispanic man, with black hair and a closely trimmed beard and mustache. This man approached Bruce and extended his hand. "Captain Mario DeSilva. Welcome to Seattle, Mister Livingston."

Bruce smiled, shaking Mario's hand and noting that he was around the same height as himself. "I hope you don't mind me being so forward but I was expecting to see a much older man. I'm very surprised to see such a young person in your position."

Mario grinned. "Well, thank you. But I've been blessed with good genes. I'm actually forty-two years old."

Bruce was amazed. "Forty-two! Wow! I thought you were in your early thirties. But, you're my age! Kudos for good genes."

Mario got a questioning expression on his face. "And what is this about a murder? Please, come into my office." Bruce and Mario walked down the hall and entered the captain's office. "Have a seat, Mister Livingston." Mario gestured to the chair in front of his desk.

As Bruce was sitting down, he commented. "No formalities needed. Call me Bruce."

"Certainly, and call me Mario. Now, tell me." He remained standing at his chair behind his desk.

"I know this is going to sound very strange but I'm expecting a murder to take place here in your city on the night of the twenty-second. A brutal and gruesome one. That is if I can't figure this whole thing out by then."

Captain DeSilva looked right at Bruce then looked down at his desk and started to snicker. "Okay, did someone put you up to this? This is a prank, isn't it?" He looked back at Bruce. "Who put you up to this?"

Bruce looked very seriously at Mario. "I wish I was joking but I am extremely serious. From what I know, I can almost guarantee there will be one on the night of the twenty-second. And it will look like this." He opened his briefcase and pulled out the photos and other papers. He handed the photos to Mario.

Mario took the photos and started looking at them. He looked at Bruce with concern and question then back at the photos. "These are horrible. And you think there's going to be a murder here? Like this? You have to be kidding me. You know this isn't funny. But how? Do you have some crystal ball?"

"Here. Sit down. Let me explain." Bruce knew this was going to take some significant convincing.

Mario took a seat at his desk and the conversation began.

Over the next hour, Bruce went into detail about previously known murders and how they all happened, during a time a concert had taken place in each city. "Now, this is what is very weird. Not only were they piano concerts but they were when the same Ethan Trendeau was performing."

Mario shook his head. "You have to be kidding me. That's so off-the-wall."

"Is there any way I can get a ticket to the concert coming up? I would like to see this Ethan Trendeau and check him out." Bruce was firm in his comment.

"Would you mind company? Think I'll go with you and see what you can tell me." He reached for the phone on his desk. "Johnny. Check around and find out where this Ethan Trendeau is playing a piano concert on the night of the twenty-second. Get two tickets, please. Thank you." He hung up the phone and looked over at Bruce. "How about some lunch? I'll ask one of the guys to run down and bring up a few burgers and fries."

"Cool. Thanks, Mario. That would be great."

They continued to go over the information Bruce had brought with him. They were interrupted, about fifteen minutes later. It was Johnny.

"Sir. I called. Yes. Mister Trendeau is playing but the tickets are gone. Totally sold out. I spoke with a Miss Jackson. Here's the number if you need it."

Mario reached for the piece of paper. "Thanks, Johnny. I'll call." He reached for the phone. "Miss Jackson, please. Oh, Miss Jackson. This is Captain Mario DeSilva with the Seattle Police Department. Yes. It is imperative I get two tickets to the Ethan Trendeau concert.

Official business. Yes. I've heard he's amazing. World's premier pianist? Yes. I have heard. But it is extremely important we attend. It's of the utmost importance. Yes. We can? That would be perfect. And would it be possible to attend the reception afterward? Great. It will be me and a Mister Bruce Livingston. You'll let them know to expect us? Excellent. Thank you, Miss Jackson, for your help. Yes. You, too. Goodbye." He looked at Bruce. "No tickets. All the seats are gone. Every single one. But. She said we can sit backstage in the wings where they are setting up seating for the overflow attendees. If we get there early, we can pick out the seats we want. She'll let the stage personnel know we're coming."

"Damn. Actually, that could be a good thing. We can peruse the audience from there. Not that we'll see anything but you never know. The reception could be interesting as well."

"I can't believe I'm going to a cultural event to try and solve a murder. Especially, one that hasn't happened yet. I haven't been to something like this since I was in college." Mario shook his head.

Bruce responded. "Hopefully, we can stop a murder by going. I really do like the piano. I studied when I was a kid but never really continued with it. Oh, I play a little for my own amusement. Have gone to several piano concerts over the years. Seems this Trendeau is the next, up-and-coming pianist of the ages, the way he's being praised by everyone I've spoken with. Those who've heard him can't seem to say enough good things about him. It should be fun if nothing else."

⟫◆⟪

The days before the concert, both Bruce and Mario did some research on Ethan. One thing that became very clear was somewhere, between his concert in March of 2007 and December of that same year, his playing became dramatically different. Before, he was acclaimed for his excellent playing and interpretations. But with his December concert, his playing took on a completely remarkable form. Everything about it was unbelievable. Everyone said it was the most incredible piano playing they'd ever heard. By attending the concert, Bruce and Mario would find out if all the adulations were warranted. Mario thought Bruce would probably be a better judge than himself.

———————⧓⧩⧨———————

Finally, the night came. They arrived backstage around seven to check things out. What surprised them was many of the attendees had already arrived and were getting seated. They immediately chose the seats that gave them the best visual advantage of the audience as well as the stage.

Mario looked out from behind the side curtain. "Bruce. Look! The place is half-full already."

Bruce glanced around the curtain. "Well, the show will begin in less than an hour. I'm very glad we got here when we did and got our seats." They sat down and waited.

The ebony piano was located about ten feet from the front of the stage and in the center. Bruce recalled an old memory. His first piano recital. The thought made him shake his head and chuckle.

Mario looked at him with a questioning expression. "What?"

"I just happened to be remembering my first piano recital and how I was scared shitless, hoping I wouldn't forget my piece."

Shortly thereafter, several people came and sat in the remaining seats near them.

It was time. From stage left, out walked Ethan. Confident and fearless. The audience applauded. He went to the front center of the stage and bowed to the audience. The applause grew in volume. He stood straight, smiled and walked to the bench. The audience was silent.

As Ethan played the first half of the program, Bruce was truly impressed. He'd heard most of the pieces before. But he had to admit, he'd never heard them played the way Ethan did. There were varying dynamic levels. Wonderful nuances were brought out. Amazing retards just in the right places emphasized the emotion and feeling of the pieces.

During the thirty-minute intermission, they talked about Ethan and his playing. "I must tell you. His playing is truly superb. I'm amazed at his technique. I'd never have thought a man of his size would be capable of playing a fortissimo as powerfully as he does. He must have the strength of an ox. Seriously. I can't wait to hear the rest of the concert. The Granados is a beautiful piece. Wait till you hear it. Many are not familiar with it."

The lights dimmed several times. The second half was to begin. Bruce and Mario went backstage and took their seats.

Again, Ethan appeared as he had before to a loud applause before going to the bench. He began. Just as in the first half, the pieces were played with perfection. When he struck the last chord of the last piece, the sound slowly faded away to silence. Instantly, the place went wild. The audience was standing, jumping up and down with raucous applause, stomping of feet, whistling, and screams. "Bravo!" "More!" "Encore!" Ethan stood, left the bench, bowed to the right, to the left and to the center then walked off stage left. The screams and yells continued. Ethan reappeared again just off stage left, bowed several times then left the stage again. The audience was relentless with their adulations and yells. "Encore!" "The *Great Gate*!" "The *Eighteenth Variation*!" Yells came, resounding from the crowd. After a few moments, Ethan reappeared again, bowed then walked to the piano bench to the continued screams and phenomenal applause. He sat down to an incredible silence.

From the first few introductory notes, Bruce immediately recognized it. So did the audience who for a split second applauded loudly then was silent. Bruce had learned the solo version of the *Eighteenth Variation* from the *Rhapsody on a Theme of Paganini* by Rachmaninoff and knew how difficult it was. The dynamic levels went from one end of the spectrum to the other. Also, retards in the right places could absolutely make the piece.

As the music unfolded, he couldn't believe his ears. This version he'd never heard before. It was much more difficult than the one he'd learned. He was astounded. Bruce watched Ethan carefully as he came to the central section of the piece. The way Ethan came down with those huge bravura chords in fortissimo was remarkable. He had no idea how he could possibly get such a powerful sound from the instrument. Then, it ended with the last set of chords played so softly, Bruce's head shook in disbelief.

The last chords in pianissimo faded into silence. After a moment of complete silence, the audience went ape. It was total bedlam in the place. You'd have thought it was Saturday Night Fights at an arena instead of a sophisticated cultural event. Ethan stood, walked up front and bowed several times, to the screams and yells of the people. He left the stage several times, returning to bow again and again. But the audience kept on.

Bruce was on his feet, clapping loudly and yelling out. "Bravo! Bravo!" He had a big smile on his face. In all his years of going to piano concerts and recitals, never had he heard such playing before. They were right. Everyone was right. Ethan was the next premier pianist of the world.

Finally, after almost ten minutes of applause, the audience realized it was over and it diminished into the combined sounds of multiple conversations and laughter. They were headed to the reception.

"You really enjoyed it, didn't you?" Mario smiled at Bruce. "I have to admit. I'm glad I came. It was something. I'm absolutely flabbergasted how such a man of his size could play such incredibly big chords with that huge sound. I thought he was going to pound the piano into the floor."

Bruce nodded in agreement. "I know what you mean. I've heard he's five-foot-six. Five inches shorter than me. And he has that kind of power and control." He looked out at the audience, moving toward the doors. "Well, we better get to the reception. After hearing this, I definitely want to meet this Ethan Trendeau."

"You know, I haven't seen anyone who looks suspicious at all tonight."

"I know. I looked at a lot of folks, during the intermission but no one stands out. But they rarely ever do. It's always the ones you least suspect who are the guilty ones."

"You're right." Mario nodded.

By the time they entered the reception hall, the receiving line had already begun to form. Mario and Bruce couldn't use police privilege here. They had to stand in line with all the rest, mainly so they wouldn't stick out from everyone else.

"Listen, I know you want to meet him. Something tells me, you know what to say and ask, being a pianist yourself. Go ahead. I'll get us some refreshments." Mario pushed Bruce toward the line.

Bruce obliged and got in it. The line did move at a fairly decent pace and finally, he was there.

Bruce extended his hand to shake Ethan's. "Mister Trendeau. There are no words to express how much I enjoyed your superb playing. I had never heard the Granados played more beautifully. It was incredible." Bruce smiled and looked down at Ethan's hand to see the unusual gold ring he was wearing. He was suddenly stricken with some notion he recognized something. But he shook his head, looked at Ethan again and smiled. "Thank you so much for an incredibly amazing evening."

"I'm so glad you liked it. Do you play?" Ethan smiled back.

"A little." Bruce gave a shy nod.

"Well, if you haven't, you should get the Granados and learn it. But remember the retards. They are very important. Feel the music."

"Why, thank you. Thank you very much. I will." He bowed slightly and moved on to join Mario.

Mario was over near the refreshment table, getting some drinks. There were cocktails but he thought since he was working he should stick to soft drinks. He handed one to Bruce as he walked up.

"Mario, I need to go back to the office. There's something I need to check."

"You've got to be kidding? Really?" Mario was surprised.

"I feel like we're wasting time here. I don't see anything or anyone that looks suspicious."

"Okay. If you say so. Let's go."

They headed out the door and to the car. As they drove along, Bruce explained. "Something about his ring reminded me of something. I'm not sure but I need to check it out. Something I saw in the photos from the murder scenes."

Soon, they entered the precinct. Several of the officers called out. "Hey! Captain! What are you doing here so late? And you're all dressed up. Looks good." Several gave a 'thumbs-up'.

"Just needed to check something." Mario and Bruce went into his office.

Bruce went to his briefcase and pulled out the photos. He started shuffling through them as he quickly glanced at them. Finally, he came to the ones showing the heads of the victims. He dismissed the one of the victim taken in December as too much deterioration had taken place on the head. "Here. Look. Look at that. What does it look like to you?" He pointed at a specific spot in the photos.

"Some sort of burn. Like some branding iron made a mark."

"Exactly what I thought. I never could understand what could make such a mark. Not until tonight. Is there any way your forensic artists can blow up those areas of the photos and make a detailed drawing of them? I think that would be very helpful."

"Not a problem. But they won't be able to do it till tomorrow. My best artist won't be in till in the morning. Let's get some sleep. I'll drop you off on the way home."

"Thanks. That would be great."

CHAPTER XII

Bruce arrived at the precinct about twenty minutes after Mario did. Bruce had walked since it was only a few blocks from where he was staying. On the way, he stopped by a small restaurant and picked up some egg and sausage biscuits, coffee and some donuts just as he had done several times before during the time he'd spent in Seattle. The coffee and biscuits were for him and Mario. The several dozen donuts were for the guys.

The folks at the restaurant were expecting him already and had everything packed up when he walked in the door. Bruce smiled and yelled out as he was leaving. "Thanks, folks. Gratefully appreciate it. You all have a terrific day."

Walking into the precinct, Bruce yelled out. "Here you go, guys!" He handed the large bag of donuts to the officer at the main desk. "Pass them around!"

"You know the guys are going to get used to this." The one officer gave a 'thumbs-up'.

Bruce just grinned and walked on, knocking on Mario's door. "Come in."

Bruce opened the door and put the bag of goodies on the desk as well as the carrier with the coffee. "A little repast for the morning."

"I know what you're doing. Trying to get me fat." Mario snickered. "Thanks. Thoughtful of you as usual. I asked Marty to work on the drawings for you. He said he should have something in a few hours."

"Cool. I tell you, there's something to that branding."

Just then, one of the officers knocked and came into the office. "Captain. Just got a call. You're not going to believe it. But it sounds like the same situation as what you and Mister Livingston are working on. Officers are on the scene right now and have touched nothing. They wanted you to see it first."

"You're shitting me!? No! Really!? Damn!" He looked at the officer. "Call them back and tell them to photograph everything before anything is moved. Especially, anything that looks unusual." He put his coffee down, grabbed his jacket and looked at Bruce. "Why don't you come along? It might help for you to see an actual scene of one of these murders.

"Great. You're probably right."

On the way, Mario shook his head. "What did we miss last night?"

"Maybe it wasn't anyone at the concert. Maybe it's someone following the tour and using it as a cover. There could be a dozen explanations right now with all we know about these damn things." Bruce was going over in his mind the locations of the murders and the fact the concerts were in the same place at the same time.

"Motive. It's not a break-in or robbery. Nothing was taken. They're beyond crimes of passion even though they all took place in bedrooms. None of the victims were related or knew the same people. I am stumped." Mario shook his head.

"Don't feel like Lonesome Louie. I'm right there with you." Bruce agreed.

Shortly, they arrived on the scene. The photographer was finishing up his pictures. "Captain. It's beyond horrible. I've never seen anything like this before."

Bruce noticed the entire apartment was in total order except for the bedroom. Not only did it look like a bomb had gone off in the room but body parts were all over the place. He did expect to see more blood. It was something that had been bugging him and had him wondering from the first time he saw the first photos. "I know this might be strange to say but shouldn't there be more blood?"

The officer from the coroner's office was there and spoke up. "You're correct. With this kind of mutilation, there definitely should be more. A lot more. Somehow, a large quantity has disappeared."

"Okay. How do several pints of blood go missing and then the body be ripped to shreds?" Bruce shook his head.

The officer looked at Bruce with a questioning expression then spoke quietly. "Vampires?"

Bruce looked at the officer and then at Mario who was moving his hand up to cover his mouth. Bruce bent his head down, shaking it. He had to admit. As ridiculous as it sounded, that would definitely explain it. But this WAS a crime scene and someone WAS dead. He and Mario finally composed themselves.

"I'm sorry, Captain. I couldn't help it." The officer said softly.

"It's okay. We get it." Mario thought the moment had broken the tension.

"Mario, I want to look closer at the head. Would it be all right if he picks it up since the photos have been taken?" Bruce pointed at the severed head on the floor.

The officer put on plastic gloves, went over, picked up the head and held it in front of Mario and Bruce. He slowly turned it in several directions.

"There! See!?" He pointed at the marks on the sides of the head at the temples. "It's those same burns. Yes. Please. Keep turning it."

The officer obliged, turning the head slowly in all directions.

"Wait!" Bruce shouted. "Stop! Look." He pointed at some marks on the side of the shredded neck. "Aahhh. Do you see what I see?" He looked at Mario and the officer.

The officer responded. "You have to be shitting me! Oh. Sorry, Captain."

"Now, let's not jump to conclusions here." Mario shook his head. "I know it does look suspicious but I'm sure there HAS to be some logical explanation. When you get this back to the precinct, you make sure the coroner checks those out thoroughly. I want to know what they are and what made them. As to the burn marks, ask him to check them out thoroughly, too. I want a full report on those questions as soon as he can."

"Yes, sir. I will."

"It's the same burn marks I saw on the heads in the photos but I never saw the other marks. They could have been hidden by the severe trauma to the necks, being ripped and shredded. It should be interesting to hear what the coroner has to say." Bruce was thinking out loud.

"Well, I think we've seen everything here unless you need to look at something else." Mario turned to the doorway.

"I'm curious. Was this guy's wallet found?"

"I'm sure. Just a second." He turned to the officers on the scene. "Did anyone find and bag a wallet?"

"Yes, sir. Right here." He handed the bag to Mario.

"Open it and see if there is a concert ticket in the wallet." Bruce looked at the bag.

Mario put on a pair of plastic gloves and opened the bag and the wallet. "By God. There it is. Bruce, you sure do have a nose for what's happening."

Another officer held up a plastic bag with the program in it. "And here's a program from the concert as well."

"When we find out more about the marks, another piece of the puzzle may fall into place."

Mario returned the evidence to the bag and they left the apartment. The police presence was fairly large and several residents were out and being interviewed. Mario turned to one of the officers. "After you get the interviews, let me know what you hear. We'll be back at headquarters."

As they got in the car, Bruce looked at Mario. "Well. I have to say. Those other marks are really interesting."

Mario looked right at him. "If you say ANYTHING about vampires! I swear to God!" He turned away, trying to maintain his composure.

"Okay. You said it. I didn't."

Both were silent as Mario turned the key and they pulled away.

CHAPTER XIII

It was early afternoon the next day when the coroner knocked on Captain DeSilva's door and entered. He had a very weird look on his face. "We need to talk. Something is really out of the ordinary here. If you can call murder, ordinary."

"What's the problem, Robert?"

"This case. I can't figure it out."

"Wait a minute. Bruce needs to hear this I'm sure." He got up and went down to the conference room. "Bruce. My office. Think you need to be in on this."

They were all assembled and seated in Mario's office. Robert began. "This is going to sound absolutely off-the-wall but I ran the tests several times. There was saliva on the body parts." He shook his head. "And I know this is not going to make sense. I can't tell you where it came from. It doesn't match anything. It's like some combination of dog or wolf, kind of human, maybe, and something else. I'm sending it off for DNA analysis to see if they can come up with something."

Bruce got up, slowly walked beside Mario and turned away from Robert. He leaned down to Mario and whispered in his ear, so Robert couldn't hear. "Vampire!" He started to giggle.

"BRUCE!" Mario bent his head down, shaking it.

"What?" Robert questioned. "Okay. Will someone let me in on what's going on here?"

"Nothing. Nothing, Robert." Mario looked up in the air, making a concerted effort to contain himself. Finally, he calmed down and resumed the conversation. "And the marks, the puncture wounds?"

"They were definitely made by the fangs of some animal."

Bruce couldn't help himself, leaned down to Mario, so Robert couldn't hear and whispered again. "Vampires!" He started to snicker.

"BRUCE!! DAMN IT!!!!" Mario hung his head and shook it. It took a few moments but he finally gathered his wits. "I'm sorry, Robert. Continue." He quickly turned, looking up at Bruce and gave an angry stare.

Robert looked silently at Mario and then at Bruce, not understanding their private humor. He continued. "The body was ripped and shredded by fangs and large claws. But there was no sign of animal fur anywhere. As for the blood. It seems the victim must have been overpowered by something. The initial bite must have been around the throat and whatever bit him, sucked out a large quantity of his blood."

Mario was serious as he looked directly at Robert. "Do you know of anything that could do such a thing? Is there any animal you know of that sucks and drinks blood? In that quantity?"

Robert cringed, glanced quickly at both Mario and Bruce with a questioning expression and spoke very softly almost apologetically. "Vampires?"

Bruce and Mario couldn't hold back and just lost it. They broke into uncontrollable laughter. Mario leaned back, laughing so hard, he almost fell out of his chair. Bruce leaned against the wall, pounding on it as he roared in laughter. Robert reluctantly joined in but was still not in on their private joke.

After over a minute, Mario pounded his desk. "OKAY! OKAY! Seriously! Let's get serious here!" He yelled out but continued to laugh. He looked back at Robert.

Robert just shook his head. "I have no answer for you. I'm completely stumped."

Finally, Bruce gathered his composure. "Okay. What about some occult thing?" He changed the direction of the conversation and tried desperately to be serious. "Could a person or a few people with connections to the occult do something like this?"

"I guess anything is possible. People these days do the most heinous things."

"Could it have been done by one person?"

Robert paused for a moment. "It would have taken a big person to overpower this victim as we figure he was just over six feet tall and two hundred and twenty pounds. When he was in one piece. And he was built well, too. Correct. It would've taken a very strong and powerful person to do this. He'd have had to be strong as an ox."

Mario and Bruce looked at one another, hearing that comment.

"Was the victim drugged? That would've helped a smaller person, wouldn't it?" Bruce responded.

"No drugs in the tox screen. He was sober as a judge."

"And what about the branding marks?"

"You know? That's just what they are. Like someone put small branding irons on his head. One on either side right at the temples. And the marks. They seem to have a definite shape."

"I know." Bruce spoke up. "I have been looking at the drawings the police artist did, trying to enhance the details. It looks like the impression of a sheep or goat's skull with horns. The artist who did the drawing said it was the closest thing he could conclude from the marks. Now, what is very interesting is the ring Mister Trendeau was wearing the night of the concert. I didn't get a real good look at it but the ring seemed to have the skull of a goat or ram on it. But I only remember one ring." Bruce turned his head, trying to recall. "I didn't see his other hand. Damn."

"And I remember you saying, you thought he had the strength of an ox the way he played. Do you think he was capable of doing this?" Mario recalled.

Bruce had a questioning expression on his face. "Trendeau is only five-foot-six and looked to be around a hundred and thirty-five pounds. Yes, he might be strong enough to play a fantastic forte on the keyboard but I doubt he could overpower a man the size of the victim. I don't know what to say. I sure would like to see his ring again, though. And see if he has another one on the other hand."

Mario commented. "Well, you said his next concert is in Portland on June first. That's eight days away and Portland is just down the road, sort of. I can contact the Portland department and have them get us some tickets or let us stay backstage as before. I'm sure they wouldn't mind us being there. Especially, when we can tell them to be alert. We could go down tomorrow and check things out and talk with the captain down there, too, and let him know what's happening."

Bruce clapped his hands together. "Damn. That would be great. I'll get everything packed up. ROAD TRIP!!"

CHAPTER XIV

Mario decided to drive one of the department cars since it was police business. The two-hundred-mile trip would also let him get to know more about Bruce. "So. How did you get started with what you do?"

Bruce tilted his head. "Let's see. Ever since I can remember, I always had a nose for detail. Guess it was about fifteen or sixteen years ago, not long after leaving college. Was writing a book and needed to get some info on how the police function. Was a good friend of the commissioner in San Francisco. Well, he wasn't quite the commissioner then but was well on his way. He got me involved with some of the things happening at the time. Soon, I got involved with a case and with my help, it was solved. Got into forensics and found I very much enjoyed the challenge and the puzzle of putting the clues together. I seemed to see things others didn't. He got me in on several cases that year. By the end of the next year, I was doing some consulting with other departments who heard about me. It got to the point where they would only bring me in on really unusual cases. Ones that were REALLY unusual or off-the-wall. And so, here we are." He gave a big grin. "Never did get to write that book." He chuckled. "Maybe one day down the road. Who knows?"

"Well, after this case, you just might have to write a book. This case is more than off-the-wall. It's downright weird as hell and extremely spooky. I know it would make a fantastic story. Especially, if we get to the bottom of it all and solve it." Mario responded.

"We shall see. We shall see. And what about you? Didn't see any wedding ring, so guess you're not married and what got you into chasing bad guys?"

"Think I always wanted to be a cop. Used to dress like one every Halloween. Loved cop shows on TV. Then, I grew up. That's when I knew, I wanted to be one. Thought about marriage but saw several end because of the job. Didn't think it fair to a woman to do that to her. And I really do love my work. Guess you could say, I'm married to it. Had some flings but that's all they were and both parties knew it. I like my single life. I can do what I want, when I want and have to answer only to me. Maybe that sounds selfish but hey. It is what it is." He stroked his mustache with his right hand.

"Same here. I was always doing this and that and never met anyone that just turned my head." He paused for a moment. "Well, there was one once. Back in college." Bruce smiled, recalling a distant memory. "But that didn't happen. Maybe for the best. I guess that sums it up in a few words. I know it sounds boring but I really have enjoyed the consulting. I love puzzles. Always have."

"I feel the same way." Mario nodded in agreement.

"Like you said, this case is truly strange and spooky. Because of that and I hope you don't mind, I tried contacting an old friend of mine. Never got hold of him but did leave a message. His name is Peter. I was hoping he'd join us in Portland if he had the time or inclination. Not sure he will with such short notice. He and I go way back. I think you'll like him. A little in left field but a really great guy."

"What does he do?" Mario was curious.

"He's a professor." He turned to watch Mario. "Now, don't wreck the car but he's a professor of Psychology and the Occult. And..." There was another pause in his voice. "He's... psychic." Bruce was watching Mario to see his reaction.

"Occult!? Psychic!?" Mario turned quickly to look at Bruce then back again to watch where he was going. "Really? You have credence in that stuff?"

"We both agree, this one is incredibly bizarre. Seriously, he is very good at what he does and I mean very good. I have followed his career over the years. Don't worry. Wait till you meet him. I think you're going to be pleasantly surprised. With what he knows about the occult, if there's anything dealing with it, he'll see it right off. As for his psychic abilities, he's quite well-known in that world. No one has ever been able to disprove anything he's said. And trust me, many have tried."

"From the way you talk about him, one would think you actually knew him. I mean almost personally."

"I told you, he and I go way back."

Mario grinned. "All I have to say is... spell my name right."

"What? Spell your name right?"

"Yeah. When you write the book. Spell my name right."

They both cracked up laughing.

It was almost noon when they arrived in Portland but they wanted to get to the hotel first and clean up before heading to the police department. When they got to the front desk, Bruce spoke to the desk manager. "My friend, Peter, might be checking in. Not sure if he will come but if he does, could you leave a message for him that we are here? Since we only have the few pieces of luggage, there's really no need for a bellboy."

The desk manager smiled. "Very good, sir. And your friend has already checked in and is in room four-o-eight. He told me to let you know when you arrived."

Bruce's mouth fell open he was so pleasantly surprised. "Really? He came and is already here? I wasn't sure he would. It's been a long time."

"Would it be possible for all three of us to be in adjoining rooms since we're all working on a case together?" Mario spoke up. "And could you call up and let him know we have arrived? Also, his bill will be paid by me since this is business. I'm Captain Mario DeSilva with the Seattle Police Department." He turned to Bruce. "I'm anxious to meet your friend."

"Yes, Mister Livingston. You're in room four-ten and Mister. Oh, excuse me, Captain DeSilva. You're in four-twelve. Yes, no problem. I will put his room on your bill. I will call Mister Solvinoski immediately and tell him you're here."

"Solvinoski? You're kidding me?" Mario was somewhat shocked at the name. "Tell me he's a gypsy, wears a turban and I will shit."

Bruce couldn't contain himself and broke out with laughter. "No! No. He doesn't wear a turban."

"But he's a gypsy?" Mario tweaked his head.

"No. No. He's not a gypsy, either." All the way to the elevators, Bruce kept snickering.

They got in the elevator and got off on the fourth floor.

"From the arrows, looks like the rooms are this way." Bruce started down the hall.

Just then, a man around forty-four years old, several inches over six feet tall, with dark brown hair, beard and mustache came out of a room ahead. He turned and his steel-blue eyes saw Bruce. "Bruce! My friend! Long time, no see! How the hell are you!?" There was a huge smile on his face as he walked up to Bruce.

Bruce put down his luggage and hugged him. "Peter! Doing well. So good to see you. Damn. Feels like someone's been working out with a vengeance." He grabbed Peter's wrists and stood back to look him up and down. "Geez. With the right clothes, we could pass you off as a Russian czar. You REALLY are looking good." He shook his head. "No. You look GREAT."

"Thanks. I've been doing well." He then turned to Mario. "So, this must be your policeman friend you mentioned in the message you sent to the college." He extended his hand. "Peter. Peter Solvinoski."

Mario shook Peter's hand. "Good to meet you, Peter. Mario DeSilva. Bruce speaks very highly of you. I look forward to getting to know you." He turned to Bruce and smiled. "As I said. I can tell. You DO know him... personally. Yeah. Just wait. I'll get you."

"What?" Peter looked at Mario and then at Bruce.

"Just something Mario and I talked about earlier in the car coming here."

Mario muttered. "Just wait. Just wait."

Bruce continued. "I wasn't sure you'd even get the message. I knew you were a professor there but had no idea if they would contact you or if you were on some adventure somewhere."

Peter responded. "Go put your things up and come to my room. I have ordered lunch for all of us, knowing you'd probably be here by this time. For me, it's mid-afternoon."

Bruce looked at Mario. "Peter's from Boston. Not sure if I mentioned that already."

After getting their things in their rooms, they joined Peter in his. They all pulled up chairs and sat down. A cart had been brought to the room with several goodies, ice and soft drinks on it. They began eating.

"I swear, I wasn't sure you'd come. It's been a long time." Bruce looked at Peter.

"Got the message at the university yesterday and almost fell over when I saw it was from you. I know there were no details but if you needed my help, you should've known I'd come." His face was full of joy. "Bruce. It truly is good to see you again. Damn!"

Mario pronounced slowly. "Sol.. vin.. os.. ki. So. You're a damn Russian?"

Peter grinned. "Oh. No. Bruce's reference to me being a Russian czar, he was being facetious. But don't feel bad. Many think I'm Russian. Actually, Polish. Guess it's like a lot of people think Chopin was French since he spent so much time in France and is buried in Paris. He, too, was Polish."

Bruce suggested. "We're headed down to headquarters as soon as we get cleaned up a bit. Thought you'd like to come along and get into this damn thing. Wait till you see and hear the details."

"Definitely. I would like to get up to speed on this. I'm ready when you are."

———————

Within an hour, all three were heading to the car and were off to police headquarters. Entering, they went to the main desk and introduced themselves and asked to speak with their captain.

"Certainly. Captain Brooks will be with you shortly. He's been expecting you."

Very shortly, a tall, stocky man of fifty-one, came out and walked up. "Gentlemen, how are you? I'm Captain Michael Brooks. Please, call me Mike."

They all stood up and started shaking hands. Mario spoke. "Hello. Captain Mario DeSilva. This is Bruce Livingston and Peter Solvinoski."

"Come into the conference room and sit down. Tell me more about what you're here for. I wasn't quite sure when you called yesterday. But it sounded rather macabre."

Bruce opened his briefcase and took out all the paperwork, setting it on the table and separating it into piles. He looked right at Captain Brooks. "If we can't find a way to stop it, this is going to happen here the night of June first."

After Mike glanced at several of the photographs, he looked at Bruce with a questioning expression. "What!? What are you talking about? You can't be serious?"

Mario looked at Mike. "Do you think we would've come all this way as a joke?"

"But how could you know? Please, explain."

Mario turned in his chair. "I will let Bruce go over it since he's been involved the longest in this thing and has a major handle on it."

Bruce started telling of what he knew and the timeline of events. Then, he mentioned Ethan Trendeau's name.

Peter immediately chimed in. "Bruce! Excuse me for interrupting. But, did you say Ethan Trendeau? The concert pianist?"

Everyone looked at Peter with surprise.

"Yes. This whole thing seems to be wrapped around his concerts." Bruce looked at Peter.

"Oh. You're probably wondering why I ask. I just arrived on the red-eye this morning and know none of the details of any of this. All I knew is, it had to do with some unusual case. This is the first time I have heard the name, Ethan Trendeau, being attached somehow. Very interesting. And from what I have heard so far, now it's beginning to make a LOT more sense."

"What do you mean? You know something we don't?" Bruce was somewhat shocked. "Before I go any further with this, maybe you should tell us why you should say that."

Everyone turned to Peter again.

"Gladly. Now, I can't believe you haven't heard the stories. About Ethan Trendeau?" Peter looked at everyone's unknowing expression. "I see. No one has a clue. Hmmm." He reached up with his right hand and scratched his cheek. "He was being called the 'Haunted House Pianist' right after all that happened at their home in Maine. It was all over the news. They even called me to come help with it, back sometime like the last week of August last year. But I was on my way to the Amazon. Being out of the country, I didn't get any information about the whole thing till after I got back in December. By then most of the dust had settled, so I never pursued it."

"Oh, wait. Yes. I do remember something in the news last year but I have no idea why I didn't connect that situation with Trendeau." Bruce scratched his head. "I also never knew any details about it."

Peter looked at Bruce. "You mean, you never heard anything about a bunch of skeletons found in their basement?"

Everyone's face was filled with shock and surprise. That event was so bizarre they had all passed it off as some prank and the names associated with it just flashed right on by.

Bruce shrugged his shoulders with an unknowing expression. "Wow. Oh duh. My bad. We never did any major research into Trendeau's background. All we knew is that the murders just happen to coincide with his concerts. Due to his physical stature, we thought there was no way he could have committed them."

"What? You're shitting me. I definitely want to hear the whole story on that?" Mike could hardly believe what he had just heard. He rubbed his hand over his clean-shaven face and bald head.

"Yeah, Peter. I'm sure we'd ALL like to hear this." Mario was insistent. "Maybe it'll shed some light on this whole thing and there really could be a connection."

Over the next hour and a half, Peter told of all he knew about the house where Ethan lived, its history and the gruesome findings. Even though he didn't go in on the case, he reviewed it closely after getting home from the Amazon. "So, there could be something to it that Ethan is somehow connected with something strange and macabre. All that happened in that basement was at an occult altar and involved a book, containing spells and curses. Why not? But since the notoriety had disappeared by the time I looked into it, I thought all was well, having been resolved. So, I looked no more into it. It seems I was wrong. Now, Bruce can continue, telling about his cases as I check out the photos he has here. I need to get up to speed on them."

Bruce continued where he'd left off and presented all he knew. Finishing, he paused and looked at Mike. "That's why we believe there will be one horrific murder here in Portland on June first if we can't find a way to stop it. The one reason I wanted Peter in on this is because of his psychic abilities."

Mike's face got a strange questioning look on it. "Psychic? You must be joking?"

Bruce added. "Peter is very good at what he does. And since this whole thing has an occult feel to it, I wanted his input."

"Interesting. I get it. I now understand why you want to go to his concert. I'll have one of the guys go down and ask." Mike shook his head and stared hard at Peter. "Psychic. Very interesting."

"I'm sure all the tickets are gone, so tell whoever is in charge, we're coming in an official capacity and can sit backstage." Mario explained.

"Will do." Mike left the room but returned shortly. "They'll get all that done for us. Four passes backstage. Official police business."

Peter looked up from the photos. "Damn, Bruce. This is one hell of a case. And to think Ethan Trendeau is somehow involved is unbelievable. You do realize, he's becoming the golden child of the piano, being called the world's premier pianist. I haven't had the privilege to hear him play yet."

"Mario and I went to his concert in Seattle and I have to tell you. He's no slouch at the keyboard. His playing is remarkable. Actually, it's absolutely fantastic. He wants me to learn the Granados." Bruce gave a big grin.

"What was his demeanor when you talked with him? Was there anything seemingly unusual?"

"No. He was very nice. What can I say? No demon eyes or gravel voice of the devil. No scene out of 'The Exorcist'. Sorry."

Mike stood up. "Okay. How about we call it for today? I'm sure you all are tired from your trips. We can get together tomorrow and see if we can organize some kind of strategy as the concert is right around the corner."

"I think Mike is right. We need to get our strategy in line and ducks in a row. But let's get back and chill out. I could use a good rest and I'm sure Peter could after coming all this way." Mario stroked his beard. "We'll leave everything here. Mike, if you want to make copies of this stuff, please feel free."

"Great. I will."

"I feel a bourbon coming on." Bruce gave a Cheshire Cat grin.

"Make that two bourbons." Peter agreed.

"I think we can make that three." Mario chuckled. "Mike, join us?"

"No thanks, guys. I still have a bunch of stuff to get done today. But I'll take a rain check if you don't mind. I can already tell, I want to get to know more about all of you. As far as a watering hole, you might check out Barnie's. Tell him I sent you. They'll treat you very well there. The food is good. They'll give you directions at the desk at the hotel."

"Thanks, Mike. Okay. Next stop, the hotel, then the watering hole. Barnie's!"

CHAPTER XV

Mario was rather surprised Barnie's wasn't rowdy. Most bars where a bunch of guys would gather were usually a little loud. Not this place.

Just then, a stocky older man came up to them. "You must be the gentlemen Captain Brooks said would be coming over. I'm Barnie. Hope you like the place."

"Thank you. This is Peter Solvinoski, Bruce Livingston and I am Mario DeSilva." They all shook hands.

"Captain DeSilva, gentlemen, right this way." Barnie led them to a small square table out of the way of traffic in the restaurant. "Robby will be your waiter and he'll make sure you have everything you need. Thank you, gentlemen, for coming." He went back to business.

A few minutes later, Robby arrived and took their drink order. Shortly, he was back at the table with the drinks and find out what they were going to have to eat.

"Anyone hungry?" Mario looked across the table at Bruce and Peter.

"If I get anything, it's going to be a salad." Bruce gave a 'thumbs-up'. "I've had my calories for the day with all that stuff I crammed in my mouth in Peter's room."

Peter agreed. "Yeah. Think I'll do the same thing."

"Well, I'm going to have a steak. Medium rare." Mario was firm. "I'm sort of on that low-carb diet and can eat all the meat I want."

Robby took the order, bowed slightly and left the table.

Bruce lifted his glass and turned to Peter on his left. "Here's to seeing an old friend again." He turned to his right to Mario. "And here's to an incredible new one."

They all raised their glasses, clinking them together above the center of the table.

"Salut!" Peter responded.

"And to two new friends." Mario smiled. After everyone sipped, he looked across the table at Peter. "So. You teach psychology and the occult. Wow. I must be honest. I have been ribbing Bruce about it ever since he told me. And Bruce says you are a…" He paused for a moment and bent his head down. Slowly, he looked up again at Peter. "A psychic, too?" He bent his head down again, trying to hide his skepticism.

"You know, I saw that." Peter giggled.

"Well, you have to admit. It's not every day I run into someone who claims to be a psychic. And I'll be honest with you. I don't want a possible friendship to start off, trying to cover up a lie. I just never put any stock in stuff like that. It just seems so… so… out there. Okay. I did ask Bruce if you were a gypsy and wore a turban. There. I said it. I confess." Mario was apologetic, hanging his head.

Peter started laughing and was joined by Bruce then even Mario.

Peter couldn't get the huge grin off his face. "Mario. THAT is really funny. Seriously. I hope you don't mind but I want to include it in some of my future lectures."

Mario shook his head. "Thanks for taking it with such grace. But you must run into such comments all the time. So, I have one request. Just to give me a sample. Is there anything, something, you could do to give me some example that could help me join the ranks?"

"Not a problem. But would you rather Bruce not be here?"

"Hey. I have nothing to hide. Bruce can stay here. Do you need me to do anything or to hold something of mine?"

"No. I don't need to hold anything of yours. If I was going to do a reading for someone, not present, I'd need to hold something of theirs. You sitting right here across from me is more than enough. Don't forget. I knew a great deal about you the moment we shook hands when we first met in the hotel." He gave Mario a big smile. "And I have to tell you. You're an open book. Too easy. Now, let me see." He paused for a moment. "All through your life, you wanted to be in law enforcement. You would wear clothes that looked like a police uniform and a badge when you would go out for Halloween. The ring you have on. It's not yours. But it's a symbol of why you finally became a cop." He stopped and looked right at Mario. "Mario. Do you want me to go on? This could be painful."

"Keep going. I have nothing to hide."

"Okay." He paused for a moment. "Your father who was a policeman was killed by a man when you were twelve. At that time, you wished you were a policeman to help find his killer. Your ring. It's his ring you wear. I'll tell you, too. Arturo is very proud of you. He watches over you every day, especially ever since you became a cop."

Mario sat straight up, silent and his face displayed his disbelief and shock. His thumb turned the ring on the finger of his right hand.

Bruce spoke softly, looking at Mario. "I told you he was good."

"Mario, I hope I didn't upset you. I didn't mean to do that."

"No. No. It's just that I am… I'm stunned. Nobody knows that. Nobody. No one knew this ring was Dad's. How did you know his name was Arturo?" He looked right at Peter.

"Mario. He's standing right next to you, looking down at you. His left hand is on your right shoulder and he is smiling. I see him very clearly. You look much like him. Same hair, beard and mustache. Same caring eyes."

Mario immediately placed his left hand on his right shoulder and turned to his right. "Holy shit. Really? Right here?"

"Yes. Right there. He's telling me to tell you. He is so very proud of you for all the things you have done in your life."

Mario spoke softly. "Will you tell him, I still love him and miss him?"

Peter smiled. "He hears you and he knows. He has always known. He is also telling me to let you know he will always be there for you. He's smiling and patting you on the top of your hand. Now, he's moving away and fading."

Mario took a quick drink from his glass. "Damn! You ARE good. Geez. If you know that, I feel like you now know everything about me. That's scary."

"Mario, not to worry." Peter looked right at him. "You're a kind and good man. I see all the good things you have done for others and never stepped into the limelight."

Mario took another drink from his glass. "Wow. Wow. What can I say? Wow. Geez." He turned his head and wiped a tear, running down his face with his right hand. "Sorry, guys. But that really hit me. I didn't see it coming. Wow. I see I am definitely going to have to rethink my concept of psychics. Hell yeah. I hope we'll talk again."

"I will warn you. Not everyone who says they are psychic is. Many are true charlatans. Tricksters. Good listeners and asking leading questions. A good reader NEVER asks questions, trying to find out information. Yes, there are a special few who have a real gift, some strong and some not so strong."

"I will tell you. Peter's abilities are right up there with the best." Bruce added.

"I can sure see that. Damn. Wow." Mario was still in shock, shaking his head.

Finally, dinner had arrived. Mario's steak looked so good both Peter and Bruce ordered one. There was small talk during dinner mainly about how good the food was. Before they left the table, they left Robby a handsome tip for his excellent service.

As they got to the front register to pay, Barnie came over. "Gentlemen, not to worry. My pleasure for the finest. On the house."

Mario spoke up. "Barnie, thank you so much for your kindness but seriously. With this economy! Barnie! I'm on an expense account. Hey! Kudos on the food, service and drinks, too. We're truly grateful for the gesture. But if you keep giving stuff away to guys like us, you'll be out of business and we won't have a great place like this to come to." He opened his wallet and paid the bill.

Barnie gave a huge smile. "I am glad you like the place and the food. You know, you're all welcome here, anytime. Thank you, guys." Barnie bowed as they all shook hands.

"Don't worry. We're here for a week. I know we'll be back." Bruce added.

"Be safe out there and don't put yourself in any danger. I like to have customers like you back again." Barnie gave a 'thumbs-up'.

CHAPTER XVI

Over the next several days, they worked together on plans of trying to figure out what to do to try and prevent another murder. From the very beginning, they decided to place several small remote cameras throughout the concert hall where concertgoers would be, including the reception area. Also, one was put at every entrance and exit where people would come and go as well as the stage entrances. Anyone coming or leaving would be recorded. They knew whatever they did would be a long shot for sure. But it was a beginning.

The police went in and placed the surveillance cameras, not letting anyone know their exact purpose as they didn't want to raise suspicion and tip anyone off. They wanted this undercover operation to be just that.

It was the night of the concert. They arrived backstage. Mike asked one of the stage crew about where they could sit without causing any problems. Several chairs were situated in the wings to accommodate the overflow attendees. They found a place out of the way but with a view of the audience as well as the piano located at front and center stage.

Bruce turned to Mario. "Just like in Seattle. There's still an hour before the concert and the folks are piling in already. They're like moths, being drawn to a flame."

"Yep. You're right. But don't worry. Everything is being recorded tonight. Maybe just maybe we will catch a murderer tonight."

As the eight o'clock hour arrived, so did Ethan to the piano. The enthusiastic reception was just as in Seattle.

"This is incredible." Peter was astounded at the reception. "Now, I REALLY can't wait to hear him play."

As Ethan's playing progressed, Bruce watched Peter who seemed to be spellbound by the playing.

During intermission, they milled among the people, looking to see if they could find anything out of the ordinary. But just as before, there was nothing standing out about the folks from the audience.

One thing Bruce brought to their attention. Ethan was wearing rather large rings, one on each hand. He made an effort to look at his hands when he first walked onto the stage at the beginning of the concert.

Finally, intermission was over and the lights dimmed several times. Everyone returned to their seats.

As Ethan played the last chord of the last piece written on the program, again, the audience erupted in a raucous display. After several leavings and comings with bows every time, Ethan returned for an encore. With the striking of the first forte chord, the audience went into a momentary loud applause and then was silent.

Bruce and Peter instantly recognized it. They saw that Mario and Mike were not sure what it was.

Peter leaned over and whispered softly to Mario and Mike. "It's Rachmaninoff. The *Maestoso* from the *Moments Musicaux*."

The piece was played flawlessly and with incredible dynamics. Again, with the fading of the last two huge, booming forte chords, the audience went wild.

Ethan got up, took several bows then left the stage. He re-entered several times, bowing each time as the applause and adulations continued. Then, he went over and sat at the piano again.

After a few moments of silence, he struck the first three forte chords. Again, there was an instant applause then immediate silence before the next three chords in pianissimo.

Peter leaned over and whispered to Mario and Mike. "It's another piece of Rachmaninoff. The *Prelude in C Sharp minor.*"

After the final soft chord faded, the place went berserk with yells, applause and jumping up and down by the audience. Peter had never in his life witnessed such a display at a sophisticated function.

Ethan got up from the bench and walked to the front of the stage. He bowed several times then turned and left the stage. With the raucous continuing, he returned to the stage and took several more bows and left. After several minutes of yells and applause, all realized it was over. It was time to head to the reception.

Bruce and Peter made a beeline to the reception as they were anxious to get close to the front of the line and talk with Ethan. Bruce wanted to see the two rings and to view them closer if possible. Peter wanted to see what he could get from reading Ethan. Mario and Mike headed for the munchies and drinks.

Bruce was in front of Peter. This would give Peter a little longer time to be near Ethan and watch his reactions as Bruce spoke to him. Shortly, they were standing near Ethan.

Ethan looked at Bruce. "It's you again. Did you get the Granados yet?"

Bruce was shocked Ethan could remember him even though it had only been just over a week since last they met. "No. Not yet." He shook Ethan's hand and looked down quickly to see the ring more closely. He could see the distinct design of the ram's skull. "I brought a friend of mine to hear you play. He had heard about you and wanted to come very badly. This is Peter." Bruce deliberately kept holding Ethan's hand, so he would have to extend the other one toward Peter.

Peter reached out to Ethan's other hand. There it was. An identical ring was on his hand. "Your playing was amazing. I've never heard those pieces played so... so... damn. There are no words to describe it." He wanted to remain calm, so as not to let his guard down.

"Peter, I am so glad you enjoyed it. Do you play?"

"Yes. Yes, I do. But not anywhere near as well as my friend here does." He glanced at Bruce.

"Gentlemen, I am so glad you enjoyed the program."

Bruce spoke again. "Well, let us not take up your time as there are so many who want to meet and talk with you. Thank you so much for such a wonderful performance."

"You're so welcome. Maybe I'll see you gentlemen at some of my future engagements. And you, sir, get the Granados and learn it. You'll be glad you did."

"You just might. I will. Thank you again for an extraordinary evening." Bruce nodded his head as he and Peter moved away.

Bruce and Peter headed to the refreshment table where Mario and Mike were standing. Peter shook his head.

Bruce saw him do it. "Did you have enough time to get anything? What's wrong?"

"I don't believe it." He spoke softly. "Nothing. Absolutely nothing. Something's not right here." Peter's face had a questioning and disturbed look.

"What do you mean?" Bruce didn't understand.

"Ethan. There was nothing. He was completely empty. Or there was some wall, preventing me from getting anything about him through it. Something's not right here. We need to watch him."

They walked over and told Mario and Mike of their discoveries. They'd all be on alert to watch Ethan and check out his actions.

Bruce and Peter noticed Ethan chatted with many people after the reception line was over. But there was one young man he seemed to pull aside and talk with a little longer than most. Peter also saw him get a piece of paper from the man. He saw them laugh then separate. Shortly, the young man left the reception.

Mike decided he and Mario would follow him. The man's connection with Ethan seemed a little out of the ordinary. The plan was if there was nothing overly strange, they would all go home and meet the next morning at the office and go over the camera footage.

Bruce and Peter would stay and watch Ethan and see where he went after the reception.

The young man left the building and walked several blocks to a multi-story apartment building. They followed along. They went with him through the main entrance and joined him on the elevators. Since they were not actual tenants of the building, it was the only way at the time. They didn't have passkeys to the front doors. The elevator went to the sixth floor where the young man got out. Mike and Mario did as well. The young man turned to the right. They turned to the left, so as not to be conspicuous.

They slowly walked down the hall yet turned, glancing to see where the young man went in. When he did, they immediately turned around and quickly walked down the hall to see what apartment number it was. Then, they returned to the elevators and headed back down to the lobby area of the building. There seemed to be nothing suspicious. Mike decided to go back up to the sixth floor and remain till the designated time they all had agreed on. Mario would stay in the lobby. Around four in the morning, there was nothing out of the ordinary. They decided to call it a night.

Bruce and Peter knew Ethan was staying at a hotel very close to the concert hall. They tailed him as he walked back to his hotel. Entering the lobby, they watched him go up in the elevator. About twenty minutes later, they saw him come out in casual clothes and walk out to the street. They were carefully behind.

"Oh, damn!" Bruce watched him get into a taxi that was waiting at the street and drive off. "Peter, see if you can get the number off that cab. We need to find out where he is going."

Even with the number of the cab, they were stuck. Their car was back at the recital hall and it would take about ten minutes to get to it.

"I'm sorry. I don't know what I was thinking. Of course, he would be leaving the hotel. Damn! How stupid of me." Bruce shook his head.

"Hey. We all make a mistake now and then. I wasn't thinking about it, either. It's okay. Mike and Mario are doing surveillance with the other guy, so I think we are covered. Let's stay until he returns. That way we'll have a timeline on his return. Then, we can go back to the hotel. We'll get with them tomorrow morning." Peter watched as the cab went out of sight. He knew they had made a grievous mistake.

They sat and waited for hours. It was around four o'clock when Ethan returned. He wasn't in the same cab. Bruce noted the number of the cab.

The next morning, all parties met in Mike's office and shared their stories. Bruce apologized profusely for not being able to follow Ethan when he left the hotel.

"I know. I know." Peter bent his head down. "I can hear you all. How is it that a psychic didn't know he was going to take a cab? Believe it or not, we don't know everything." He shook his head. "But, we did see him return around four in the morning. And there was nothing suspicious." He paused. "One thing very interesting. You would think if he committed such a horrendous murder, his clothes would be covered in blood."

"Maybe we're off base on this." Mario looked puzzled. "We watched the apartment building of the guy till four in the morning and there was nothing."

"No. Something's not right." Peter insisted. "I couldn't read him. That NEVER happens. He was there but it's like he was an empty shell. This is not right. Something's very weird here. It was one of two things. Either he wasn't there in his body or there was some kind of invisible wall around him, not allowing me to get through to read him. I know of no one who can project such a wall. Not unless there is something…" He paused and looked at everyone. "I know this is going to sound off-the-wall but there could be something supernatural here. And I'm thinking demonic."

"Peter, this is the twenty-first century, not the seventeen hundreds. And this is Portland, Oregon, not New England. You have to be kidding." Mike just shook his head.

"Unfortunately, I'm not kidding. This may be the twenty-first century but the evil that existed in the seventeen hundreds as you put it is still out there. We never know where or when it will raise its ugly head. And I must say, I'd love to know where Ethan went when he left the hotel." He looked up in the air as if searching for some answer.

Mario stroked his beard. "So, you're telling us these murders may have something to do with demons and not just some occult shit?"

Peter responded. "Correct."

Mike commented. "Well, before you all got here this morning, I went by the young man's apartment to see if I could check on him. Interestingly enough, he was coming out of the building as I was headed in. He's fine. I don't know what to tell you."

At that moment, one of the officers knocked on the door. He had donuts and coffee for everyone.

Bruce gave a 'thumbs-up'. "Thanks, Jeff, for getting them for me. Give the big bag of donuts out to the guys."

The officer smiled and nodded then left, closing the door behind him.

Bruce yelled out. "Okay, gentlemen. Dig in. Maybe it'll help our thought processes."

Mario looked at the donuts. "I have to say. This case is NOT helping my waistline."

Everyone broke out in laughter and clapping.

They were going to check the surveillance footage later that afternoon but first, they wanted to talk more about all the cases and the details surrounding them. It was about four hours later when there was another knock at the door. An officer walked in. "Sir. There has been a murder across town. And it seems to fit the ones you briefed us on."

"Oh, crap! It happened again. Geez." Mario scratched his head.

Mike took the paper from the officer and looked at the address. "It's nowhere near the address the cab took Ethan to last night. He must have been dropped off and then got another cab. Very shrewd. Very shrewd. Maybe he realized we were on to him." He paused in his moment of thought then spoke again. "Gentlemen, would you like to accompany me to the scene?" Mike stood and reached for his coat. "I know I have no proof but I just know he's involved." He looked at Peter and chuckled. "Maybe I'm a little psychic, too."

Everyone just shook their heads accompanied by quiet moans and groans.

Within forty-five minutes, they pulled up in front of a small house. Standing on the front steps, was a very distraught young woman with several officers consoling her.

One saw them pull up and came over to talk. "Sir. This is the sister. She came by to meet her brother for brunch and found him. Or at least, she thinks it's him. I've been inside and it is not pretty. The coroner is on his way. Nothing has been disturbed."

Mike looked at the three. "Okay. I guess we can go check this out."

Just as before, nothing seemed out of place in the whole house. It didn't look like a break-in or the like. It seemed the victim knew his killer. Again, the bedroom was the scene of the event. Even though they'd seen it before, it was still difficult to think such horror could be done to a human especially, if it was being done by another.

"I want to see if the burn marks are there." Bruce went over to the place where the mutilated head lay on the floor. He got down to look, so he wouldn't move anything. "I see one mark. The other one if any is on the side against the floor." He got up and headed back to the door with the rest of the guys.

The police photographer arrived and took his pictures before the coroner started his work.

In the meantime, the four went to talk with the sister who was sitting in the living room. Her name was Sharon and was still very distraught but knew she wanted to cooperate in hopes it would help with the investigation.

Answers to all the obvious first questions were negative. Her brother had no enemies, no people who hated him and no angry girlfriend. Then, questions as to his activities and whereabouts were next. Finally, she indicated they had talked on the phone the day before and were going to meet for brunch today. "He was going to tell me what he thought of the concert he was going to attend last night."

"Concert?" Peter chimed in.

"Yes. He was going to see this up-and-coming, very popular concert pianist, playing in town. I think he said it was an Ethan Trendeau."

"Really?" Peter was slightly taken aback. "Do you have a recent photograph of your brother?"

She went into her purse and pulled out her wallet. Going through it, she took out a picture and handed it to Peter. "This was taken a few months ago. Jack and I had gone to New York for a week to see the sights."

Peter looked intensely at it and handed it to Bruce. "Did he go to the concert with anyone or meet anyone there?"

"Oh. No. He told me the tickets were rather expensive. David is out of town, so there would've been no one else."

"David?"

She looked into the faces of those standing there listening. "David is… Jack's best friend. He lives across town." She was pleased to see no judgmental looks.

After passing the picture around, so they all could see it, Bruce returned it to Sharon.

"Sharon. Thank you so much for your help. Again. We're so sorry for your loss." Mike took her hand and patted it. He turned to the others. "Do we need anything more here? Forensics will finish up and we can review it all later."

All agreed there was nothing more they could do until others had done their work. It was back to the office.

Entering the office, they all sat down. There was a short silence before Mario spoke up. "I remember that guy last night. I didn't want to say anything around his sister."

"I saw him, too." Mike added. "My thoughts were the same."

"I was watching Ethan the whole time last night and all those who interacted with him. Jack was one of them." Peter continued, staring blankly in remembrance. "They spoke in a very friendly manner. I couldn't hear what they said. But there were smiles and laughs. I saw or felt nothing to indicate they were going to meet later."

"Yes." Bruce recalled. "Nothing suspicious. And Jack left long before Ethan did." He looked at the rest. "I still find it almost impossible to think Ethan is somehow connected. He seems to be a personable guy. I think we need to interview him. I think Peter could really get something from him if we could sit and talk for an extended time."

"I think you're right." Mario agreed.

"Where is he now?" Mike wasn't sure.

"We can check with his agent. It's how we knew he was performing here." Mario added. "His number is in the paperwork." He began to shuffle through the pages. "Yeah. Here it is."

"Let me have it." Bruce wrote the number down. "I have talked with his agent before. I'll be right back." He left the room. Shortly he returned. "Since his next concert isn't for another three weeks, he's going to be at home. In Maine. I didn't say anything about going for a visit yet as I wanted to check with you guys first." Bruce turned to Mario and Mike. "Okay, guys. Since you're into this thing, I think it would be great for you to come with us."

Mario looked at Mike. "Okay. What do you say? Since we're into this thing up to our necks, it might be a good idea to tag along. I know it's out of our jurisdiction but what the hell. Maybe we can get the help of the local guys. And I have to admit, I sure as hell would like to see the house where all that shit happened."

Mike responded. "I agree. Let's do it."

Bruce clapped his hands. "Excellent. I'm going to contact his agent again and arrange a visit. I'll tell him about Peter and his abilities and how he wants to see the house where all the crazy shit happened. I will phrase it more delicately than that." He looked over at Mario and Mike. "I won't say anything about you two. That way he won't know you're with the police." He looked at Peter. "Could you see about making reservations, if you don't mind since that area of the country is your territory?"

"No problem. We can stay in one of the dorms at the university in Boston. It's summer and the campus has a lot fewer students. We can drive up from there."

"Hey! 'All for one and one for all!'" Mike chuckled.

"Ah. There are four of us, not three." Mario challenged Mike's comment.

"Excuse me. Actually." Peter added. "There originally were four musketeers but one was killed, leaving just the three."

Mario rolled his eyes. "Of course. I should have known Peter was not only psychic but also a Mister Know-It-All. And I mean that in a kind way."

They all began to laugh and clap their hands.

Peter looked over at Bruce. Then, they yelled out in unison. "Road trip!!"

All continued laughing and exchanged high-fives with one another.

CHAPTER XVII

Ethan and Shawn were rather surprised when Bob called to see if a visit could be arranged. Especially, with Ethan just getting back from his concert in Portland. They were very interested when they heard of Peter and his background. Maybe he'd have some insight no one else was able to find, regarding the room in the basement. Ethan thought it would be very exciting.

Since Bob indicated there would be four visitors, Ethan and Shawn went grocery shopping to make sure they had enough food for everyone for at least a week or more, knowing it would take some time for Peter to get everything settled. They were sure it would be a process that wouldn't happen overnight and they wanted to be prepared.

Peter had no problem getting the troops settled in the dormitory. All organized the next morning, they took Peter's SUV to make the long trip up the coast from Boston. All were pleased that getting to see Shawn and Ethan hadn't been a hassle. Peter was sure the visit would shed a very bright light on everything.

Mike and Mario were rather surprised when they found out Ethan had a partner. When Peter was telling what he knew about Ethan, they realized they just hadn't heard it when he'd said 'their' house.

It was going on twelve-thirty when they pulled up to the house. Peter spoke as he looked through the front windshield at the façade. "I can't believe it. The evil that's been done here. Even from here, I can feel the whole spectrum of horror. Damn! I should have come when they called me last year! Damn! This is a powerful center and I know we're going to get much answered here. I have a feeling they'd never have bought the house if they knew. Bruce was smart not to tip our hand as to who you and Mike are." He looked at Mario. "I doubt Ethan realizes you and Mike are in law enforcement. Bruce told his agent about me and thought it a great idea to see if I could make any sense of the happenings here. I doubt he would remember you and Mike from the concert receptions."

Mario commented. "I think you're right. Mike and I never got in the 'meet and greet' line. We went to the refreshments."

Shawn came out to greet them as they got out of the car. "Gentlemen! Welcome! I'm Shawn McAllister." He started shaking hands. "Please, come in. Ethan's fixing a little something. I'm sure you could use it after your long drive up here from Boston."

"I'm Mario DeSilva. This is Bruce Livingston, Peter Solvinoski and Michael Brooks."

Peter immediately broke into the conversation. "Nice to meet you, Shawn. Yes. We're very interested in the house. I've been hearing much about it. My colleagues and I, all wanted to see for ourselves. Maybe we could shed more light on what has happened here. I must also admit, I'm a great fan of Ethan's. He truly is an exceptional pianist."

Shawn was happy to hear the compliments regarding Ethan as he opened the front door and they all entered.

Ethan came from the kitchen to greet them. "Hello, gentlemen and welcome! I've been looking forward to this visit ever since Bob called me. I hear Peter is very into this type of strangeness. After Bob called, I did a little research on him and know he's top of the line in this sort of thing. I've always wanted to go to a psychic but was a little skeptical. Sorry, Peter. Just being honest with you." He extended his hand in Peter's direction. "The only reason I know who you are is from your picture on the computer research I did."

Peter extended his hand. He immediately recognized Ethan wasn't the same man they'd met before, during the concert. He was totally different. No walls surrounded him. He was an open book but Peter could also sense that Ethan was hiding something. It was also obvious that there was no recognition of Bruce. This was strange since he got the impression at the concert, Ethan had a keen sense of memory. As he shook Ethan's hand, he saw no rings. "Peter. Peter Solvinoski."

"Nice to meet you, Peter." He turned to the others. "And who do we have here?" He then extended his hand toward Bruce.

"Bruce. Bruce Livingston." He shook Ethan's hand but realized Ethan had no idea who he was. He quickly glanced over at Peter.

Peter saw the questioning look on Bruce's face and instantly interrupted. "And this is Mario DeSilva and Michael Brooks." He gestured in Mario and Mike's direction.

Bruce completely understood Peter's break into the conversation. He didn't want to give it away, regarding the lack of recognition.

Ethan shook hands. "Gentlemen, please, come into the dining room and get something. I've put some things on the table. Help yourselves." He led them into the dining room and then headed to the kitchen. "Shawn! Would you mind helping me with getting the glasses? And gentlemen, when you fill your plates, please, go sit in the great room. We'll bring your drinks in a few minutes. I hope no one minds that the tea is already sweet and with lemon."

Shawn spoke up. "Okay, folks. Dig in. And by the way, Ethan is a really good cook." He left the room.

The instant they were out of earshot, Bruce spoke softly. "He didn't know who I was. What's with that? He recognized me at the concert but now, I'm a stranger to him. I don't get it."

"Yes, I know. I didn't want you to spill the beans. That's why I interrupted before you could say anything. Ethan is NOT the same man we met in Portland. I think we need to tread cautiously, so we can get some footing here. Don't let the cat out of the bag. Let them talk and maybe we'll learn something we wouldn't by letting on. And did you see? He doesn't have the rings on."

Soon, they were all seated in the great room around the large coffee table. Shawn came in, carrying a tray with ice-filled glasses and a large pitcher of tea, placing it on the table. "Okay, folks. No need to wait for us. Use the coffee table and side tables to put your glasses and plates."

With everyone finally situated in the great room, Peter started the conversation. He wanted to get close to them by asking something personal. "Ethan. I see you have a Bösendorfer Imperial Grand."

Ethan's face lit up. "Yes. Yes, it is. Shawn gave it to me. I thought it rather extravagant since they're so expensive. But he told me the best should have the best." He turned to Shawn with a look of love on his face.

Mike looked at Peter. "Ethan makes it sound like it cost a king's ransom."

Peter replied. "Yep. You could use that as a comparison. We're talking here, not to be crass but like two hundred grand."

"WHAT!!??" Mario and Mike yelled in unison.

Mike yelled out. "Are you shitting me!? Two hundred grand!?" He looked around. "Oh. Sorry. It's just that..."

Everyone roared with laughter.

Bruce added. "That's correct. A nice chunk of change. I've heard it takes over seven years from start to finish in making one."

Mike shook his head. "Seven years!? Damn!"

"One of these days, I'll have to tell you all about how it's done and why it takes so long."

Ethan was surprised. "For you two gentlemen to know that information, you must play." He looked at Bruce and Peter.

Bruce jumped in. "I play a little. Basically for my own entertainment."

Peter turned back to Ethan. "It's the same for me. Nothing special. I do wonder. What about the salt air here? The strings I know will rust."

Ethan explained. "Shawn had plated strings put on it before it was delivered. They're very rust resistant."

Peter shook his head. "Interesting. Excellent. Well, I do hope before we leave, you might play something on it. It truly is a beautiful instrument."

"I would love to. And you are going to have to come to one of my concerts. I'll see about getting you all tickets."

Mike, Mario and Bruce glanced at Peter after hearing the last comment by Ethan but said nothing. He had absolutely no recollection of any of them from his previous concerts.

Bruce quickly spoke. "Please, tell us how you ended up buying this house. It looks amazing."

Shawn and Ethan shared in the story and how it happened. Then, they got into the part about the discovery in the basement and the notoriety of it all.

All the while, Peter sat and took in all he could from Shawn and Ethan's conversation.

Shawn was a straightforward guy. There was nothing hidden in him. His love and pride for Ethan seemed to glow inside him and there wasn't the slightest bit of jealousy, regarding Ethan's fame. Peter could sense the true pride he had for Ethan when things turned to Ethan and his abilities at the keyboard. He sensed Shawn's heart beating a little faster when Ethan expressed his gratitude with the gift of the piano.

Peter knew from his sense of Ethan, something was truly amiss. Ethan was an open and happy man, giving and kind. He could tell his love for Shawn was quite profound. But he had no idea what it was that prevented him from reading Ethan at the concert and why Ethan presently had no idea who he and Bruce were.

Peter continued to direct the conversation so it revolved around Shawn and Ethan. This wouldn't let them in on the fact that Mario and Mike were with the police who were investigating gruesome murders they thought Ethan could somehow be involved.

There was also a sense of the house and all that went on there in the past. A trip to the basement would definitely prove to be very informative. But he didn't want to push it. He waited until Shawn or Ethan made the suggestion to go there.

"Well, Peter, I'm sure you're interested in seeing the basement." Shawn finally suggested. "Maybe there's something you can sense no one else has been able to do."

All headed to the basement. Once assembled there, Peter asked if he could go into the room first. He didn't want any outside influence.

He walked through the opening in the wall. Lights installed, during the investigations almost a year prior, now lit the room. Immediately, Peter was overwhelmed with the horror of the room and the power of evil that once played out there. He let out an audible gasp.

"You all right, Peter!?" Bruce yelled. He headed to the opening.

"I'm fine! I'm fine! It's unbelievable, everything that's here. Give me a few more minutes." Peter could feel the residual presence of evil. Even after all the time that had passed, a demonic source was still permeating everything. He could sense the great number of sacrifices that took place in the room. All the victims were used to elevate a demon along with the one doing the sacrifices. Peter walked around the room, looking at the symbols and markings on the walls. His hand touched the altar and immediately, a flash of horror pierced his mind. He knew he had to get out of the room and not return for a while. But. It would be necessary to return. The center of the evil was here. If it could be stopped, it would have to take place here. He needed time to think.

Mario saw Peter come out of the room. "Damn! You look like shit!" He turned to Shawn and Ethan. "Sorry. Excuse my French."

"But he does look like shit." Shawn was concerned. "Sorry, Peter. Are you all right?"

Peter commented. "Maybe we should go upstairs and talk about this."

E. THORNTON GOODE, JR.

"I wouldn't mind a drink, either." Peter nodded.

"How do Bloody Marys sound? Ethan makes a killer Bloody Mary." Shawn spoke with enthusiasm.

Mario, Mike, Bruce and Peter looked at one another, hearing the comment and all gave a 'thumbs-up'.

All were finally seated in the great room again with drinks in hand. Mike took the first sip. "Have to admit. This is damn good. Venture to say one of the best I've ever had." He turned to Shawn. "Keep this one. Not only can he cook but he's a damn great bartender."

Everyone clapped their hands and snickered.

Ethan smiled. "My father once told me, I would make someone a great wife."

Everyone cracked up with raucous laughter.

Bruce looked at his glass. "Yep. A great Bloody."

Mario added. "Usually don't get into mixed drinks but this one is refreshing and tasty and has one hell of a snap. To our hosts." He raised his glass.

All joined in. "Hear! Hear!"

Peter looked at Ethan and Shawn. "I'm not really sure how to explain this and I don't want you to be alarmed but there's something very strange yet demonic still here. And it's centered in that room. I could sense all the horror and sacrifices that took place there. But it's not gone. I can't explain it or describe it. It's just something I know." He looked at Ethan. "I have no desire to frighten you about this but this needs to be addressed. I must ask questions and I hope you don't feel overwhelmed by them. Your answers may provoke newer questions. We must take our time with this, too, to make sure we discuss and cover every facet. I hope you don't mind."

"Will it create any trauma here? The house isn't going to burst into flames, will it?" Ethan seemed terrified. "You know. Like in the movie, 'Carrie'."

There was a moment of silence with everyone, finally realizing what they'd just heard Ethan say was the same vision everyone imagined. The house going up in a blast with everyone in it. The mental image caused all to get a nervous expressions on their faces.

Peter shook his head. "No. No 'Carrie'."

"Well, I didn't mean for it to sound so dramatic." Ethan bent his head down.

"Not to worry. I'd first like to do something to start the ball rolling here." Peter spoke in a calm voice. "Does anyone have any problems with being hypnotized?"

Shawn shook his head. "If it will help, no problem here."

Ethan was a little skeptical. He was afraid something could come out about the rings. "Well, I'm not sure I'm really up to it."

Shawn looked right at him. "How could you not want this thing put behind us? I don't know why you wouldn't want something done if it will help."

"I guess. I know you're right." He hoped nothing would be mentioned, regarding the rings. But he then realized, he had never met them before and they had no idea about the rings.

"Ethan, I see you're still reluctant. Don't worry. It doesn't hurt and I won't make you stand up and act like a chicken, clucking around the room." Peter added. His comment broke the tension in the room.

"Okay. Okay." Ethan blushed slightly. "You're right."

"First, I want to do this to get a handle on what happened the day you both opened the room."

Shawn interrupted. "But we were not the only ones."

Peter looked surprised. "What!!? What do you mean!? There were others!? When you said, 'we' broke into the room, I just assumed you meant you and Ethan."

Shawn spoke with apology in his voice. "I'm so sorry. We talked about the discovery so quickly, we never mentioned there were others involved with opening and checking out the room. Geez. I guess it did sound like Ethan and I did it by ourselves. Seriously. I'm so sorry."

Peter smiled. "No problem. I do understand. After all, it's been nearly a year since it happened. So, there was someone else here at the time?"

"There was Hank." Ethan looked at Peter. "And later Jake."

"Hank? Jake? And who are Hank and Jake? I definitely need to have them here, too. Please, tell me they aren't far away."

"Oh. Hell no. Hank helped us break the opening and get into the room that day. He lives in town." Shawn commented. "And Jake is the local sheriff. They're like right around the corner, kind of."

"Do you think they would come? It's very important that I get their input." Peter paused for a moment. He turned to Shawn. "Jake? He's the sheriff? Is that Jake Banister?"

Shawn was surprised. "Why, yes! Yes, it is! But how could you know that?" He paused for a moment then chuckled. "But of course. You're a psychic. Stupid me."

Peter smiled and shook his head. "No. Not to worry. I'll explain later how I knew his full name."

"Let me call Hank. I know he will. He can call Jake and ask him. I'm sure they would love to help. You should hear Hank's stories about this house when he was young and how he used to sneak into the basement." Shawn got up and headed to get his cell phone in on the kitchen counter.

"He used to sneak into the basement? When Jeremiah lived here? Wow. I DEFINITELY want to talk with him." Peter called out then looked over at Ethan. "Would it be possible to get another Bloody Mary? That last one was so good."

Ethan took Peter's glass and headed to the kitchen.

Shawn came back into the great room. "Hank wants to know when you want him to come over." He looked right at Peter.

"How about around nine tomorrow morning if that's good with you and Ethan."

"He said he'll be here and will drag Jake with him. He actually sounds excited on the phone." Shawn called out to Peter. "He wants to know if he needs to bring anything with him."

"Tell him to do me one favor. On his way over, to stop by the Catholic Church and get eight blessed candles. One hundred percent beeswax if at all possible. And a quart of holy water. Whatever it costs, tell him I'll reimburse him."

"Hank said he heard you and it's no sweat. He can't wait." Shawn hung up and walked to the kitchen to put the phone back on the counter again. Returning to the great room again, he commented. "Wait till you meet him. Wait till you meet both of them. They really are such cool older guys."

Peter apologized. "I hope you all don't mind, but I'm too tired to do anything today and I don't want any Bloody Marys under my belt, either, when I'm doing it. This is going to take all my concentration."

At that, Ethan returned with Peter's drink and handed it to him.

Peter took the glass. "Thank you, Ethan."

"You need candles and holy water?" Bruce was curious.

"I have a stash in my bag of tricks in the back of the SUV. I just want to make sure I have enough. Never hurts to be truly prepared."

Shawn looked at his watch. "Ethan fixed some fried chicken, potato salad and some slaw for dinner. I'm going to go put the chicken in the oven. I'll wrap it up, so it doesn't dry out. Should be ready in about an hour. How does that sound?" He quickly got up and headed to the kitchen.

Mario clapped his hands. "Sounds good to me. And I love fried chicken."

Peter turned to Ethan. "I don't want to impose but I'd love to hear you play something now. If you don't mind."

"I would be glad to." Ethan got up and headed to the piano. "Yes. Shawn was so loving to get it for me. But I can't help saying it again. I absolutely love it."

Peter looked at Mike and Mario. "It is said, they are the finest pianos made. Wait till you hear it. The sound is amazing."

Mike snickered. "Well, for two hundred thou, it should be. At that price, I'd almost expect it to play itself."

Everyone giggled and clapped their hands.

"Does anyone have a request? I'll see if I have it under my fingers." Ethan turned to everyone.

Bruce spoke out. "Play whatever suits you." He paused a moment. "No. Wait. Do you happen to know The *Maiden and the Nightingale* by Granados? It's a truly beautiful piece of music. But wait till Shawn gets back here."

Peter was extremely pleased Bruce was playing the game exceedingly well.

Ethan sat at the piano and played the piece spectacularly.

Bruce couldn't believe it but it sounded as new and as fresh as it did at the concert in Seattle. Yet, Ethan was not wearing the rings. He found that very interesting.

Finally, the sound of the last chord faded. Everyone applauded.

Peter spoke. "Yes. Yes, it's a stunning piece and you played it flawlessly."

"Thank you, Peter." Ethan looked at Bruce. "I'm surprised at your choice of music. Not many are familiar with it. For you to know of it, it's obvious to me, you must play well."

Bruce responded. "I'm familiar with that piece. I've contemplated getting the music and learning it as I always thought it was so beautiful. Thank you so much."

Ethan turned on the bench and looked at Bruce. "Well, since you play, you must come play something and see just how wonderful an instrument the piano really is."

"Oh, no. I'm not very good." He bent his head down.

"Oh, come on, Bruce. You can do it." Mario called out.

Everyone joined in the calls of persuasion.

Ethan called out. "We'll do a duet. And I know Bruce knows it. Come on, Bruce."

Bruce got up and walked to the bench.

Ethan looked up. "You sit in the treble and I'll do the bass."

Bruce sat down at the upper end of the keyboard. "Okay. What is it?"

Ethan hit the first several chords of the piece and stopped. "I know you know it." He looked right at Bruce.

"Yes. Yes, I do." Bruce chuckled. "I'll nod when I'm at the end."

At that, they both played several runs of *Heart and Soul*. Ethan varied the bass accompaniment as Bruce ran through several melody lines in the treble with octave chords and harmonic note clusters. Bruce nodded to Ethan when he had run out of variations, indicating it was at an end. And as Ethan held the last chord, Bruce played the 'we do mean you', ending with a tremolo chord.

Ethan and Bruce smiled, stood up, gave each other a high-five and then a few short bows to the raucous applause and cheers of the others. "Thank you. Thank you." They chimed in together.

Ethan immediately spoke up. "Bruce. You'll have to come to one of my concerts and I'll call you up on stage. We can play that piece together. The audience will love it, I know."

Everyone broke out in cheers and began clapping in approval of the suggestion. There were several loud, 'Oh, yeah's, as well.

Ethan smiled. "I would love for you to play something solo when you like. I want to hear you play by yourself."

Bruce nodded. "Well, all right. But not right now. Maybe another time."

Ethan gave a 'thumbs-up' and clapped his hands. "Okay. Now, let me get to the kitchen and get everything ready to eat."

"Shawn, do you happen to have the number of the local inn in town? I wanted to call and see about accommodations for all of us tonight." Peter stood up and started getting his cell phone out of his pocket. "I should have done this much earlier."

"You'll do no such thing! You all are our guests until we get this whole thing taken care of. Ethan and I went grocery shopping and have enough food for an army for at least a week or more. We stocked up on everything. You should have heard the folks at the store when we basically bought them out of eggs, bread, sandwich stuff and other things." He chuckled. "And before coming home, we hit the booze store, too. As for sleeping, we have four bedrooms upstairs and two down here. Ethan and I can sleep down here in one of the rooms south of the great room. And you all can each have a room upstairs."

Bruce chimed in. "That's ridiculous. You and Ethan can stay in your own room. Mario can have a room. Mike can have his. Peter and I can share the other one. We were roommates in college. It's not a problem." He looked over at Peter.

Peter nodded. "No problem here. We can pretend we're back in school."

"Really?" Shawn verbally expressed the surprise on everyone's faces. "But there are two bedrooms down here and there's only one double bed up there, not twins."

Bruce snickered. "Hey. We can put pillows down the middle of the bed like in 'It Happened One Night' with Clark Gable and Claudette Colbert. We can fight over who'll be Clark Gable."

"Now. THAT's funny!" Ethan laughed.

"Yep. We became roommates Winter Quarter of my Freshman year. Peter was a Junior. We stayed roommates till Peter graduated."

Mario shook his head. "I guess you really HAVE known each other for a good while. I knew it. I just knew it."

Shawn spoke up. "Great! That's all settled. Now. Let's eat. Mario, just so you know. Ethan fixes a damn good fried chicken."

CHAPTER XVIII

Peter sat on the edge of the bed, removing his boots. "Heading to take a shower. Back soon." Peter left the room. He returned some twenty minutes later, wrapped in a towel and carrying his clothes and toiletry case. "Had to wait a few minutes for Mario. Mike's in there now. Wait a few. He should be done shortly. I really do want to talk anyway. I know now how important it is. But not till you get back from your shower."

Bruce picked up his toiletry case and went down the hall to the bathroom. He saw Mike coming out and heading to his room. He nodded a goodnight. He returned after about fifteen minutes to see Peter still sitting on the edge of the bed. He looked down at him. "Okay. What happened?"

"What happened?"

"You know what I mean. When you left school? You disappeared into thin air." Bruce sat down on the other side of the bed.

Peter looked down at the floor. "Yes. As I said, I do want us to talk. I guess I should explain from the beginning."

"Ah. Yeah. That would be a good start." Bruce was miffed.

"After I graduated, I went to grad school in Boston. I had a grant."

"You never wrote to me. What happened? I'm ready to hear." Bruce spoke with disappointment in his voice.

"You know." Peter shook his head and looked at the floor again. "I guess I was unsure and immature. I didn't want to build something for the wrong reasons. I had no idea how it would play out. I wanted to get away, get my education finished and my career started. And remember, it was another time. I knew it wouldn't be easy back then."

"Peter, when you left, I tried to find you. It took several years. But I finally did. And when I did, I saw you were well on your way in your field and a noted academic. I was happy for you. Do you know, I went to one of the conferences where you were speaking just to see you? I was going to come up to meet you afterward but had second thoughts. I was sure a handsome guy like you had moved on and found that special someone. And I wasn't about to come interrupt your life and open old wounds. I cared too much to do that."

Peter looked at Bruce. "As time passed, I thought the same of you. I wondered how you were and how you were doing." Suddenly, a surprised expression crossed his face. "Was that possibly the conference in Saint Louis about ten years ago?"

Bruce nodded and was amazed that Peter knew exactly the one he was referring to. He just grinned. But then he realized Peter's abilities.

"Damn. Now, it makes sense. It was the only time I've ever been flustered when talking in public. Something kept creeping into my head, breaking my concentration and I never could put a finger on it." He bent his head down, shaking it. "It was you."

Bruce continued. "Yeah. Over the years, I went out looking. Had a few short encounters. But every single one of them was lacking that 'something'. I knew shortly, they'd never last. So, they ended. I kept searching, really not sure what for and just couldn't find it. But I knew deep inside me what it was. I just couldn't admit it to myself."

"I guess we were both caught in the same dilemma. I was doing the same damn thing. Searching for that... 'something'. It finally came to me a few years ago. I was reflecting back to our time at school." He looked right at Bruce. "To what we had. The fear I had back when I was young. Afraid I had built a relationship on the physical. I realized my fear was totally unfounded. Bruce, we had so much more than just something physical. We had a connection that's so difficult to find. A mental and emotional connection as well as a physical one. I had thrown it away because of fear and uncertainty. And it was too late. I had lost you."

Bruce smiled. "Damn! What can I say? I had the same revelation a few years ago myself. Every time I met someone and tried to start something meaningful, it didn't work. I kept comparing it to what we had back then. None of them came anywhere close to what we had. That person wasn't the one I wanted or was looking for. I now know. I was constantly, looking for you." He paused a moment before continuing.

"Do you know, I can remember when I first saw you at that pep rally at school? You in those white pants and your letterman sweater. Yeah. You. The head cheerleader. I thought you were the cat's meow, so good-looking with that dark hair, beard and stache. Geez. I can see you now in my mind." He paused in his memory. "I almost shit a brick when a few days later there came that knock at my dorm room door and you were standing there, asking me to go have a cup of coffee with you. Peter, I had an instant connection with you. I thought it was the same for you. True. There definitely was that physical connection. Wow. Hell, yeah. But I could feel something stronger even more important, something more lasting."

Peter nodded. "Funny you should say that. I remember that day all too well myself. I was leading a cheer and looked up in the stands in front of me. And there you were. Eighteen, clean-shaven, your hair blowing in the wind. And you smiled. Something happened. Something clicked. Yes. There was that physical thing. But you're right. There was also something else. Something I couldn't put a finger on. I knew I had to meet you."

Bruce continued. "I think it was then it happened. But when you left and I didn't hear from you, I thought maybe what we shared for almost two years wasn't the same for you as it was for me. Maybe it had been just the physical for you. And when I finally found you and saw you were happy and doing well, I didn't want to upset the apple cart by barging in. Especially, if you were with someone. Yes, I followed your career and your success but stayed at a very long arm's length. I didn't want to pry into your private life. I'd have been happy if you were with someone. Of all things, I wished you happiness. I always wanted you to be happy."

Peter stared out into the emptiness of the room. "I was so afraid what we had in school was possibly just physical for you. I mean, we were young and the young have no concept of what a real relationship is all about. I, too, felt so much more but was reluctant to express it. Hey, it was the mid-eighties. Stonewall had happened some sixteen years before? But then the AIDS epidemic began to explode and coming out of the closet was totally crushed. It wasn't like we could all go around and sing *Kumbaya* anymore. Things were only just beginning to change socially but the AIDS crisis didn't help the situation at all."

Bruce agreed. "You're right. It truly was another time. And maybe we wouldn't have had the strength to hold it together then. Maybe it took us this much time to realize what we had and how truly real it was. I now know I loved you then and when I saw you in Portland, my heart went crazy. I knew I loved you more than I did in school. I wanted to grab you and kiss you to show you how I felt."

Peter looked across the bed and into Bruce's eyes. "When I saw you coming down the hall, I was almost overwhelmed with wanting to grab you as well. All those old feelings came rushing back like a damn tidal wave. It was instantly crystal clear to me. YOU were the one I'd been searching for all my life. I swear if Mario hadn't been there. Well. Just think about it."

"What if I'd had a significant other?" Bruce teased.

"Hey, I'm a psychic. I could feel you when you arrived at the hotel. I knew you, your mind. I knew your heart. We were destined to be together. It just took us time to figure it out."

"So, it's not too late? You still love me?" Bruce gave a smile and flexed his eyebrows several times.

"I didn't realize it but it's you I have loved all my life. I never want to lose you again. I believe there has always been a connection, a string, holding us together, distance and time couldn't break. It only took the Fates to finally shorten the string and bring us back together again." Peter leaned over the bed and started to sing softly. "'Betcha by golly, WOW. You're the one that I've been waiting for forever.'"

Bruce gave a big grin. "I do love you. I can't imagine, being without you now. You're right. We're finally mature enough to understand it. And as you can see with Shawn and Ethan, we don't have to hide it anymore." He leaned toward Peter and kissed him.

Peter grabbed Bruce and they rolled to the middle of the bed in a passionate embrace.

CHAPTER XIX

The smell of bacon and sausage cooking woke everyone. It was a little after eight. Hank and hopefully Jake would soon be coming up the road.

Mario came out of his room, dressed in his casual wear, shortly joined by Mike. He leaned over the railing of the balcony to the great room. He called out. "Okay! Smells good down there!"

Mike agreed. "Yes, it does!"

Peter and Bruce were soon joining them. The 'Four Musketeers' headed down the stairs together to breakfast.

"Good morning. Good morning." Shawn and Ethan spoke in unison as the four entered the kitchen. "Hope everyone slept well."

"Like a damn log." Mike smiled. "I want to know what kind of bed that is. I want one."

Mario agreed. "I'll second that. My bed is so damn comfortable, too."

"Hank and maybe Jake should be here in a while. Thought we'd wait on them to join us for breakfast." Shawn had the coffee pot, pouring cups for everyone.

Shortly, there was a rap at the front door. "Hank's here." Shawn went to open it.

"Morning, Shawn. And look who came with me." He turned to Jake.

"Hey. After what I heard and saw last year, I wouldn't have missed this for the world. It's been bugging the back of my mind ever

THE RINGS OF SODOM

since. I wanted to see it through." Jake gave a 'thumbs-up'. "Glad I was invited. Thanks for including me."

"Jake, good morning. Glad you could make it. Come in. Come in. Meet the guys."

Hank stretched out his hand, holding a satchel. "Here you go. It's the candles and water. All I had to do was tell the priest we were heading out to the old Raines place and not to ask." He handed it to Shawn. "And there's no charge. He gave me three jars of water." He chuckled. "He even made a cross sign in our direction."

"Hope you're ready for some breakfast. Ethan is cooking it up right now." Shawn added.

"You know I can't resist Ethan's cooking." Hank nodded.

They all entered the house and headed to the kitchen. As they did, everyone stood up from the table.

"These are the guys." Shawn placed the satchel Hank brought over on the counter then made introductions. "Mario, Mike, Peter and Bruce. Guys, this is Hank who is one incredible carpenter and plumber. And this is Jake who is our great sheriff." Hands shook and greetings made.

Peter saw the satchel on the counter. "Hank, thanks for bringing them." He looked hard at Jake. "Jake, you may not remember but you had one of your deputies call me the last week of August last year about all this. His name was Jerry. But I was headed to the Amazon."

A look of surprise came to Jake's face. "So. You're Peter..... Solivinski. Solatrotski?"

Raucous laughter filled the room. After a few moments, it calmed with everyone shaking their heads.

"Solvinoski." Peter turned to everyone. "See. It's just like in 'Night at the Museum' when Custer is trying to say Sacajawea's name. It happens all the time."

Jake continued. "So, you made it after all. I knew you were the man for the job. Hank said you were the one who should have been here. He knew about you before I did. They pulled in someone else back then but I knew he didn't have your credentials. Too bad you weren't here from the beginning of all this. But you're here now. That's great." He turned to Hank. "Since then, I did some more research on this guy. He really is supposed to be something else. And he's a psychic."

Hank looked Peter up and down. "A psychic? How did I not pick that up on some of the stuff I found out about you? Hmmm. Interesting."

Peter turned to Hank. "Thanks again, Hank, for bringing everything. Let me run them down and put them by the doorway in the basement." He left and quickly returned.

Shawn lifted the coffee pot. "Okay. Everyone fill your plates. And I will pour."

"Ethan, I swear, if Shawn didn't have you, I'd take you home." Hank had a big grin on his face. "No one can cook like this young whippersnapper can."

Everyone clapped in agreement and all ate their fill. It was going on ten o'clock when they were finishing up.

Peter spoke up. "Okay, guys. I don't want caffeine interfering with what needs to be done. No more refills of coffee." He looked at Bruce, Mike and Mario. "This doesn't apply to you guys."

They all got up from the table and went into the great room. Shawn pulled a few chairs from the dining room, so there was enough seating for everyone.

Mario looked at Jake. "Jake, you look like you have about ten more years and you can retire."

Jake shook his head and chuckled. "Mario, you are too kind. I'm seventy-seven."

"WHAT!? What!? Seventy-seven!? You're kidding me! You look great for seventy-seven. And you haven't retired yet?" Mario was shocked.

"I have tried several times but the folks keep re-electing me to the post. Hey, it's not some big city or a place with a lot of crime. Things here go from a missing cat to a fender bender. What can

I say? So, I stay on. I like it but if it ever gets a burden, I'll stop. Probably see about having Jerry take my place."

Bruce sat with his mouth open. "Jake, I swear. I thought you were in your mid-fifties. Wow! Looking good, man. Damn!" He gave Jake a 'thumbs-up' with his right hand. "I should look so good when I get your age. Geez."

"Thanks, Bruce. And again, thanks for the kind words."

Bruce looked over at Mario. "To be honest, when I first met Mario, I thought he was in his twenties but he's actually forty-two. Yeah."

Mario grinned as everyone called out. "Wow!" "Really?" "Lookin' good!"

Ethan jumped right in. "Well. One more surprise. Look at Hank. Guess his age." He looked at Mario.

Mario scratched his beard. "Okay. I have to be honest. I'd say sixty. Maybe sixty-one. But now, I know you're going to drop a bombshell and tell me something else after what was just said about Jake here."

Ethan looked at Bruce. "What about you?"

"I'd say just what Mario said. Sixty or sixty-one. Max, sixty-five."

Ethan turned to Hank. "Okay, Hank. Tell them."

Hank hung his head, chuckled and spoke softly. "I'm eighty-three. Be eighty-four right around the corner this year."

Mike yelled out. "You have to be shitting me!!! Eighty-three!! Damn! You guys look fantastic. Damn! Is it the water here? I want several gallons to take home with me."

Everyone roared with laughter.

After the laughter calmed, Peter spoke with commitment. "Okay, gentlemen. We really should get started. No time like the present. But let me tell you how this is going to work. You all are going to sit in the kitchen. I'm going to bring each of you back here to the great room. One at a time. And put you in a comfortable position. You can sit or lie down on the sofa. We'll do a little bit at a time. Once I have a start and get enough information, we may all sit together and compare notes to see if everyone is on the same page. And don't worry. What you say to me will be in strictest confidence. I'm only interested in information, regarding happenings related to the basement. Those will be the only things discussed among everyone. So, any deep secrets that might come out unrelated to all this, will be between each of you and me. Remember. I'm a licensed psychologist and hypnotherapist. You know. Doctor-patient confidentiality and all that."

"Oh! Wow! I didn't know we were getting hypnotized. I love it." Hank clapped his hands. "Now! Promise me! You won't make me cluck around the great room like a chicken."

Everyone cracked up as Hank got up, imitating a chicken with his arms tucked back and jerking his head back and forth and strutting around the room, clucking.

Jake snickered. "I was going to say the same thing."

They all could not stop laughing.

Peter shook his head. "Guess I won't have to make him do it since he has just satisfied our curiosity about that."

After a few moments, Peter tapped the coffee table. "Okay. Okay. Let's try to get serious here. But I must admit, I'm glad everyone has a terrific sense of humor and levity. I have a feeling we're going to need a lot of it before we're through here. Now. Before we start that, I'd like Hank to tell me about events when he was a young boy concerning this house. It'll help me in asking the right questions of him. Hank, do you mind sharing your story with everyone or would you rather it be in private?"

"Hell. No problem. I've got nothing to hide. And they all know it already. Just you, Bruce, Mike and Mario don't know it all." He turned and looked at the others. "You have all heard the story several times. So, if I leave anything out, let me know."

Over the next almost two hours, Hank told of his adventures when he was young. Peter did ask appropriate questions of him at the time to clarify certain points. Finally, it was time.

Peter turned to Jake. "Do you have anything to add to the past history?"

"Yes. But first, I have to say, Hank always was the adventurer back in those days. Hope you don't mind me saying but he seemed to always have the balls no one else did. Never told him but I've always admired his ability to stand up and do things. He's six years older than me but I always thought he had... balls." Jake began to chuckle as he glanced over at Hank.

Hank looked over at Jake and smiled. "Really? I didn't know. Thanks, Jake. I appreciate that."

"Yeah. From what I've just heard, I'd totally agree." Mario grinned. "I like a guy with brass ones. Shows he has 'moxie'."

Peter turned to Jake. "So. You have additional information for us?"

Jake nodded. "I thought you might like to know some of the information that's in the journals that were found inside the altar downstairs. They are at my office in a secure place."

Peter responded. "Yes, I very much would like to hear that information as it could be helpful."

Jake immediately told of the story Jeremiah had written in the journals. When he was finished, he looked over at Peter. "I hope that was helpful."

Peter nodded. "Thank you, Jake. That information could be very useful." He paused for a moment then continued. "Okay. Who wants to be first?" Peter looked around the room. "We can draw straws if you like. I mean we have four people here and four straws are not a problem."

There was a reluctant pause of silence.

Finally, Shawn shouted. "Me! I'll go first."

Peter turned to the rest. "Okay. All of you to the kitchen. I'll let you know when it's time for someone else. And remember. No Coffee!"

Everyone headed to the kitchen and sat around the kitchen table. They all knew this was going to be very interesting.

"Would anyone like anything more to eat?" Ethan looked around the room to no takers.

Everyone sat silent, listening. The quiet was almost deafening.

After some fifteen minutes, Mario quietly spoke. "Some coffee would be great. I'd like a cup since I'm not hitting the couch." After a brief pause, he continued. "Got to tell you. Peter is amazing. When I first met him, he did a reading on me and it shocked the shit out of me. Let it not be said he doesn't know what he's doing. He's unbelievable at what he does. I was very dubious about such things until I met him."

Ethan got up and poured a fresh cup for Mario. He also put out some cheese and crackers just in case.

It had been nearly forty-five minutes when Shawn returned to the room with a smile on his face. "Well, that didn't hurt at all. Not sure what happened as Peter thought it best to make it that way, so as not to bring up anything traumatic into my memory. He's ready for Hank. He said he wants to work with Ethan last."

Hank got up and headed out of the room. He turned and looked at everyone. "Now. If you hear clucking or other chicken sounds coming from in there, don't any of you start laughing."

Everyone bent their heads down, trying to stifle their giggling as Hank turned and left the room.

Ethan poured coffee for Shawn and started another pot.

They all looked at Shawn.

Shawn looked at everyone. "What? I have no idea what he asked me. All I know is I went in there, laid down on the sofa and we started talking. Then, he said everything was fine and I could leave. I asked him if he was going to ask me anything special. He said he had all the information he needed right now. It was like I was in there for a second then got up and left the room. But from the clock, it looks like I was in there for some three-quarters of an hour. Wow. I don't remember the time at all. Wow."

"Peter is very good at what he does." Bruce spoke up.

Again, it was about another forty-five when both Peter and Hank walked into the kitchen. Everyone looked right at Hank. There was a moment of silence when Hank looked around. "What?" He looked at everyone. "No... he didn't?"

The room erupted with laughter as Bruce yelled out. "No! Seriously, Hank. He didn't. But we did hear oinks and squeals from in there."

The laughter got even louder.

"Just kidding!" Bruce laughed. "Just kidding! Just kidding!" He slapped the top of the table.

It took a few moments for the laughter to stop. Everyone was shaking their heads and big grins filled all the faces.

Peter shook his head. "What a group! What a group! What can I say? I love you guys."

"Have a cup of coffee, Hank." Bruce got up and poured a cup for him. "You're a good sport. I really like you." He turned to the others. "Anyone else?"

"Think I'd like one but I really must wait." Peter responded. "A short break would be good right now. Then, it will be Jake and Ethan's turn.

Coffee break over, Peter and Jake left for the great room.

It was only a little over twenty minutes when Jake reappeared.

"Wow. That was short." Hank slapped his thigh. "What's with that?"

"What?" Jake stared at everyone.

"You were only in there for twenty minutes." Hank responded. "Guess it's not the length of the session. It's the info gathered. You bet. Quality is so much better than quantity." He smiled as he glanced at Jake.

"When he finished, Peter said he had all he needed from me." Jake turned to Ethan. "Peter said it's your turn now." He shook his head. "Maybe I'm not as interesting as everyone else."

Ethan looked at Shawn with a touch of fear on his face.

"It's going to be fine. You'll see." Shawn spoke in a reassuring manner as Ethan left the kitchen.

Hank turned to Jake. "Now, don't say you're not interesting. You're one of the most interesting men I know. So, don't sweat it. Never forget that."

It was well over an hour before Peter and Ethan returned to the kitchen. Peter glanced over at Bruce. It was a knowing glance. Bruce knew all was not well.

"Well, how did it go?" Shawn smiled at Ethan.

"I guess all right. I don't remember anything. So, I guess it was okay." Ethan looked at the clock. "Since we haven't eaten any lunch, I thought I would start an early dinner. If you all would like, go chill out in the great room and I'll get started. Hank. Jake. You ARE staying for dinner. And we're not taking 'no' for an answer."

"Thanks. I'd love to." Hank was pleased with the invite. He looked at Jake. "If you need to get back, take the car. But you should stay. Ethan's cooking is fantastic. What he served for breakfast is just a touch of what he's capable of." He gave a 'thumbs-up' with his right hand.

Jake clapped his hands. I'd love to stay. Always great to get a terrific meal I couldn't begin to cook even if I had the recipe. These kids are so nice and considerate."

"Sounds good." Shawn also did a 'thumbs-up'. "Eight for dinner." He looked at Jake and smiled. "Thanks for the kind words."

Peter commented. "I need to get some things written down and organized right now, while it's still fresh. Would like to discuss it with the guys, too. While Ethan and Shawn are fixing dinner, we can powwow up in the room. We'll be down later."

"Great." Shawn responded. "We'll see you guys later."

They all headed up to Peter and Bruce's room. Mario and Mike sat in the two chairs in the room. Bruce, Jake and Hank sat around on the edges of the bed. Peter leaned against the dresser. Peter spoke softly, breaking the quiet. "Ethan is hiding something." He paused for a moment. "Everything was fine, during the session until I got it out of him. He found a set of rings in the room in the basement."

Hank spoke quietly. "So, that's where they are."

"Really?" Bruce was surprised.

Peter continued. "Yes, and he never told anyone. Not even Shawn. It's his secret. He did say he feels so very bad about lying to Shawn but something has prevented him from saying anything. He found them in a small box in a niche in the wall by the door to the room. This was never mentioned in the report I read about the house."

Jake spoke up. "There was an unanswered question about that niche. Everyone thought something was supposed to be there but nothing was ever found that seemed to fit. A small box and the missing set of rings makes sense. That's why there was no conclusive comment in the report. We all knew the rings existed somewhere as they were mentioned in the journals. But they were never found. Now, we know why."

Peter continued. "He revealed to me that when he touched the rings for the first time, there was a strange overpowering feeling that raced through his body. I also found out he has no memory of anything from the moment he puts the rings on until the time he takes them off."

"Wow. That's weird. Very interesting." Bruce was putting puzzle pieces together in his mind.

Mike was shocked. "Are you telling me he played an entire concert and has no recollection of it? You have to be kidding me! How can that be?"

"I'm not sure." Peter continued. "But one thing I do know. I want to hypnotize him and talk with him while he's wearing the rings. I think the best place to do it would be in the room in the basement. That room is the center of everything."

"I have a feeling the rings had something to do with what went on here in the basement those many years ago." Bruce was adamant.

"How are you going to get Ethan to put on the rings?" Mario was curious. "And if he was the one actually doing those murders, shouldn't we be taking some kind of precautions? I mean. Geez. You saw those bodies. Or should I say... body parts."

Hank interrupted with a big question on his face. "Ah. Murders? Body parts? What are you talking about?" He looked over at Jake. "Do you know what they're talking about?"

Jake shook his head. "No clue!"

Peter spoke up. "Okay. The cat's out of the bag. We need to fill them in on what this is REALLY all about. Jake. Hank. Nothing has been mentioned yet because we wanted to talk with Shawn and Ethan and didn't want them to have a guard up. If we had told them everything, they may never have opened up to us like they have. But now, you both should know the whole truth. I think Bruce, Mario and Mike can fill you in very well. And so you understand, Mario and Mike are in law enforcement. Mario is Captain of the Seattle Police and Mike is Captain of the Portland Police. Portland, Oregon, not Portland, Maine."

Jake nodded. "You know, I had a feeling there was a lot more to all this. I mean, why would Peter come here with three others if he was the one wanting to investigate just the house? I knew something was not quite right with it all. And now, you are saying there were murders? Wow. I am all ears."

Hank added. "You bet, I'd like to know the whole story as well."

Peter turned to Bruce. "Explain as quickly as possible to Hank and Jake the high points of all this. Then, we can get down to business."

Bruce told most of the story with periodic points of interest from Mario and Mike. They mentioned the gruesome details but not with every murder. Just enough for Jake and Hank to get the basic picture.

Hank spoke up. "And you think somehow, Ethan is involved? Okay. True. The murders took place during the times of his concerts but you've met Ethan. He's a fine young man. He's kind and sincere and caring. I so hope he isn't involved. I just can't believe he could be guilty of such things."

"Hank is right." Jake nodded his head. "I can't imagine Ethan hurting a fly. For crying out loud."

"Well, I tell you now. Somehow, he IS involved. But I don't know to what extent or in what capacity. It's one reason I want to talk with him when he has the rings on. Please, remember. Don't mention the rings and don't let on that Mario and Mike are with law enforcement. I don't want him spooked."

Hank chuckled. "Interesting word you chose there. Spooked. Yeah." He grinned and flexed his eyebrows.

"Peter, if you are going to do this in the basement, maybe we should tie him to a chair first." Mike was blunt. "That should keep him in place should he try something weird."

"Geez. Yeah. With chain, not rope." Mario added.

Mike shook his head. "Chain. Great idea." He snickered. "But you know if he does become violent, I think the rope would help keep him in one place."

Jake twitched his head. "You really think that's necessary?"

Mario looked at Jake. "If you saw what we have seen, you'd completely understand. Who or whatever did these murders was strong as an ox to overpower the victims as he did."

"Yes, but I think we need to think this through a bit." Bruce shook his head. "We need to make sure we cover all the bases here. Whoever committed those murders was one strong dude."

"What if I have a big stick ready just in case?" Mario pounded his right fist into his left palm.

Everyone just shook their heads, trying not to laugh at the image in their heads.

Hank bent his head down. "Ethan is a fine man. I think it's sad someone like him could be involved with such stuff."

Jake responded. "Hank's right. The time I was here back then, both Shawn and Ethan were so gracious and hospitable. I swear, they're good kids. Throughout my career, I've seen many who got the raw deal when it wasn't even their fault. Sometimes life just isn't fair."

Peter looked at Hank and Jake. "If either of you has like four lengths of rope you can bring tomorrow, I'd appreciate it."

Jake spoke up. I could bring several sets of handcuffs if you'd like."

Peter grinned. "No. I really need rope."

Hank spoke up. I know I have some rope at the house. How about four pieces around two feet long?"

Peter smiled. "Perfect."

Peter had listened to Hank and Jake and sensed their hearts. Both were compassionate men, caring and loving. But there was so much more. But it was time to head back downstairs. "Okay. Let's go see if we can help out downstairs. And remember. Nothing about who Mario and Mike are or about the rings."

After dinner, Hank and Jake thanked everyone and headed to the door. "We'll see everyone around nine tomorrow. Sure appreciate letting us see this through."

"Don't eat. I'll be fixing breakfast for you." Ethan called out.

The night was still young but Peter suggested that he wanted everyone to be well-rested. He knew that the next day was going to be very trying and he wanted everyone to be alert and ready for anything crazy that might happen.

They all knew that tomorrow was going to be even stranger since Peter told Ethan he wanted to have another session with him. Ethan was apprehensive but Shawn came to the rescue with reassuring words.

The 'Four Musketeers' gathered in Bruce and Peter's room. They discussed several ideas before breaking up and heading to bed.

"Tomorrow, while everyone is getting ready for breakfast, I have a few things I want to do in the basement." Peter pulled the sheet back.

"You need any help in setting anything up? You know I'll be glad to help and it might go quicker." Bruce plumped his pillow.

"I'd appreciate that. We can get up early, get my bag of tricks out of the SUV and take it down to the room and get started. I have the candles and water already by the door down there. I'll tell you, I feel it in my bones. Tomorrow is a day we are ALL going to remember for the rest of our lives. Trust me. And it's not going to be pretty, I'm afraid."

"What do you think is going to happen when Ethan has on the rings since he doesn't know anything after he has them on?" Bruce seemed nervous.

"That's why I'll put the rings on him after we tie his arms and feet down to a very heavy chair as Mike suggested. I'll wear my white gloves dipped in holy water to put the rings on Ethan. I think that big wooden armchair in the great room near the fireplace will do quite well. Then, I'll wet his ropes with holy water. I'm also putting a ring of salt around the area of the room where we all will be situated to prevent any evil that might show itself from escaping." Peter explained. "I keep a big bag of it in the back of the SUV. Never know when it might come in handy. Yes indeed. Also helps when I get an order of French fries that's not salted enough." He looked at Bruce and began to snicker.

"Okay. I do use it to sprinkle when there's ice on the driveway. Okay?" He continued to explain.

"Now, let's get serious here. What do you think about this? You might want to sprinkle some holy water on the salt as well." Bruce added.

"I plan to. It couldn't hurt." Peter nodded. "The candles I'll light to purify the area and keep them lit. The one hundred percent beeswax is the purest of holy candles. Might hang a crucifix on the front of the altar just in case. I have a rosary blessed by the Pope. I think we're as ready as we can be."

"I sure as hell hope so." Bruce got in the bed.

Peter leaned over and turned off the bed light. All was quiet for several minutes. Then, he spoke quietly. "I have to tell you. So much is happening here and some of it has nothing to do with the room in the basement or the rings."

"Oh? Like what?"

"It's Hank as well as Jake. When I shook their hands, that's when it really hit me. And then, when I talked with them, during their sessions. Trust me. I think we're going to witness something wonderful that's been long overdue."

"Seriously? Like what?"

"I'm not going to say anything else. Just watch each one of them. You'll see. At least, I hope it unfolds. It should." He smiled to himself in the dark. "But enough. We need to rest. Tomorrow is going to be very trying. I just know it. Goodnight, Bruce."

"Goodnight, Peter." The darkness was quiet. Then, suddenly, Bruce loudly yelled out. "GOODNIGHT, JOHN-BOY!!!"

Just then, they heard two distant responses in unison, obviously from Mario and Mike. "GOODNIGHT!" This was followed by loud laughter from their rooms as Peter and Bruce joined in.

CHAPTER XX

Light was just creeping in the window when Peter awoke. He got up and headed to the bathroom. Returning to the room, Bruce was awake. He, too, headed to the bathroom. When he got back, Peter was nearly dressed. Bruce quickly dressed. They were out the door, down the steps and out to the SUV. Peter grabbed up the big zippered bag and the big bag of salt. He handed Bruce a very large black suitcase. They went back into the house and to the room in the basement. He also grabbed the satchel Hank had brought the previous day and placed them all together out of the way in the room.

Within the hour, they had taken the necessary items out of the bag, suitcase and satchel and had them set out in the room. They definitely needed the large chair from the great room and some other chairs. Peter would put items in place just before they began the session.

"Are you going to leave the lights on during all this?" Bruce looked up at the electric lights.

"Yes. They'll have no affect on the process." Peter looked around to see if there was anything else he needed to do. He checked the line of salt. "I left one break in the line. It's at the doorway. I won't finish it until everyone is inside the space. That way, if evil enters with Ethan, it won't be able to leave. Remember to have me tell everyone the importance of not breaking that line once I complete it. It's extremely important. That salt is like a set of prison bars to evil. It must not be broken."

"I will. Don't worry."

"Okay. Let's get upstairs and see if anyone is up yet."

Opening the door from the basement, they heard Ethan rummaging around in the kitchen.

"Well, good morning." Bruce called out.

"You two are up rather early, aren't you?" Ethan looked at Peter and Bruce coming from the basement.

"Just wanted to get a few things ready for later on." Peter responded.

Just then, Shawn, Mike and Mario walked into the kitchen.

"Guess everyone's up early today." Mario looked over at Bruce. "Hey. Mike and I heard you yell out 'Goodnight, John-Boy' from *The Waltons* TV show last night." He snickered. "Haven't heard that in a long time."

Suddenly, there was a loud knock at the door. "Even Hank and Jake are early." Shawn headed to the front door.

"I think some nice omelets are called for today." Ethan started getting all the ingredients out of the refrigerator. He turned and yelled out. "Is there anything you all don't like in your omelets?" He saw everyone looking around and shaking their heads. "Okay. It's everything but the kitchen sink."

Shawn went and started the coffee. "It'll be ready shortly."

"Ethan, I don't want you to have any coffee until after the session. Caffeine tends to interfere. I think I mentioned that yesterday." Peter commented.

"No problem. I can wait." Ethan kept working at the counter, prepping the things to go into the omelets.

Hank walked over and handed Peter a paper bag and spoke softly. "It's what you wanted me to bring."

Peter took the bag. "Thanks, Hank." Then, he looked at everyone. "We're going to do the session downstairs today. In the room." Peter looked at everyone to see their expressions. "I thought it would bring us closer to the source of the problem here and probably get many questions answered. Shawn, we need that big chair from the great room if you don't mind. And some other chairs, so everyone can sit down. None for me since I'll be standing."

"Not a problem. Would anyone like to help?" Shawn smiled at everyone. "We'll get the big one from the great room and six of the side chairs from the dining room."

They all got up. Mario and Shawn got the big chair. Mike and Bruce got two of the dining chairs each. Jake and Hank each got one. They headed down the stairs and went to the room.

"I see someone has been busy here." Mario saw the candles stuck in holders, standing near the doorway and the line of salt.

Peter led Shawn and Mario with the big chair to a spot out in front of the altar and some fifteen feet from it. "Here will be fine." They set it down, facing the altar. Peter placed the paper bag on the seat of the chair. "Bruce, if you all will place the chairs you have next to one another, facing the ones Mike has. Leave a space about six feet wide down the middle." He led Bruce to a place about four feet from the big chair toward the altar. Bruce and Mike placed the chairs appropriately. "Hank, you and Jake put your chairs near to one another just in back of the big chair and facing the altar. But make sure you both will have a clear view of everything." He placed a candle at each end of the sets of two chairs out front of the big chair. "I have a few more if we need them." He placed his bag, suitcase and the satchel next to one of the chairs behind the big chair. He took the paper bag and opened it. He took out the four lengths of rope and placed them on top of his zippered bag. "Mike, you and Shawn will sit on this side. Shawn, you in the chair closest to the big chair and Bruce, you and Hank will sit on this side, facing Mike and Shawn. Mario, you and Jake will be back here behind the big chair." He directed with his hand. "I'll be on my feet most of the time." He looked around the room again to make sure everything was in place. "One last thing." He took a rosary out of the bag and headed to the altar. The instant the rosary touched the altar, it flew out of Peter's hand and across the room with the reaction of same poles of two magnets trying to touch.

"Whoa!" Mike called out. "Did I see that?"

"Yes. Yes, you did." Peter shook his head. "I sensed energy in this room but I wasn't sure it was THAT powerful. I had no idea anything like this could still be here in the house."

Shawn looked worried. "Is everything going to be all right? I don't want Ethan to get hurt." He walked over and picked the rosary off the floor, returning it to Peter.

"Guess I don't dare put the holy water, crucifix or candles up there." Peter jested nervously.

"Trust me. Peter is very good at what he does. He's probably one of the best in the whole world." Bruce tried to reassure Shawn. He wondered if he wasn't trying to convince himself as well. "If I were in this situation, HE is the one I'd want to be taking charge."

Peter was curious. He went to where he had placed the three jars of holy water, opened one, poured a small amount in his hand and walked toward the altar. Everyone stood still in suspense. He walked around to the back and then threw the water into the air above the altar. As it fell back and landed on the surface, loud bangs and pops along with bright flashes of fire and sparks erupted from every place a drop hit the altar.

"Holy shit!" Mario yelled out. "Whoa!"

"Guess you're not using any holy water today." Bruce tried to be funny but no one laughed. "Well, I see that went over like a lead balloon."

Mike, Mario, Shawn, Jake and Hank just gave an unforgiving stare.

"Yep. This is going to be a tough one for sure." Peter stroked his beard and looked at Shawn who looked apprehensive. "Don't worry, Shawn. I'll do my best to take care of this situation." He looked at the rest. "I just might need all of your help in doing it. If I do, I'll tell you what to do. Mario. You, Jake and Mike are in law enforcement.

You probably will have some idea what to do if the situation arises. I'm sure you have dealt with tough guys, during apprehensions."

A questioning look came over Shawn's face. "I didn't know that Mario and Mike were cops. Is there something I should know?"

Peter looked at Shawn. "Okay. Yep. We thought it best not to reveal that at the beginning. I didn't want you to become apprehensive. We weren't sure how things were going to go in the beginning. You need to know. But Ethan must never know. We are here, trying to get to the bottom of several gruesome murders. I can explain more later but it's sufficient for you to know the rings are all a part of it and Ethan is intertwined with the rings."

Shawn had a sadness in his voice. "Please, don't tell me my Ethan has committed murder. Ethan has the rings? He never told me. Those must be the ones he had but said he had bought them in Portland and was going to return them."

"Shawn! Listen to me! Listen clearly and carefully. The Ethan you know is hurting badly inside because of the lies he told you about the rings. This came out when he was under hypnosis. Know this. He could not help it. He has a great love for you. As much as he wanted to tell you the truth, the power of the rings would not let him do it. Not to worry. More of this will become clearer after all this is over." Peter spoke reassuringly to Shawn. "Just remember. What has happened is not Ethan's fault. This will be resolved when we have finished here. Does everyone agree and understand?"

"Okay. You got it." Jake agreed with a 'thumbs-up', using his right hand.

"Mario and I are here with you." Mike added.

"And you know you can count on me." Hank nodded his head. Jake and I may have a few years on you younger fellas but trust me, I know we can hold our own." He smiled at Jake.

"Peter, you know I'm with you." Bruce nodded.

"If it will help clear this house and help my Ethan, you know I'll do what I can." Shawn gave a positive 'thumbs-up' with his left hand.

"One last thing that is extremely important." Peter took the time to look right at everyone. "The line of salt. I want Bruce to complete it once Ethan and I enter the space here. At no time, let it get broken after that. Under NO circumstances. NEVER let it get broken. Salt is like prison bars to evil and it cannot cross it. It will not be able to escape the circle."

They all nodded their heads, understanding the importance of the demand.

Just then, they heard Ethan, calling from the top of the basement steps. "Soup's on!"

"Guess we can go eat." Shawn directed the guys to the stairs.

They were all filing into the kitchen.

"After what I just saw, I think I could use a drink!" Hank was emphatic.

There was virtually no conversation during breakfast. No one wanted to send up alarm bells about what happened earlier in the room. Everyone ate rather quickly but made a few comments about how delicious it was. Soon, it was over.

"Guys. You go down and get seated. Ethan and I are going to start in the great room." Peter instructed. He and Ethan went to the great room where he told Ethan to lie on the sofa and relax. Shortly, Ethan was under hypnosis.

"Ethan. Again, I don't want you to remember anything. It will be unimportant for you to remember. Is that clear?" Peter spoke in a calm and reassuring voice.

"Yes."

"When I talked with you before, you told me about the rings." Peter spoke softly but Ethan became agitated. "Relax. Everything is going to be all right. Do not worry."

After a moment, he began again. "Ethan. I want you to go get the rings and we are going to go downstairs. Do you understand?"

"Yes. You're not going to take my rings, are you?" Ethan became agitated again.

"No, we're not. Not to worry. When we're done, everything will be all right. Now, let's go get the rings and leave them in the box."

They got up and headed up to Ethan and Shawn's bedroom. He walked over to a set of drawers, opened the bottom one, dug into the back and pulled out a small box.

"That's good, Ethan. Leave them in the box and we will go downstairs to the room in the basement."

Once they were inside the room, Bruce immediately completed the salt circle and sprinkled holy water on it.

When he entered the room, Ethan instinctively walked over to the altar and placed the box in the center.

"Ethan. Come, sit here in this chair. Everything is going to be just fine." Peter directed him to the big chair where he sat down. "Now, for your safety, I am going to place some restraints on your hands and feet."

Ethan became agitated. "Why are you tying my hand and feet? Did I do something wrong?"

Shawn immediately responded. "Ethan! Ethan, it's all right. It's for your safety. I am here for you and won't let anything happen to you."

Ethan became calm. "I know you will. I love you so much."

Peter turned to Shawn. "Thank you so much for that." He then directed Mario and Jake to get the lengths of rope, sitting on top of the bag by the chair and told them to tie Ethan's wrists and legs to the chair. "Is that too tight?"

"No. It's fine." Ethan just stared straight ahead.

"Mike. Mario. Light the candles for me, please." He watched as they lit the candles then returned to their seats. "Now, Ethan. I will go get the rings and put them on your fingers. I want you to listen to me. Is that clear?" Peter went to get his gloves as they would insolate him from actually touching the rings.

"I'll try but you don't have to get them. I'll do it." Ethan stared at the box on the altar.

Suddenly, the box on the altar snapped open and the two rings flew out like rockets, across the room and were instantly on Ethan's fingers.

All looked at each other to make sure they'd all seen the same event. None made a sound.

Peter immediately sensed a drastic change in Ethan. Ethan seemed to disappear. It was the same impression he had when first meeting Ethan at the concert. But before he could prepare, there was an extreme sense of total evil within Ethan's body.

Peter yelled out. "Ethan! Take the rings off! Right now! Put them back in the box! NOW!"

Just as they arrived, they flew off Ethan's hands and were back in the box which snapped closed again.

Peter was silent for a moment. He concentrated on Ethan who was back to himself again but still under hypnosis. "Are you feeling all right, Ethan?"

"Yes. Everything is fine now. But for a moment, it seemed I was with someone."

"Do you know who it was?" Peter was surprised Ethan could recognize the difference under hypnosis. He was glad. It meant Ethan was still there somewhere. This could be a huge advantage.

"No. I'm not sure. But he is here when I have the rings on. And when he is, he won't let me say anything."

"So, he's not with you when you have the rings off?"

"Right. He is only here when I have the rings on. And it's funny but I'm just realizing it. He's in the rings. Does that make sense?"

"Could you tell me more?" Peter was amazed.

"In the past, I never knew he was here. But for some reason just then, I could feel him. I knew he was here."

"Ethan. Listen to me carefully. Remember. I will be here with you, during this entire session. Shawn is here as well. I don't want you to think you are alone. Call out to me if you need anything. Do you hear me?"

"Yes, I do. I will."

Peter looked at Mario and Jake. He spoke softly. "Take off the ropes before I bring him out of it and blow out the candles." He looked at the others. "Do not say anything of what has happened. Ethan must not know anything. We are going to take a short break. I'm going to tell Ethan to go lie on the sofa in the great room and rest while I talk to you all about what we're going to do in the next session. Shawn. You're going to be very important in all this. You're his anchor. Ethan loves you more than life and I know you love him the same way. That bond is more important than you could ever imagine. I know it may sound cliché but love is the strongest force for good that can be imagined." He looked at everyone. "Step over the salt line at the doorway so not to disturb it."

He turned to Ethan and spoke calmly. "Ethan. You and I are going upstairs again and you're going to take a short rest on the sofa. Is that clear? As we leave here, do not step on the line of salt at the doorway. Do you understand?"

"Perfectly. But what about my rings?"

"They will stay in the box on the altar till we get back. They are going to be just fine. No one will bother them." Peter spoke with authority and calmness.

Ethan stood up. He and Peter went up to the great room.

"Now, I want you to lie down on the sofa and when you do, you will come out and be relaxed as if you had a really nice nap." Peter spoke quietly.

Ethan did as he was told and almost instantly, turned his head with a smile. "Did I do all right?"

"You did just fine. Now, stay here and rest for a while. I will be back shortly." Peter left and went back to the basement.

"Okay, guys. We definitely have our work cut out for us here. Shawn, please, go to the kitchen and see if you have any small cups or containers." Peter started giving directions.

"Would small paper cups be all right?" Shawn questioned.

"Those would be perfect. Hurry as we need to talk about some things."

Shawn was gone only a few minutes when he returned with a whole package of paper cups, handing them to Peter. Peter handed two to everyone. He then went and got one of the jars of holy water and poured some in each cup. "Hank. You know, it's probably the Fates with us that the priest gave you three jars of water." He put the empty jar down next to the full one and the empty one used to sprinkle water on the salt line. "Put the cups by your chairs. I feel we're going to need them later on." Peter went into his bag, grabbed several small crucifixes and handed one to everyone. "Hold on to these. You may see they could come in handy as a powerful weapon."

"Weapon? I don't like the sound of that." Jake cringed.

"What about you?" Bruce looked at Peter.

"I'm going to wear the rosary around my neck. I'll be fine." Peter looked around the room again. "Make very sure no one breaks the salt line. If something major happens here, it will keep it within the circle. If there is a break, it will get out. As you can see, the line goes around the settings of the chairs and the altar. If I tell you to step outside the circle, do so immediately. Once outside the line, nothing should be able to cross it. Try not to step on the line and disturb it."

"Definitely don't want that to happen." Hank responded nervously.

"Are you sure Ethan is going to be all right?" Shawn was very concerned.

"As long as everyone keeps their heads everyone will be fine. Regardless of what happens, just don't panic and listen carefully to me. If there are any problems, it's essential no one panics. I believe with the kinds of backgrounds you all have, you will be able to hold your own and take action. Our strength is in our solidarity. But above everything else, Shawn's and Ethan's love will be the most powerful thing we have going." Peter looked around again. "When I bring Ethan back down here, Mario, you and Jake tie him as before. Hank will light the candles. Then, everyone take your places as before. Okay. Is everyone ready?"

All shook their heads and all gave a 'thumbs-up'.

Peter went to the great room, speaking to Ethan. "All right. We're going to do this again. Are you ready? Make sure you step over the line of salt at the doorway."

Ethan had been quietly lying there. "I guess so. Yes. I'm ready."

Within a few minutes, Peter had Ethan hypnotized again and they went down to the room. Ethan sat in the chair. Mario and Jake tied him as before. Hank lit the candles. Finally, they were in their places, seated and quiet.

"Ethan. Please, put on the rings."

"All right."

Immediately, the box on the altar snapped open and the two rings flew to Ethan's hands.

"Ethan, can you hear me?" Peter asked in a calm voice.

All heard the affirmative. "Yes." But it sounded like Ethan was miles away.

"Is there someone else with you?"

"Yes. He is here." Ethan's voice still sounded distant.

Suddenly, there was a loud gravelly voice from Ethan's mouth. "Shut up, you damn little bitch! No one said you could talk! Hey! You! Out there! What the HELL do you want? No pun intended." Then, there was a burst of loud evil laughter.

CHAPTER XXI

Everyone's eyes opened wide in shock upon hearing the voice. They all looked at one another. No one uttered a sound.

Then, Shawn whispered. "What was that? That wasn't Ethan."

Peter picked up one of the cups, containing the small amount of holy water in it and walked over to Ethan. He spilled a small amount on Ethan's left hand and on the ring there. There was a loud pop and bang and a flash of fire. Sparks exploded from his hand where the ring was. A loud scream issued from Ethan's mouth.

Shawn jumped up. "He's hurt! He's hurt!"

"SHAWN! Sit down! SIT DOWN!" Peter immediately wiped the water off Ethan's hand. It had only burned him slightly.

"You damn BITCH! What the fuck are you trying to do to me? You BASTARD! Who let you in here?" The deep ominous voice spoke again from Ethan's mouth.

Peter heard every word just spoken and realized what had happened. Then, he spoke with authority and directness. "Who are you!?"

"Wouldn't you like to know, you damn pansy ass?" The voice let out a loud sinister laugh.

"Oh. So, you're afraid to let me know who you are?"

"Look, you damn bitch! I have nothing to hide. And I'm not afraid of anything. Especially, from some damn faggot pansy like you."

Peter was not going to be provoked. "Then, what is your name?"

In a mocking whiny voice, he uttered. "'A rose by any other name.'" He was silent for a moment. "You damn BITCH! My name is..... Balzar! There! Satisfied?"

"Well... Balzar. I'm sure you have a reason to occupy the rings and you have some plan for those who wear them. Maybe you can enlighten us."

"Hmmm. Very interesting. I see you're one of 'those' people who can see and know. Unlike most walking this planet. It might be interesting to hear your take and opinion on the reason I had the rings created. Yes. It might be very interesting." There was a pause. "Wait a minute! It's YOU! Yeah! You're that damn whore, bitch faggot! Yeah! I remember now. You came to the concert in Portland. I could feel you, trying to read me then. Yeah. You damn fucking cunt, bitch, candy ass! So! What the hell do you want to know?"

"Trust me. I'd truly like to know what it's all about. And yes, I believe it will be very interesting. I certainly wouldn't mind giving you my opinion about it." Peter walked between the altar and Ethan. "Do you have to be inside Ethan to communicate? Don't you have a form of your own?"

"Yes, I have a form as you put it. But I usually don't come out unless... unless I'm completing a mission."

Peter was curious. "Oh. So, you have a mission?"

The deep gravel voice responded. "Yes. But I'll get to that."

"I'm surprised you're so willing to discuss it with me. Aren't you afraid it could jeopardize your mission?"

"Do you seriously think a candy ass like you, your companions and a few trinkets and candles are a threat to me?" There was loud roaring laughter. "Get serious!"

Peter immediately spoke in a stern voice. "Ethan. How are you doing?"

Ethan's distant voice answered. "I'm here. I'm fine."

Then, came the loud harsh voice. "I told you to shut up, you little shit-bitch! I didn't tell you, you could say anything!"

Peter smiled. He immediately realized, Balzar didn't have total control of Ethan while under hypnosis. This was a good thing and would be extremely helpful and important down the line. "So. Balzar. Tell me about yourself and how you are here. It should be a very intriguing story. I do want to hear it. We all want to hear it." He wanted to boost Balzar's confidence. Overconfidence could cause a slip-up and give him an edge. "Why don't you come out and join us, so we can talk face-to-face? Then, you can start at the beginning with your whole story." Peter walked and stood behind Hank's chair.

"Certainly. It will be my pleasure." There was a sinister chuckle sound from Balzar. "You thought I was going to say 'no', didn't you?" He laughed again. "Your trinkets and baubles are no threat to me. Come on! Get a life. Yeah. Cause you won't have one shortly. And neither will those fucking assholes, sitting there with you." He roared loudly again with laughter. "Okay, you asked for it. You got it! But it's not a Toyota!" He laughed loud again. "Does anyone remember the Toyota commercial?" He continued to laugh.

Suddenly, a smoky, sparking image began to emerge, directly from Ethan's body and was finally standing, full form in front of Ethan. Quickly, the form became solid. It was that of a creature, similar to that of an undernourished, naked human. About five feet tall and covered with a reddish scaly skin. The hands and feet were gangly and elongated with long pointed nails on each finger and toe. The head was larger than normal, pointed, with very sharp features and sunken cheeks. The mouth exhibited a set of fang teeth. The intense, completely black eyes were oversized and bulging out. There was no hair anywhere on the creature.

Everyone was shocked at what stood before them but no one said a word or moved. They knew to let Peter do all the talking.

"I see you don't have on the rings. They are still on Ethan. I don't understand." Peter's face twisted in his question.

Balzar looked right at Peter. "It's because I'm not going to kill you… yet!" He walked over to the altar and climbed up on it, sitting, facing everyone. A twisted smile came to his face and his eyes squinted. "Now, I can begin to tell you all about it. Are you bitches ready? Yeah. Sure you are." He leaned back, using both arms to support himself and crossed his legs.

"Many ages ago, my Lord and Master came to me with a proposition. He had a sense I was ambitious and had a desire to be closer to him in position and rank. He wanted me to collect some five thousand souls, bring them to him and he would raise me up. I couldn't resist the challenge. He wanted me to work out a plan, bring it to him and explain how it would work. If it did work, I would be raised high and have great rewards. Of course, he also told me that being ambitious had its consequences. If I were to fail, I would be sent to the bottom of the ranks and have to work my way up again or worse."

"I finally came up with a plan. I thought it quite exceptional. It was flawless. There was no way it could fail. Two rings would be forged of solid gold. Being of this metal, so coveted by men, it would be a cinch whoever saw them would desire them."

"Once they were on someone's fingers, I had them. Each person who had the rings would be assigned by me a specific number to achieve. The number would vary for each person. When that number was finally reached, I would make it possible for the person to realize it and go for his final reward."

"Also, with me in control, the rings could never be destroyed. If they were melted down, the gold would reform back into the rings again, destroying nothing."

"The plan was perfect. Whoever was wearing the rings, whatever talent that individual had would be enhanced to the point of incredible excellence. If he was an artist, he'd become the greatest of artists. If he was a writer, he'd become a most famous author. If a builder, he'd become the most famous of builders. Now, he could wear the rings anytime and nothing would happen, regarding the mission. Only when he made or created one of his masterpieces would the mission come into play. You get the idea?"

"Ah. Not to interrupt. But I have a question." Peter was curious.

"Ask away, pussy fag. What?"

"What about the size of the hands and fingers? How could the rings fit?"

"Interesting question." Balzar gave a big grin. "It didn't matter. The rings would immediately adjust to fit any finger perfectly. Not too tight and not too loose."

"Ah. Just one more if you don't mind."

Balzar became flustered. "Are you trying to try my patience?"

"No. Just wanted to make sure we were all on the same page here. It has to do with the person's ability or profession. What about someone like me? Who can see the dead and know about people? How would the rings affect someone like me?"

Balzar screeched then spoke. "That person would be one of the greatest psychics in the world. And he would never be wrong. Also, he'd be able to see an alternate path should the one projected be one of an undesired outcome." He paused for a moment. "But there would be consequences."

"Well, as you indicated, there would be consequences and all this would not come for free. There would have to be a payment of some sort for the individual. So, what would that be?"

"One of the consequences would be, he could never see anything, regarding his own life and future." He screamed out. "Sorry, Deary. You can't have it all." Balzar laughed again. "Oh. Damn. You're so perceptive to know about consequences and payment. I swear. You damn homos never cease to amaze me. You can take that as a compliment and know that I rarely give compliments." He nodded. "Yes. Yes, there are. As to what those payments would be, I'll get to that."

"But let me not digress. Now. You asked how it all got started. I'm sure you all know the stories about Sodom and Gomorrah. Sodom is where I wanted the rings to first come out. It was the perfect place with all the corruption and deviance there. Even my Lord and Master thought it was a great place to begin. The very first one to get the ball rolling was a man from Sodom who discovered the rings while out one day, looking for vegetables for a dish he was preparing. I had them placed in a small box out in a field of vegetables. It was obvious. Sooner or later, someone would come along and find them. Once he had them and put them on, he was hooked."

"Very soon, he was cooking the most amazing dishes in his little restaurant and people were flocking to eat there. Not long afterward, the king heard of him. So, he went to work for the king. He became very wealthy, creating exotic dishes in his kitchen. He also became known throughout the land and people from far and wide would come to the city and palace to eat at the table of the king."

"You said there were consequences. What was his?" Peter broke into the conversation.

"Did I mention? The whole purpose of this was for me to gather up five thousand souls? Yes. I know I did." Balzar snickered. "Well, how do you think I was going to get these souls? You do realize to get one, that person has to die." He clapped his hands together. "Right? What can I say? I have a feeling since we are all sitting here talking, you have some idea of that."

"Well, for our famous chef while cooking, he would have on the rings in order to create his famous dishes. And every time he created a major dish of significance, there was a price to pay. A penalty. A consequence. After the celebration at the house of the king and all the adulations, the chef would find someone to be... how should I say... the payment." Balzar paused again. Then, he yelled out. "And you know what that means!" He clapped his hands and roared with laughter.

"So. You had the chef murder someone?" Peter interjected again.

"Au contraire. No. No! No! The chef would still have on the rings and go to the house of someone and somehow, get that person alone. This was usually not difficult as he would find those who lived alone. The chef was totally unaware. As long as he had on the rings, he was completely unaware of where he was, what he was doing and would have no sense of the time. After a while of conversation with the soon-to-be victim, I took over. I came out and the rings transferred to me. But the chef had no idea of what was happening because he was still under my influence and remembered nothing. I immediately attacked the individual and collected his soul. Sucking out several volumes of blood was just a lucky side benefit. I love human blood. It's so… tasty… tasty." He roared with laughter, rubbing his hands together. "I know you have seen my handy work. And the poor chef had no idea what was going on. Once I had what I came for, I would go back and occupy the chef with the rings back on the chef's fingers, until he returned to his place and removed the rings. All he ever knew was somehow, when he had the rings on, he always created great and wonderful recipes. He never had knowledge of anything that took place. He never even knew he had been where the killing took place. Since there was no blood on his clothes, he had no clue. He did realize a span of time had passed that he didn't remember. Now, once I had collected enough souls allotted to this individual, it was time for HIS reward." Balzar tilted his head back and screamed with laughter. "He thought his reward would be to become the great renowned chef and be given great wealth and recognition. Unfortunately, he had no idea that what he thought was a complete lie. It was me collecting his soul as well with all the rest stored in the rings."

"So, you would kill him, too?"

"Oh, no. A power within him would make him return to the place and area where he had discovered the rings. I would make sure the authorities connected him with all the killings. He would be dragged off, kicking and screaming, denying any knowledge of the crimes. Of course, I had the great ability to make him commit suicide before there was ever any further inquiry or trial. It was perfect."

"Would he be wearing the rings when he took his life?"

"Oh. No! I'd be in his head when that happened. And when he killed himself, his soul would be drawn to the rings and kept there with all that had been collected. The rings would be wherever he placed them before going to the original location where he discovered the rings. The rings were in a place that would eventually be discovered by some other unsuspecting fool. I was very pleased how this first collection happened. It went like clockwork. Time was all I needed to collect the full five thousand. Time is irrelevant when you're talking about... eternity. All I had to do was wait for the next someone to find the rings and it would begin again."

Balzar paused for a moment then gave a sinister chuckle. "While we're talking about Sodom and Gomorrah, let me tell you about one of the huge lies that exists, so dearly cherished by those dumb fuck, moron, religious fundamentalists. It's the story told by that lying, punk-ass bitch, mother-fucker, Lot. Yeah. The story he told is a total fabrication. Let me just refresh your memories regarding the way he told it."

"Because the cities were so corrupt and evil, they were going to be destroyed along with all the sinners and evil-doers. Lot was told to get his family, leave the cities and not to look back or there would be consequences. They were far away when the destruction began. The death and destruction Lot describes are similar to the ones that occurred at Pompeii and Herculaneum when Mount Vesuvius blew up. He said because his wife turned and looked back to see what was happening, she was turned into a pillar of salt. Got that?"

"Because asshole, dumb fuck fundamentalists are more stupid than a pile of shit, they never question. Well, ponder this. If Lot's wife saw what was happening and was turned into a pillar of salt, how the FUCK did Lot know what was happening to write about it if he, too, didn't turn and look back? Answer me that question, boys and girls! I'm waiting. What's the answer? He was psychic? Oh, he looked in a mirror, the same way Jason did with Medusa? Sorry. WRONG! No mention of a mirror in the tale. Yeah. Lies. Total BULL SHIT! So, now I'm going to tell you the real story."

"Lot was a cheating whore fucker. His wife finally found out about what he was doing and threw his fucking ass out of the house, telling him never to come back. Actually, that was a good thing for him. Why? Because he left and got out before the real shit hit the fan."

"He alone had gotten out just in time when a purely natural event occurred. It was an event similar to Pompeii. That makes perfect sense because that whole area of the world is seismic. He was in awe, watching the cities and everyone in them become crispy." Balzar roared with laughter. "Yeah! As you would say... Crispy Critters! Don't you just love it!? Crispy! Yeah!" He continued his laughter.

"Lot realized he needed to cover his lying fucking ass, so folks would feel sorry for him. That's when he conjured up the story that is known. Yeah. Why no one has questioned the fact that if he saw and knew what was happening, why didn't he turn to salt as well? Just goes to show you how fucking stupid most evangelical fundamentalists are."

"There was a plus to all this though. Lot's story was so impressive that he is now one of Lord and Master's best storytellers. That's right. That lying piece of shit is NOT where everyone thinks he is." Balzar laughed and clapped his hands.

Peter responded. "I must admit that is a very interesting side tale but could we get back to the issue at hand? I have a question about the person who wore the rings. You say that person would commit suicide and his soul would fly back to the rings. What about distance?"

"Hell. Distance is not a problem. How do you think Jeremiah died in Paris but his soul flew right back here to this room and into the rings? Distance was never an issue."

"Very interesting. Yes. And what about Jeremiah?" Peter continued to question.

"I'm getting there. Geez. Don't rush me, faggot! Guess you don't want to hear all the details. And some are so wonderfully creative. Okay. Okay. I'll pick up the pace a bit. Okay. Needless to say, there were many between the guy from Sodom and Jeremiah. But since you insist."

"Jeremiah. Yeah. Now, he was one piece of work. He was smart but such a damn greedy bitch. I loved him. He had no idea what he was getting into. He was the first to have the book and the rings, working together in almost two hundred years. The first smart thing he did was kill the old geezer who came to him in Paris and had the rings."

Peter was well aware that everyone knew the story from the journals. He let Balzar continue.

"The old man knew the power of the rings by themselves but knew if put in combination with the information and incantations held in the pages of the book, he would be a true force. It's why he sought the book, before putting on the rings. Yeah. He'd have killed Jeremiah if he found the chance first and if he'd been stronger."

"Another thing Jeremiah had in his favor was his age. Part of the initiation into gaining the power of both the book and the rings was the need to marry and have two children to sacrifice. Yeah. The man in Paris was too damn old to even think about that. The slimy, codger bastard. He could never have done what Jeremiah did."

"I'm curious. What was Jeremiah's special talent? Everyone said he was a financier but he never did any significant or notable transactions. What is that?"

Balzar roared loudly, writhing on the altar. "Jeremiah's talent. Finance had nothing to do with it. HE WAS A DAMN MURDERER!!!!" He roared again. "And he did it so well and so gruesomely. No one in the past had his knack. His panache. And he really didn't know it until he killed the old man in Paris. I have to say, he's the only one I let be with me when we killed the sacrifices. He loved it. You should have seen him when we killed his family. It was glorious. Especially, the kids, all screaming and yelling as we ripped them apart. It was spectacular." Balzar twisted with glee on the altar, clapping his hands together as he roared with laughter.

Everyone slightly twitched in their chairs and looked at one another with disgust but said nothing.

"Jeremiah would capture his victims, during the night most of the time. He was totally aware of what was happening and what he was doing even when he wasn't wearing the rings. The only other who came close was the Italian merchant. He also was another bloodthirsty bitch. But he was a sniveling pussy when compared to Jeremiah. Hell no. When I take everyone to meet the Lord and Master, I'm going to see about having him raised up in status. He doesn't belong with all those other wimpy ass bitches. Yeah. Might even put in a good word for the Italian merchant. But I doubt it."

During Balzar's telling of his story, Peter had moved and was now standing behind Ethan, sitting in the chair. He turned to Bruce. "Bruce. I am sure you have a question for Balzar. Why don't you ask it."

Everyone was completely thrown off guard. Even Balzar. They all looked at Bruce who tried not to look flustered. He realized Peter had something up his sleeve and wanted him to distract everyone for a moment. He stood up and slowly walked across the room. All eyes were on him, including Balzar's. He put his left hand up to his face, pulling on the left side of his mustache then stroking the beard on his chin, looking down as he walked around toward the far wall. "I'm very interested in how the ones for sacrifice were chosen. What made them special? None of the ones we investigated, seemed to have any notorious backgrounds." He looked right at Balzar to engage his vision.

Balzar was full of himself. He leaned back and laughed. He looked right back at Bruce and spoke just matter-of-fact. "I guess you could say they were… collateral damage. They happen to be in the wrong place… at the RIGHT time… for ME!" He slapped his right hand on the top of the altar and laughed. "And what does it matter anyway. Most were useless pieces of shit, doing nothing of significance with their lives."

Bruce chimed in. "But they were people loved and cared for. They were brothers, sisters, mothers, fathers."

"Oh, don't hand me that shit!" Balzar was annoyed. He stared right at Bruce. "What is it with all this lovey-dovey shit! I have never understood it. All it does for all of you is get you in trouble. It seems to be one of the greatest reasons for all the problems you humans have in your life. I swear! It makes me sick. I could puke."

Suddenly, Shawn rose to his feet and yelled out. "You son-of-a-bitch! Don't tell us about something you know nothing about! And don't say a damn word about it because you will make it sound sordid and ugly!"

Balzar turned quickly to look at Shawn. A big grin came to his face. "You. You and that piano player. It's disgusting. All your perverted physical writhing with one another. It's obscene." He shouted. "Disgusting!"

"I knew you'd make it sound twisted and ugly!" Shawn yelled out. "What Ethan and I share is real! It's true! It's genuine! No one will EVER make me think something is wrong with it!!"

Just then, Ethan cried out in a strained weak voice. "Balzar! Return to the rings! Balzar! Return to the rings!"

Everyone was shocked at the interruption. They all turned to look at Ethan, still sitting in the chair with Peter's hands on his shoulders.

"Balzar! Return to the rings!" Ethan was louder this time.

Balzar had been taken totally by surprise. His face became angry and frustrated. Then, in a split second, he became a smoky image again, flew through the air and disappeared back into Ethan's body.

Immediately, the rings flew off Ethan's fingers and into the box on the altar. The lid snapped shut.

Peter spoke quietly. "Ethan. I want Jake and Mario to untie your hands and feet. When they do, I want you to go upstairs and lie on the sofa. And don't forget to step over the line of salt at the doorway. Do you hear me?"

"Yes. Yes. I do." Ethan's voice was back to normal again.

Mario and Jake moved over to untie Ethan. Ethan stood up and headed upstairs.

Mike scratched his head. He looked around the room and spoke quietly. "Wow! What just happened?"

"Thank you, Bruce. I couldn't have done it without your help. And Shawn. Wow! That couldn't have been better scripted. That REALLY distracted Balzar." Peter smiled at Shawn and then at Bruce. Everyone was on their feet and Bruce was walking back to join the rest.

Hank scratched his head. "I think I missed something. Something really important."

Peter looked at Shawn. "Now, do you see why the murders that have happened are not Ethan's fault? Let's head up to the kitchen, so we can talk." Everyone followed and sat in the kitchen as Peter went in and pulled Ethan out of his trance. Then, they returned to the kitchen.

Ethan was clueless as to what had just happened in the basement. He looked at his left hand. "Somehow I have a burn on my hand."

Shawn immediately when over and grabbed Ethan's hand. "I can get something to put on it."

Ethan commented. "Not to worry. It's not that bad. I think everyone needs some coffee." He started fixing a pot.

"While Bruce had Balzar engaged, I leaned down and whispered to Ethan to say what he did."

Ethan turned from fixing the pot of coffee. "Who is Balzar? What have I missed, being in my trance?"

Shawn got up and walked over to Ethan, putting his arms around him, hugging him tightly. He looked right at Ethan. "Damn, I love you. And don't you forget it."

Ethan laughed, in slight embarrassment. "Peter, whatever happened, maybe you should put me under again and bring me out if it gets this kind of reaction." He chuckled. He hugged Shawn tightly and whispered. "I hope you know how much I love you, too." He pulled away and looked up at Shawn and smiled. "Okay. Let me get the coffee going here."

Mario shook his head. "What if Balzar had heard you?"

"I had to take that chance. I sensed since Ethan was still himself and separated from Balzar, my whisper would be heard by only him." Peter twitched his head. "And Shawn. Have to tell you. Your outburst surprised even me. But it made what Bruce was doing even easier. Thank you."

Shawn shook his head. "Well. It pissed me off. I'm so sick of people thinking that the love shared between two men is not genuine or real. How dare they."

Jake looked at Peter. "Okay, I have to say. He was none too kind to you, calling you all those names. Think I'd have punched him out if it had been me. I hate it when I hear people use derogatory slurs, regarding others who are different. I mean, not that you are. Sorry, if I gave that impression."

Hank chimed in. "I'll second that."

Ethan was returning to the group and sat down. "Wow! I must have really missed something to get you all riled up. Especially, about relationships between two men."

Hank smiled. "You know. Seeing what Shawn and Ethan have together kind of makes me sad that I didn't take the chance when I was younger." He quickly glanced over at Jake.

Peter spoke up. "Hank! It was another time. A time extremely less understanding than today. But I agree. It's sad people couldn't share companionship and love with someone because of social mores, ignorance, bigotry and intolerance. I have a feeling with your personality, you would have made a great husband. And let me tell you. You are still a very attractive man. I can only imagine how handsome you were when you were thirty."

Jake spoke up. "You should have heard the ladies, talking about him back then. You're right. He was a 'looker'."

Shawn spoke up. "Well. Jake, you're still one handsome guy, too. Hope you're not offended by a gay man telling you that. I'd love to see what YOU looked like at thirty."

Peter added. "But you know, whatever someone's persuasion, it's never too late."

Hank nodded. "Well, since we're sharing, I'll tell you. Once, there was someone. And yes, I still know this person but I'm not sure how it would be received today if I approached the subject. I mean, I'm not even sure that person might punch me out or even if that person would have similar feelings." He quickly glanced at Jake.

Peter responded. "Hank. What are you trying to say? You're in good company here. No one here is judgmental. You should realize that. Don't just skirt the issue. Come out with it. Maybe we can help."

Peter paused for a moment. "Okay, guys. To break some ice, I'm going to tell you all something." He quickly glanced at Bruce who was nodding his head.

Bruce spoke up. "What Peter is trying to say is that he and I are just like Ethan and Shawn. And yes. We, too, love each other."

Mike stood up, looking back and forth at Peter and Bruce. "Nah. You're kidding? Really? I know there were those references by Balzar but I thought those were just taunts." He then sat down again.

Mario slapped the table and laughed. "I knew it! I knew it! And you guys just said you only knew each other for a long time." He shook his head. "I knew it! I knew it! I knew it!" He clapped his hands together several times.

Peter added. "It started for Bruce and me back in college."

Mike looked over at Mario. "Okay. Do you have anything to say?"

Mario shook his head. "No. No. I like women but I just like being single."

Everyone broke up in laughter.

After a few moments, Hank blushed, then spoke in a soft but calm voice. "Damn it! You're right! I've missed out by keeping silent for so long. I see what Ethan and Shawn have and it hurts me I never got to share and know what they have. Now, don't get me wrong. I'm not jealous. I'm just sad for me. Yes. There was someone way back then. I fell in love with... him. There. I said it. I fell in love with... him... from afar. I was afraid. I just knew that such a man could not possibly be in the same corner as me and I didn't want to create problems."

Peter was ecstatic. What he had sensed from the first handshake was coming out. The dam was breaking and Hank was coming into his own. He had hoped he would. He started to ask a question of Hank but he already knew the answer. And not just from his first meeting with Hank but his session exposed a wealth of deep internal secrets. "Hank. Do you still know this person? This man?"

"Yes. Yes, I do."

Peter looked at Hank. "Hank, why don't you say something? You just might be surprised. Jake says you have balls. Well. Remember, I'm a psychic."

Suddenly, Jake raised his hand. He bent his head down for a moment then looked directly at Hank. "Truth. Hank. I have watched you for years and wanted to tell you how I felt. Hank. You're so handsome to me. You're the bomb."

A huge grin came to Hank's face. "Jake. Really? Really? If I had only known. I've had a crush on you for over sixty years. Wow. When I was twenty-two and you were sixteen. I thought you were the tops and so damn handsome. To me, you're more handsome now, than when you were sixteen."

Peter turned to Bruce. "I told you there was more here than just what was happening in the basement."

Mike shook his head. "You have to be kidding me. Six out of eight of us. I don't believe it and I'd never have guessed. Seriously. I'd have never guessed. Now, Shawn and Ethan, yeah, cause they have made it obvious. They aren't afraid of who they are. But you guys. What can I say?"

Ethan stood up. "Okay. I think the coffee is ready. How many?"

Everyone raised their hand.

Peter looked at Ethan. "Remember. You'll have to wait for your coffee."

There was a moment of silence. Then, Mario spoke softly. "Six. Six out of eight. I think I need a drink."

Everyone's snickers grew into loud laughter again.

Mike spoke as Ethan poured coffee for all. "Okay. I'm going to be honest here. I'm telling you. For me, personally, I think I'm among a fantastic group of guys and I consider you all friends for life, regardless of who you sleep with. You are all incredible men. I'm extending an invite to you ALL to visit me whenever you like. I'm proud to know each and every one of you. And Ethan, it's not for you to feel obligated to play the piano. I want you and Shawn to visit just to visit." He paused for just a moment. "But it would be great if you'd cook."

Everyone roared with laughter, as they raised their coffee cups and clinked them together. Ethan had water. All called out. "Hear! Hear!"

"Okay. I hate to break up the party but we still have something extremely important to resolve here." Peter was serious but optimistic. "There are a few things that need to be done first. Ethan. I want you to go lie on the sofa. I'll come to help you relax."

Ethan got up and went into the great room. Peter followed and placed him in another trance.

He returned to the kitchen. "There are things I didn't want Ethan to hear. I can't take the chance the information I'll share with you all won't get snatched by Balzar when Ethan puts the rings back on again. As long as Balzar has his hooks in Ethan, it will continue. Ethan is still under his influence when he has on the rings. Ethan is not Ethan. That's why he had no knowledge of what was done. But when Ethan has the rings off and Balzar is in the rings, Ethan is fine. That said, I have an idea. I believe Balzar in his over-zealousness, exposed a secret and I don't think he realized it. Of course, the final solution is something I'm not sure of. What I have in mind is only a stopgap. I just hope it works."

"Shawn. You're going to have to be very attentive until we complete this segment. You cannot let Ethan out of your sight. Is that clear?"

Shawn nodded his head.

"Hank. I want you and Jake to drive back into town and get a very large jug with a twist cap. One with a fairly large mouth on it. Like a big gallon mayonnaise or pickle jar. Then, I want you to run to the church and ask the priest to fill it with holy water. Do it now, as there is no time to waste."

"I have a big pickle jar at the house. I think it will be just what you want." Hank and Jake got up and headed for the door.

"I think that'll be all we need. When you all get back, I'll tell you the plan and we'll begin." Peter was very optimistic.

CHAPTER XXII

It took Hank and Jake a little over two hours before they returned. When they did, Hank had one large jar and Jake had another one. As they entered the kitchen, Hank grinned as he held up his jar. "Wanted to make sure we had enough for whatever you have planned."

Jake held up his and smiled. "The priest asked if we were having some baptism. But knowing we were coming here, he gave it a double blessing and said he'd pray for all of us the rest of the day."

Peter looked at the two jars. "That's great. I'll tell you what we're going to use them for. I thought one would be sufficient but two couldn't hurt. Well, maybe just a little for Balzar. Just wait. Now, everyone sit down. I want to tell you the plan."

He quickly covered how he hoped things would go. But everyone could use their judgment should things seem to be running amuck. He then directed them all to go to the basement and take both gallon jars with them. "Shawn, don't forget the wooden spoon. And put it with my stuff in back of the big chair. Use one of the big jars to fill up all the paper cups."

"Got it." He held a long-handled wooden spoon up in the air.

Shortly, all had taken their places in the room, sitting just as they had before. Peter made sure everyone's paper cups were completely filled. All the jars were placed back behind the big chair.

Peter returned upstairs, went into the great room and spoke softly to Ethan. "Ethan. We are going downstairs again. I want you to sit in the chair just as before. This time I won't tie your hands and feet. I just want you to sit quietly. I'm now going to tell you what I need you to do." Peter calmly gave Ethan his instructions. "You will do what I've just instructed you to do immediately when I yell out. 'Ethan! Now!'" He paused for a moment. "Is that clear?"

"Yes. I understand."

"Good. Now, let's go downstairs. And again, do not step on the salt at the doorway."

Everyone was seated when Peter and Ethan entered the room. Ethan went over and sat in the big chair. The candles were lit and all were quiet.

Peter looked around at everyone. "Is everyone ready? This is definitely going to be something to see. Remember the game plan. If this doesn't work, we may all end up in bits and pieces. I know Balzar looks like some emaciated weak thing but I tell you all now, from the horrors some of us have seen, he is far from that. He definitely has the strength of an ox. So, if any of you want to bow out, I'll understand because I need all who stay to be strong." He looked into the face of everyone there.

Mike stood up and spoke softly. "Let's do this." He raised his right fist in the air. Everyone except Ethan, stood, raising their right fists in the air with an expression of determination on their faces. As they looked at one another, they bumped fists with the other hand. Shortly, they all sat and were quiet.

Peter went over and put on the white gloves. Then, he spoke with authority. "Ethan. Put on the rings."

The box on the altar snapped open and the rings flew as before right onto Ethan's fingers.

"Ethan. Can you hear me?"

A voice from far away answered. "Yes, Peter. I hear you."

"Good." Peter walked around behind the big chair and he called out. "Balzar. I'd like to talk some more. Will you come out?"

Instantly, the smoky image appeared, materialized and was standing in front of Ethan between the seated men. He was staring right at Peter. "You damn bitch! What was that business of having me return to the rings? I wasn't finished with what I wanted to say. Think I'm a damn toy you can throw around like some yo-yo?"

Peter quickly looked down at Ethan. Just as he had hoped. The rings were still on his fingers. "Balzar. I must apologize for the rudeness and hastiness of the ending of our last meeting but I knew everyone was tired and needed rest. I wanted everyone to be alert, so they could understand all you had to tell us. My sincere apology."

Balzar's angry demeanor changed. "Well, you should have told me this. That really pissed me off." Balzar walked over and sat as before on the altar. "So, you want to chat some more? Why not. Ask whatever you want. It matters not as you will all be dead before the day is over." He laughed loudly.

"You indicated that Jeremiah and the Italian merchant were the only ones who connected the book and the rings. Why? What happened in between?"

Balzar grinned. "Yes. The merchant was very much into the occult and had the book written to go with the rings. He and I worked fairly well together and we both collaborated on writing the book. His apprentices helped do the artworks within the pages. He wanted to teach and make his apprentices understand the workings of the book and the rings together. They were present at many of the sessions held by the merchant. He wanted the connection to continue when he had reached his goal and it was time to get his final reward. Later, because of what the apprentices knew, many in occult circles became aware of the power of the book and the rings, working together."

"It was finally time for the merchant's final reward. He left the villa and returned to the location where he originally discovered the rings. Unfortunately, when the merchant realized his final reward was not power and wealth but to die, he was not happy. Yeah. I took his soul to join me in the rings when he committed suicide."

"Thinking he would be returning to the villa, he had left the rings and the book together on the floor in his chamber right in the middle of a pentagram there. What's so ironic is that it wasn't one of his apprentices who discovered the rings and book on the floor, it was an idiot servant who entered the room. He saw the box, opened it and saw gold. He was a poor slob who needed money to feed his family and took the rings without knowing the value of the book. The moron. He could have been incredibly powerful if he had known the connection with the book. But he couldn't read."

"As for the book, one of the other servants came into the room the day after the rings disappeared and saw the book on the floor. She picked it up and took it, thinking the merchant didn't want it. She was another imbecile, taking the book and selling it for virtually nothing, so she could buy a little food."

"When the apprentices eventually came for another lesson, they discovered the merchant was not there and assumed he had taken the rings and book with him. They had no idea what had happened. It was only because of the passing of time, they realized something was not right. The merchant's body was brought back to the villa which alarmed the apprentices. They had no clue as to what had happened. After much searching, they realized the rings and book were gone."

"That's how the book and rings got separated and stayed separated for two hundred years. The story of the book and the rings together did not die. The apprentices told the stories of how powerful the rings were with the incantations in the book and kept them going. Many in occult circles, hearing these stories, had searched high and low for the location of the book and the rings with no success. Not until Jeremiah came along."

"From the time of the merchant, the rings passed from one to another over the many years and the book just fell into obscurity. It was Jeremiah who happened to stumble upon the book. Because he was educated and sensed its value, he wanted to know about the book and what information it held. If he hadn't sought information about it, he'd never have come in possession of the rings. I'm so glad he did. As I said before, it was the first time I ever got to work with someone and not just use them. I hated that I had to end our relationship but he had reached the number assigned." Balzar gave a sinister laugh. "He so thought his trip to Paris was culminating in his great reward. Funny. Everyone thought there was going to be some great reward for them. Little did they all realize the reward was just mine. Every time." He clapped his hands and laughed again. "I will say, when it's all over and I reach MY reward, I'm putting in a good word for Jeremiah. He deserves it. I wouldn't mind working with him again."

"Excuse me for interrupting but how long is it before your mission is over?" Peter stood firm with his hands on Ethan's shoulders. Jake and Mario were sitting in the chairs behind him.

A huge grin came to Balzar's face. "When I finish with all eight of you, I will be over the amount. Actually, three of you will be..." He looked up in the air. "What you call... collateral damage." He roared with laughter.

Peter was pleased that everyone kept their composure and remained seated. He didn't want Balzar to become alarmed. He knew the moment was coming for action to be taken.

Balzar got off the altar and started walking slowly between the four men seated in front of Ethan's chair. He looked down at each man as he walked by. "Let me see." He placed his left hand up to his face and stroked it with his long fingers. "Who should be first? Hmmm."

Everyone intensely watched Balzar. No one moved.

"I know." Balzar looked right at Peter. "What more fitting than to have our piano player watch his bitch-mouthed lover go first."

Peter called out. "But you don't have on the rings. Don't you have to be wearing the rings?

Balzar paused and looked at Peter. "Wow. You really are astute. I do need the rings."

At that, Peter yelled out. "GO, GUYS!!!"

Mario and Jake were already prepared. While conversation was going on, Jake had picked up the big half-empty jar of holy water and had it ready in his lap. At the call, he immediately dumped it on Ethan's head, covering his entire body with holy water.

"ETHAN! NOW!!" Peter yelled.

Ethan let out a scream as the water washed over his body and he stood up. As it hit the rings, there was a popping sound and sparks began to fly. Ethan yelled. "BALZAR! RETURN TO THE RINGS!"

The figure of Balzar flew toward Ethan's body but just bounced right off.

Peter was ecstatic. His plan was in motion and happening just as he had thought it could.

All the guys sitting up front grabbed their two cups of holy water and threw them on Balzar.

Balzar screamed out in anger and pain. "YOU DAMN BITCHES!!!" He raced toward Shawn again and grabbed him around the throat and started ripping at him. "I'LL KILL YOUR ASS!!" Blood flew from the cuts on Shawn's neck and arms where Balzar's sharp fingernails scratched him.

Mike, Bruce, and Hank jumped in, joining the melee. Mike and Jake ran at Balzar like some quarterbacks and slammed into him, knocking him to the floor and away from Shawn. Bruce and Hank each grabbed one of the large candlestick holders on the altar and started beating Balzar in the head and body with them while Mario delivered major right and left hooks to Balzar's body and face. All were getting their knocks in the brawl.

Peter called out. "Ethan, wake up! Just like I told you! Ethan, wake up!"

Ethan immediately came out of his trance, saw what was happening and ran toward Balzar yelling out. "DON'T YOU DARE TOUCH MY SHAWN!" He reached to try and strangle Balzar.

Mike ran and grabbed the full big jar of holy water and thrust it toward everyone. The water flew out of the jar and soaked the whole group.

A loud scream of agony came from Balzar and he worked himself free of the group. He jumped up and down, using his hands to try and wipe off the water. Ethan screamed as well. Shawn grabbed Ethan and pulled him free.

Peter had already slipped on one of the white gloves from his satchel and ran over, pulling the rings from Ethan's fingers. They fell to the floor.

The rings popped and bounced as they landed in the puddles of holy water all over the floor. Bright sparks flew as well. Finally, they bounced to a place on the floor where it was dry and about ten feet apart. They remained motionless.

Balzar was yelling out while still jumping up and down, trying to wipe off the water. "YOU DAMN FUCKING WHORES!!! BITCHES!!!! SLUTS!!! YOU CUNTS!!!!"

Peter ran to the spot where one of the rings was located. "MARIO!" He yelled.

Mario was ready. He ran over and set the last of the quart jars full of holy water on the floor in front of Peter and handed him the wooden spoon. Peter still had on the gloves and picked up the first ring, using the long handle of the spoon by slipping the handle through the ring. He quickly ran over and got the second ring on the handle of the spoon. Carefully walking over to the quart jar of holy water, he dropped them both into the jar. Everyone watched as the water seemed to boil and pop. Sparks flew like fireworks out of the top of the jar as the rings fell to the bottom.

Balzar was now laying on the floor, writhing and screaming out in agony. "YOU DAMN BITCHES!!! SLUTS!!! WHORES!!!"

They all stood back. After a few moments, the sparks from the jar slowed to a stop as did the bubbling and popping. On the floor in front of the altar where the shackles and chains were set in the floor, a vortex began to form, swirling from a pinpoint, getting bigger and bigger in circumference until it was almost four feet across. Immediately, the shackles and chains were pulled into the swirling hole.

Suddenly, Balzar screamed out. "NO! NO! YOU BITCHES!! NO! NO!" He kept screaming and flailing in total agony. At that, he became a smoky form. In a split second, the image flew into the air, exploded into a million pieces of sparks and flashes and was sucked into the whirling vortex.

The jar began to bubble again. The ethereal image of Jeremiah flew out of the jar and into the air, screaming and writhing. It, too, burst into flashes and sparks and was sucked into the vortex.

Just as that faded, another ghostly image flew from the jar and into the air. It repeated the same sounds of agony and pain, exploding into sparks and flashes and was pulled into the vortex.

At that moment, the vortex immediately slammed closed. There was no indication it ever existed in the floor.

The room was finally silent. Everyone stood speechless. Shawn held Ethan and could see the severe burns on his fingers where the rings once were located.

Then, just as everyone thought it was over, the jar bubbled one last time, catching everyone's attention. They stood quietly, staring at the jar. Suddenly, the bubbling stopped. Within a moment, wispy images began to rise and swirl from the jar, one after another, flying upward into the air and disappearing. Hundreds and hundreds of images flew out, causing swishing sounds as they rose and vanished.

All watched in amazement. "It's all those souls who were captured in the rings." Peter spoke softly. "They're now free and going to a better place and peace. They were the ones who had no idea what they were getting into when they either wore the rings or were the victims of them."

It took just under ten minutes and then there was nothing. The room was silent.

Mario spoke up. "Okay! I don't know about any of you but seriously, after all that, I need a drink! And I also have a few cuts and bruises I need to attend to."

Everyone was in total agreement. All the guys realized they had cuts and bumps they had to take care of, too. Sounds of quiet sighs came from the group.

Peter could tell it was the sounds of relief from a major, unbelievably stressful event. He took off the gloves and placed them with his satchel.

They all slowly went upstairs.

Mario patted Mike and Jake on the back. "Those were some damn good tackles. Geez! Jake. I'd never guess a guy your size could pack such a wallop."

Jake snickered. "What you're trying to say is you'd never guess a guy my age could pack such a wallop. Thanks for being kind."

Mike shook his head. "Reminded me of my college football days. And Mario. Damn. Those right and left hooks. Wow! What was that?"

Mario responded. "Did a little boxing in my time. Guess I haven't completely lost it."

"You all know where the booze is located. Bring it to the table. I'll be right back to join you. I think I have enough stuff in the safety kit for you all. I'll run up and get some gauze and stuff. Be right back." Shawn called out, as he ran up to the bathroom.

Bruce and Mike went to get the bottles of liquor and mixers from the bar and pantry. They took them to the kitchen table.

Shortly, Shawn returned and placed the first aid kit on the kitchen counter. "Okay, guys. Go to it. Help each other out." Everyone pitched in to clean and bandage all the cuts and bruises. Finally, that taken care of, all were seated around the kitchen table except Shawn who was being tended to by Ethan.

Bruce looked at Ethan. "Wow! That was courageous of you down there. Peter is right. Love can be a conquering force."

Ethan stood there with a dazed expression. "Okay. Someone is going to have to fill me in on all that just happened. The first thing I remember is seeing some ghastly creature trying to kill Shawn and jumping in to attack and my hands felt like they were on fire. I feel like I came in on the tail end of some damn horror movie." He continued to try and clean Shawn's cuts.

Shawn then started seeing about the burns on Ethan's fingers.

Jake nodded his head. "Have to say, Ethan's right. I think this whole story would make a great horror flick."

Sounds of agreement came from the group.

"How about some sandwiches, if that's okay with everyone." Ethan walked to the fridge. "I'll put everything on the table, so you can help yourselves."

"I'll help." Shawn started organizing plates and utensils then went for the bread after setting everything on the table.

Soon, all had made a sandwich. Drinks were already being poured.

Mike was pouring his drink. "What was that last image that blew up in front of us? I knew the first one was Balzar and pretty sure the second was Jeremiah. I could tell from the old photos of him."

Peter took a sip of his cocktail. "It had to have been the Italian merchant. I'm sure. And the way they all disappeared, I'll bet 'Lord and Master' is not happy or pleased with any of them." He turned to Shawn. "How are Ethan's burns? I hope it won't be detrimental to his playing."

Ethan looked down at his hands. "I think they'll be fine. I won't let it get me down. But I don't think I'll be able to touch the keyboard for a while." He looked at Peter. "Well, someone needs to tell me what has happened."

Bruce looked over at Ethan. "Now, we all get it. Every time you had the rings on, you had no idea what was happening. We know you have no recollection of any of your concerts or anything that happened afterward."

Ethan saw everyone looking at him. "Geez. The way you all are looking at me, you'd think I committed murder or something." He snickered nervously.

Everyone was silent.

A question came to Ethan's face. "What? Did I do something terrible when I was wearing the rings?"

Mario sat up straight in his chair. "Let's just say this. Whatever happened, it wasn't your fault and you can't be blamed. Only the seven of us here know the truth and I believe we will all agree. We will keep it to ourselves and it goes no further. There is no reason for you to know. Mike and I know the answers now and I know I'm satisfied with them. I'm sure he will agree. This case is now closed."

Mike raised his glass. "Hear! Hear!"

Shawn looked at Mario. "You mean there will be no punishment or repercussions?"

Mike spoke. "I believe Ethan has literally had his trial by fire and has come out the other side alive. I pray those burns on his hands won't affect his playing." He stared at Ethan's hands. "Nothing was or could have been his fault. As Mario said, this case is closed."

Soon, all cuts and bumps were on the mend. Everyone had their cocktails and sandwiches, sitting at the kitchen table.

Peter cleared his throat. "Okay. But I hate to stick a pin in the balloon but this case is not completely closed. We do have the rings. Since they are in a jar of holy water and all the souls have left them, they pose no threat. But. Where is the book?"

Bruce interrupted. "You mean all this could start all over again?"

"Actually, I don't think so. What I figured out came to be." Peter continued. "Balzar dropped his guard, during conversation. In all his self-assuredness and self-adulation, he made a fatal slip. He kept indicating the souls were with him as he continued to collect them. The only place they could have been was in the rings. And when I saw how Ethan and the rings acted when I doused his left hand with holy water and Balzar's immediate comment about 'what are you trying to do to me', I knew it was the answer. Holy water was the ultimate weapon as simple as it seemed. Regardless of what Balzar said about being immune to our trinkets and baubles, he said nothing about the holy water. I was truly pleased to see Balzar could not re-enter Ethan when Ethan was doused with holy water. He couldn't re-enter the rings, either. That was the answer. It was the time he was vulnerable. The rings were his refuge but he couldn't get to them, especially after they were dropped in the holy water. Later, I want to go down and throw some more holy water on the altar. How it acts will let me know if the room is clear or not." He took another sip of his drink.

"All right, I don't know about anyone else but I'm bushed." Mike raised his hand. "Is there any way we can call it till tomorrow?"

"I agree." Peter set his drink down. "I think everyone needs a good night's sleep."

They all finished eating their fill and their drinks. Each picked up his plate and glass, placing them in the sink.

"We can do those tomorrow." Shawn mentioned.

Hank and Jake started to the door. "We'll be heading home."

"Hell no!" Shawn insisted. "You're not driving home after all that has happened. No way! You're staying right here."

"But we don't want to put anyone out."

"You're not. I can pull out the cots for you both and put them in the rooms on the south end of the house." Shawn headed to the back storage room. "We haven't had time to set them up officially as bedrooms yet."

Mario, Jake and Hank went to help Shawn get the cots, taking them to the rooms.

Suddenly, Hank spoke out. "Shawn, put them both in the same room." He looked over at Jake and smiled.

Jake smiled. "Yes. Put them in the same room."

"Guys. You've got it." Shawn had a pleased expression on his face.

Everyone's face beamed with happiness.

"Now, you two have dibs on who's first in the shower. Then, it's the powder room down here for everything else." Shawn commented. "Hope that's all right."

"Hank joked. "Hey. Jake and I have lived this long and made it this far. No complaints here."

Eventually, all were going to their rooms. They all needed the rest but would they all be able to sleep after what they'd seen that day?

CHAPTER XXIII

The next morning, the entire group seemed to congregate at the same time in the kitchen. They were all aware of a major revelation. Their aches were still there but the bumps and bruises were gone. So were all the cuts. Even the burns on Ethan's hands were gone. Everyone was shocked.

"I have no explanation for it but maybe it's because the curse is over." Peter commented.

Everyone tended to watch Ethan to see if there were any residual effects from his experience. Peter even pulled Shawn aside to ask if he had noticed anything. Shawn indicated Ethan slept well and had no strange episodes during the night. Peter was glad.

"Okay. I know it's the same thing but how about omelets this morning?" Ethan headed to the fridge for the eggs and ingredients.

Hank chuckled. "I don't care what you fix. I know it's going to be good. Never pass up a good meal from Ethan."

"Hank's got that right." Jake agreed.

All nodded their heads and sounds of approval rose from everyone.

As everyone got seated, Mario started a comment, looking at Mike. "I was truly impressed with those body slams you and Jake delivered yesterday. That took some damn balls to do that."

Mike chuckled. "I think it was automatic. Something leftover from college football days. Just seemed like the thing to do. But I must tell you. I'm paying for it today. My bumps and bruises may be gone but I feel like I was hit by a truck."

Jake agreed. "Just seemed the thing to do. I was following Mike's lead. And have to say. I feel the same way. Feel like I've been beat with a stick."

Bruce jumped in. "I have a feeling Balzar was not expecting that. But all of you did get your bumps, cuts and bruises. I'm really glad somehow, they have all disappeared."

Shawn spoke up. "If you hadn't done it, he might have ripped my throat open instead of the miscellaneous cuts and bruises I did get. Thanks, guys. I owe you all my life."

Ethan started bringing plates to the table. "All right, everyone eat up. And who wants more coffee?" He poured cups full, they all ate and finally finished breakfast with little conversation.

Ethan cleared the table of the plates but refilled the cups. Then, he sat down to join everyone. "Someone is going to have to fill me in on all that happened and what it all entails. I keep hearing about a Balzar and have no idea what you're talking about. Was that the weird thing that had hold of Shawn?"

Peter looked over at Ethan. "Not to worry. It doesn't matter now. I believe it's all over. Balzar has failed in his mission and as I said, I don't think 'someone' is going to be too happy about that. I feel Balzar has a long road up from the bottom again. And I doubt he'll use the same game plan."

Bruce added. "I sure hope so. But what about the rings and the book?"

Ethan had a queer look on his face. "What is this about rings and a book? I do feel totally in the dark."

Shawn turned to Ethan. "The rings you found. The ones you wore. Don't you remember? The book is the one that was on the altar down there in the basement."

Ethan shook his head. "I have no idea what you are talking about. What rings? But yes. I do remember the book. It was on the altar the day we went into the room."

Everyone looked around totally in astonishment. Then, they looked at Peter.

Peter just shook his head. "Maybe it's a blessing. I think it best he has no idea and it stays that way. It would serve no purpose."

"But what is to happen to them?" Hank asked quietly.

"I'm going to put a lid on the jar and take them to a safe place for a while. I'll do some research and see if anything needs to be done in a special manner with them. I believe from what we all witnessed, the rings are just rings now. They contain no entities or spirits. We watched them purge. I believe if I have them melted down, they won't reconstitute. They are finished."

Mario questioned. "I hope you'll keep us all informed of the outcome. And what about the book?"

"Right. The book." Mike joined in. "It's still out there. It may be old and possibly valuable but I think it should be destroyed. In the wrong hands, it could be incredibly dangerous."

Jake commented. "Sorry. I was waiting my turn. I know where the book is."

Peter was ecstatic. "Really?"

Jake shook his head. "Yep. It's in my office at the station. In the evidence locker. Along with all Jeremiah's journals. I put it in a plastic bag. Took it there, after all the craziness was discovered in the basement. Didn't want anything to happen to it. The FBI wanted to take it but I told them it would stay here till I knew what was to happen about closing the case."

Peter was emphatic. "Jake. Seriously. I need to get hold of that book."

Jake gave a 'thumbs-up'. "Consider it yours. I know if anyone knows what to do with it, you do. Not a problem."

"Excellent. Now that I know where it is and it's safe." Peter was happy.

"I'll have Buddy or Jerry bring it out here. I'll give a call to the office." Jake added. "What about the journals? They're in my office, too."

Peter responded. "I only want the book right now. The journals pose no threat. But I'll give you a call down the road about them and come up here one day and get them from you. What's in them might make some interesting lectures on the occult and paranormal."

Shawn interrupted. "Jake, I hope you don't mind but I want to hear about you and Hank. I think it's so sad you both had feelings for one another, going so far back but could never act on it. To me, THAT is a tragedy and is so sad."

Jake looked at Hank. "Do you mind if I tell them?"

Hank nodded. "Go for it. They're great friends. They should know our story."

"Well, I want you to jump in when you want."

"I will."

Jake began in a quiet voice. "Things were extremely different way back then. It was the forties. Now, I couldn't figure out why I was never attracted to women. Then, at sixteen, I saw Hank in his military uniform. That's when I knew why." Jake lowered his head and began to chuckle. "Damn. He was so handsome in it. Every time I saw him, I couldn't help but stare. I was so afraid he would see me."

Hank broke in. "Actually, I did see him. And I couldn't believe my eyes at what a sexy guy Jake was then. We were both looking but not wanting the other to know."

Mario interrupted. "I have a question. You both seem to know the whole story. How can that be? You only knew about one another yesterday."

Hank grinned. "Do you really think Jake and I could sleep last night, finally realizing how we felt about one another? We talked virtually all night long."

"Oh. Wow." Mario nodded his head. "Damn. Of course. Sorry for interrupting."

"No problem." Jake responded. "From then on, I couldn't look at anyone else. I thought Hank was the cat's meow." He looked over at Hank. "I still do."

Hank added. "As Jake said, we became aware of one another back then but could never act on it. Eventually, we became great friends. Jake is a great guy. I'm glad we've been the friends we have been to one another over the years. We've basically had a relationship but it was Platonic. I know now, things will be different." He gave a big grin. "I can say it, now that everyone knows. I knew he was the one and always wished he felt the same way. Now, I know he did."

Shawn commented. "You know, you said something the first night you came to dinner. I had a sense but never said anything more. Now, what you said then makes perfect sense."

Jake shook his head. "I'm just so sorry for all the time we have let slip through our fingers. We missed out on so much, not being together. But as Hank said, we actually did have a relationship. It was just Platonic for all those years."

Mike spoke up. "Guys. Okay. Here's a comment from a straight guy. Stop your bitching, grab the bull by the horns and go for it. You both know what you want. Do it. You have waited long enough. Two good men who care about one another should be together. And that's from the heart of a straight guy."

"Wow! Did I just hear what I think I heard? And from a straight man?" Ethan's face was filled with amazement. He looked at Shawn. "Don't let any of these guys get away. They are really and truly our friends. Wow."

Jake looked at Shawn. "Let me call the office for the book. Is there anything else we need out here?"

Peter looked up. "Yes. Could someone stop by the church and get another large jar of holy water? I need more."

Jake stood up and pulled out his cell phone. "Harriet. Jake here. I'm still out at the old Raines place. Stop laughing. Yes. It's been crazy. Yes. Do me a big favor. Tell Jerry or Buddy to grab that big book in my office. Yes. It's in the evidence locker. It's in a plastic bag. Correct. That's right. The one from the Raines House and also tell him to run by the Catholic Church and pick up a very large jar of holy water. Hopefully, a gallon jar if at all possible. No. I'm not telling you what I need it for. Great. Thanks. If all goes well here, I should be back in tomorrow. Okay. Goodbye."

Bruce chuckled. "You do realize we're going to have to come up with a good story for your deputy."

Jake smiled. "It's all right. Both of the deputies were in on all this from the beginning. It'll be old hat for whichever one comes."

"Jake's right. His guys kept things from getting out of hand here in the very beginning." Ethan added. He got up. "Guess I'll put another pot of coffee on for everyone."

They could hear the sound of the deputy's car, pulling up in the drive. Jake went out to meet him. "It's Jerry."

Jerry got out, carrying a large rectangular shape wrapped in a black plastic bag under his right arm and a big gallon jar under his left. He saw Jake and Hank. "Hey, guys. Good to see you. How have you been?" Then, he saw Shawn and Ethan. "Hey, guys. Hope you have been well." He handed the wrapped item to Jake then looked at Ethan. "Been hearing incredible things about you and your playing."

Jake started the introductions. "Jerry. This is Captain Michael Brooks of the Portland Police Department. Portland, Oregon."

Jerry shook Mike's hand. "Hello, Captain. Jerry Blake. Welcome to the neighborhood."

"Call me Mike." Mike smiled.

"This is Captain Mario DeSilva of the Seattle Police Department."

"Welcome, Captain." They shook hands. "Hope you don't mind me saying it but you look awfully young to be a captain. Wow. Maybe there is a chance for me after all." A big grin filled his face and he looked over at Jake.

Jake nodded. "Yep. You're next in line."

Jerry thrust his right fist in the air. "YeeeHaw!"

"This is Bruce Livingston. He's a consultant for the police." They shook hands.

"And last but not least, is Peter Solvinoski. He's from Boston and is connected with the University there." They shook hands.

"Thanks, Jerry for bringing everything. Do appreciate it."

"You're so welcome, Peter." He paused for a moment. "Solvinoski. Russian?"

Everyone laughed.

Peter responded. "Polish, actually."

"Solvinoski. Solvinoski. I know that name somehow." Jerry shook his head as if trying to find some lost piece of information. "Yes. I remember now. I was the guy Sheriff Jake asked to call you way back last year when all the insanity was here but you had a prior commitment and couldn't come. I'm glad you got to finally get here. I know you have to realize how incredible this whole thing is."

Peter raised his eyebrows. "Trust me. I'm very familiar with what has happened here. I do regret I didn't get to come in the beginning. I think if I had realized the gravity of the whole thing back then, I'd have dropped everything and been here."

"It's all right. You're here now." Jerry looked at Jake. "I thought everything was over and settled? What are all these guys doing here now?"

Jake's face cringed. "Well. Not settled yet. But it's almost finished."

"You're kidding? What now?" Jerry looked up in the air.

"Let's all go in. I think Peter would be the best one to fill you in on everything." Hank led the group into the house.

Peter turned to the others. "I'll take Jerry downstairs and fill him in. It may take a little while. No use trying to keep him in the dark now."

Shawn spoke up. "Ethan and I can stay up here and start fixing something for everyone for lunch. That way, you all can go down and help Peter tell what happened."

Jerry carried the jar of water and Jake had the book. They headed to the room in the basement.

Mike and Hank pulled the two chairs from in back of the big chair and Mario helped arrange them all in a group between the altar and the big chair. They sat down. Peter remained standing. Jake had the book on his lap and he sat next to Jerry.

Peter took the jar from Jerry and set it down beside Bruce's chair. Everyone was quiet.

Peter went and leaned against the altar and began to tell it all from the beginning, right after the discovery in the room. Finally, ending with what had taken place the night before. "And that's it. Till now."

"Holy shit!" Jerry scratched his head. "That's unbelievable. Too bad you didn't have a camera to record the whole thing. You know no one will believe it. It's just too fantastic to be true. That's what they will say." He looked over at the book in Jake's lap. "But what about the book?"

Peter continued. "It's the last link. It has to be destroyed. Then, no one can use it ever again for evil." He looked at Jake. "I hope this won't cause problems for you as to destroying evidence."

Bruce added. "I think Mike and Mario will agree. Destroying that book would be the best thing and I'm sure there would be some way to explain it. I mean, everyone knows the book is associated with some weird-ass event and if something bizarre happened to it, it wouldn't be unexpected."

"I think you're right. Not the first person has asked about the book since we took it to the department last year. I don't think anyone wants to hear more about it." Jake grinned.

"One thing that's very important." Peter softly spoke. "Ethan must never hear what happened as he doesn't remember any of it. That kind of possible guilt wouldn't be fair since he had no idea he was even involved."

Mario added. "Peter is correct. He truly has no knowledge of anything. Mike, Jake and I have agreed there is no reason to bring charges because he actually didn't do any of the actual killings. Yes. He happened to carry the rings but he really never knew he was doing it. Some might say he was an accessory to murder. I don't think so. The guy has been through enough. He as well as the rest of us would've been among the dead if what we did hadn't succeeded. We would have all been victims."

Mike continued. "Peter was very shrewd to figure it out. He's the one who picked up on the weakness in the armor. He told us the plan and it worked."

"But if you all hadn't followed it to a tee, the results would NOT have been what they were." Peter added.

Jerry looked at the quart jar, containing the rings. It had been placed on the floor in front of the altar. "So, those are the rings. Do you think they're still a threat?"

"The water would have boiled completely out of the jar if they were." Peter looked at the jar. "Going to take them to get melted down. Then, they will be just pure gold again."

"What are your plans for the book?" Jake walked over and handed the package to Peter.

"We're going to burn it and the ashes we will put in holy water and stir till there is nothing left. I'm going to pour it over the spot where the vortex formed. That should keep it from ever opening again. Mario, will you go up and ask Shawn or Ethan for a very large metal tray and a big bowl? When I burn this thing, I don't want any of the ashes to get away."

Mario bounded up the stairs. Almost instantly, he reappeared with a big round aluminum tray and a large glass bowl. "Shawn said to use them however you need."

Peter took the tray and placed it in the middle of the altar. He set the bowl down on the corner. The book was unwrapped from the plastic bag, placed on the tray and then Peter opened it. Everyone gathered around the altar to watch. Peter went to his suitcase behind the big chair. He returned to his place behind the altar again, holding a bottle and a small brush. "It's holy oil. It will burn. Water won't." He placed the brush in the bowl then slowly poured some oil on the pages of the book.

Everyone was amazed. There was no ignition source but the book began to smolder and finally started to burn. Peter continued to pour on the oil. The pages charred and burned, one by one, shrinking to ashes, pulling to the middle. The hotter the flames got the faster the pages burned. Within five minutes, there was nothing left except a pile of ashes and the pile was rather small with regard to the size of the original book. Peter took the brush and swept the ashes into the bowl. "Jerry, if you will do me the honors." He pointed at the gallon jar of holy water then picked up the bowl and walked around to the front of the altar where the vortex had occurred. He set the bowl on the floor. "Mario, if you would get the crucifix from my suitcase. The one that's about ten inches long. Thank you."

Mario retrieved the crucifix and handed it to Peter.

"Jerry, I want you to very slowly pour the water from the jar into the bowl as I stir. Try hard not to get any on the floor."

As Jerry poured, Peter stirred, using the crucifix. The ashes seemed to just fade into nothing. At Peter's direction, Jerry stopped adding water. Peter continued to stir for a while as all gathered around. Finally, he removed the crucifix from the mix and handed it to Hank. Everyone was surprised. There was not one speck of ash on the cross. Peter picked up the bowl. Right where the center of the vortex was located, he slowly poured the mixture on the spot.

The small area of the floor began to glow and steam rose. Everyone moved back. The spot on the floor became red hot. The few remaining ashes seemed to fade into the floor. Within a few moments, the glow faded and the floor appeared normal again.

"The ashes are gone. Wow! I'm impressed!" Jerry was surprised.

"That's nothing." Hank spoke up. "You should have seen the other things he did. I know you heard about them but seeing them was a totally different thing."

Jerry looked at Peter. "You do this stuff? And you teach it, too?"

"Well, it's not quite like this." Peter nodded his head. "Teaching and knowing about it isn't like actually being involved in it for real. Now, hand me the jar of water. I want to see if the altar is clear."

"How will you know that?" Jerry handed the jar to Peter.

"Oh! You'll know." Bruce started to giggle.

Everyone began to chuckle nervously, remembering the last time holy water hit the altar.

Peter walked over to the altar, holding the jar of holy water. Everyone else followed behind but not too closely. He picked up one of the empty cups, lying on the floor from the previous night and filled it with water. He set the jar down and walked to the front of the altar.

Before he did anything, something popped into his head. His mouth twitched, trying to keep from laughing. Of course, no one could see because they were all standing behind and back from him.

He saw it all in his mind. At the moment he threw the water at the altar, he would quickly turn around with a distorted ugly face, roll his eyes, raise his arms up with his hands out like claws and he would make loud growling and snarling sounds as he twisted his body and arms in contortions. He was curious how everyone would react. He just had to hope no one would slug him.

He had to compose himself to sound serious. He spoke with authority. "Is everyone ready?"

There were soft affirmative replies from all the guys, then silence.

Peter threw the water from the cup at the altar. There were no sparks or pops but he jumped quickly around and performed his plan.

Everyone jumped back yelling loudly. "Shit!" "Damn!" "Jesus 'H'!" "Holy Shit!"

Peter lowered his arms and bent over, laughing and slapping his upper legs. Everyone instantly realized they'd been had.

"You damn BITCH!" Bruce yelled. "You absolute asshole BITCH!! You scared the immortal shit out of us all! You Bitch! You damn Bastard!" Then, he started to laugh.

Everyone, seeing it was a joke, joined in the laughter but muttered under their breath. "You damn Bitch! You absolute Shit!"

Mike yelled out. "THAT WASN'T FUNNY!! You almost made me SHIT myself!"

Hank was doubled over laughing. "Yeah! Yeah, it was! It was funny as shit! And I almost shit myself, too!"

Peter could not stop laughing. "You should have seen all your faces!!" He doubled over again. "I wish I'd had a camera!"

Mario could not help himself. "Just wait. You're going to get yours one of these days. I'll see to it." He nodded his head but couldn't stop laughing.

Bruce entered the joke. "Mario! Don't worry! I'll get him for you! And in the worst way, too! Trust me!"

"Good thing I didn't have my damn gun. I might have shot your ass." Jake laughed. "Holy Shit!"

Peter finally gathered his wits. "Sorry, guys. I couldn't resist it. It was too good to pass up. No hard feelings I hope. I was a little concerned Mario might slug the shit out of me, though."

Mike muttered. "Yeah. Almost gave me a damn heart attack."

Finally, they all calmed down and returned to the subject at hand.

Hank cleared his throat. "Okay. What next?"

Peter got serious. "As you saw, there were no sparks or detrimental happenings when the water hit the altar. It is clear. That being the case, the room is now clear. It's over."

Hank questioned again. "Over? Completely over?"

"Yep. Completely over." Peter answered.

"Guess we can go upstairs now." Jake stroked his mustache. "Okay. NOW! This case is CLOSED!"

Everyone nodded their heads and started clapping their hands and cheering.

Peter spoke up. "Bruce and I will get the things together from down here later. Now, we can all go home."

They all headed up to the kitchen.

As they appeared in the kitchen, Shawn was curious. "Did everything work out? And what the hell happened down there? I was expecting to hear screams of terror but NO! I hear uncontrollable roaring laughter. What the hell happened?"

Hank looked over at Peter. "Peter. Peter happened and scared the ever-living shit out of all of us. A joke on his part. We'll tell you about it later. But he says it's all over. The altar is clear, the room is clear, so I guess the house is now clear."

Peter looked at Shawn, nodding his head. "But I think Mike has to go change his pants."

Everyone began to snicker again.

Mike called out. "Yeah. Yeah. I'll get you. One of these days." He shook his head and kept snickering.

Ethan was surprised. "Wow! Whatever happened must have been REALLY funny. But for now, everyone sit down and eat. I fixed a nice lasagna. Shawn, if you will pour the wine, I'll serve." He looked at Jerry. "Can you have some wine? Didn't know if you were still on duty."

Jerry looked at Jake.

Jake looked at Jerry. "Sit down, boy, and have some damn wine. After all this shit, you deserve it."

Everyone clapped their hands.

Shawn questioned. "So. It's over?

Bruce looked at Shawn. "Yep! It's over! Finished! Done!"

Mario grinned. "I'm so glad it's over and closed. If it had lasted much longer, I'd be the size of an elephant with all the good food. I swear, I'm going to have to go on a damn diet when I get home. And not just this low-carb one I use now and then. Damn! I might even have to do some exercise!"

Everyone shook their heads and giggled.

Hank added. "It's true. Ethan is one hell of a good cook."

They all turned to Ethan and applauded as he took several bows. "Thank you, guys. I appreciate the compliments."

As they started eating, Bruce turned to Jerry. "Not trying to put you on the spot but you're the only one we don't know much about. Give us a synopsis of your history."

Jerry felt somewhat the focus of attention but understood. "Geez. Where to begin? There's not much to tell. I've lived here virtually all my life. Jake will tell you. Went to work with him and the other deputy, Buddy, when I got out of high school and I love it. Was kinda hoping I might become sheriff one day when Jake retires. That's about it. Oh. Been seeing this girl over in Trenton. What can I say?"

Jake joked. "Jerry's still young. He has a lot to learn. But he's getting there."

Everyone made sounds of approval.

Mario interjected. "That's great. But remember, a cop's life is not an easy one. Your girlfriend needs to know and realize that. Seems I was always married to the job."

Mike nodded. "That's right. Mario is right."

No one wanted to put Jerry on the spot with more questions.

Peter spoke. "Well, we are very grateful for your help today. You don't know just how helpful you really were. Without that book, we couldn't have closed this situation and I sure didn't want it left open-ended."

Jerry responded. "You're welcome. Glad to be of service. And speaking of service, I do need to get back." He turned to Ethan and Shawn. "Thank you, guys, for being so kind with lunch." He got up and headed to the front door. "Jake, see you tomorrow?"

"Yep. See you then."

Shawn accompanied Jerry out. Soon, the car headed down the drive.

Hank suggested they go down and bring the chairs back up and help Peter gather his things. "And maybe it might be time to seal off that room again." He suggested nervously.

In about twenty minutes, Peter's things were out in his SUV and the chairs back where they belonged in the house. All gathered in the great room and sat down.

Ethan spoke up. "I truly don't know how to thank ALL of you. I realize I have no idea as to the true dimensions of what has taken place but from Shawn's reactions, I know they are significant. I have no way to thank you except to say thank you."

Hank stood up. "Ethan. There is a way. Would you play something for us?"

Everyone clapped and cheered.

Ethan got up with a smile and walked to the piano. "I guess I should play something pertinent to what's happened." He chuckled. "I was going to play Rachmaninoff's *Prelude in C Sharp minor* but instead, I'm going to play another wonderful piece by the same composer. It's called the *Maestoso*. It's the sixth piece in the *Moments Musicaux Opus Sixteen*."

Ethan played it with the greatest of dynamics and style. Both Peter and Bruce realized the ability of his performance had not diminished. The excellence of his playing was still there. It was obvious that even though the rings were no longer in control, Ethan's playing was incredibly superb. They both smiled in their approval.

As the last two forte chords faded, all jumped up with applause and cheers.

Ethan stood up and gave a quick bow. He looked at Bruce. "All right. Now, it is your turn." He gestured in Bruce's direction with his right hand.

Everyone clapped and cheered.

Bruce stood up. "Okay. Okay. But please don't compare my playing with Ethan's. Remember. He's a concert pianist." Bruce sat down on the bench and sat silently for a moment. He reached for the keyboard but stopped. He turned, looked at everyone and smiled. "I know Ethan and Shawn will know this one and most likely Peter. But for you others, it's called *Oh, Do Not Grieve* from the *Twelve Romance Songs* by Rachmaninoff." He went back to the keyboard again and was quiet for a moment. Then, he began. As the piece progressed, the huge chords boomed through the room.

Peter was astounded at Bruce's incredible playing, knowing full well the difficulty of the piece. A smile filled his face, he was so proud of him.

As the last chord faded away, everyone jumped to their feet, clapping and whistling. "Bravo! Bravo!"

Ethan spoke. "Bruce. That was not only magnificent but incredibly beautiful. You played with such amazing dynamics and feeling. Excellent. And that is a critique from a concert pianist! I think you should play at least one more."

Everyone stood and applauded, cheering and whistling. "Yes! One more! One more!" The cheers and clapping continued.

Bruce stood up and smiled. "All right. All right. There is a piece I'd like to play. It's not a classical piece in the sense of Chopin, Debussy or Rachmaninoff. It is a more modern piece that to me, will always be a classic. And from now on, every time I play it, I'll be thinking of all of you. If any of you know it, please join in with me."

Bruce sat down on the bench again and was silent for a moment. His hands extended over the keyboard and he began to play. The introductory melody line gave the piece away. Bruce sang the melody in his very good tenor voice. All were familiar with it and joined in. "'I'll be seeing you… in all the old familiar places… that this heart of mine embraces… all day through…'" They all continued singing as Bruce played the melancholy melody with great emotion until finally coming to the end. "'I'll find you in the morning sun… and when the night is new..… I'll be looking at the moon… but I'll be seeing..… you.'" His right hand moved up the keyboard in broken chords to a pianissimo with the final last octave notes in the bass.

As the sound faded, everyone was silent in the room but had big smiles on their faces. Bruce turned his head to the right and smiled. "I love all you guys."

Everyone stood up with cheers and raucous applause. Mario and Mike even whistled a few times.

Bruce got up from the bench and returned to the group, everyone patting him on the back, thanking him for his wonderful tribute.

"If that doesn't call for a drink, nothing does." Shawn got up and fixed a cocktail for everyone. He handed one to each.

Peter stood and smiled. "Who would have ever guessed such an event would bond a friendship between eight men such as us like it has? I feel I have added six new brothers to my life, not to mention a wonderful partner." He smiled at Bruce. "How lucky is that? I drink a toast to you all and thank you for being in my life." He raised his glass.

They all stood and glasses clinked together.

Mario then spoke. "I'll second that. But I must tell you. If someone had told me a year ago I would have an incredible friendship and brotherhood with not only another straight brother but with six terrific gay guy brothers and one who's a psychic, I would have laughed them off the planet. Just goes to show you that you never know what's around the next corner. Here's to a bunch of incredibly great guys." He raised his glass. All the glasses rang out as they touched.

Mike also had to have his say. "Mario, I know what you mean. I'd have done and said the same thing. But I say it again. I have never met such an outstanding and finer group of men in my life and I consider myself the lucky and fortunate one to know all of you. I'm a better man for it. To all of you and thanks for being my brothers." He raised his glass. All the glasses touched.

Shawn looked around at the men standing there. He reached over and grabbed Ethan around his back, pulling him close. "Ethan and I feel the same way. Who would have ever guessed? You guys have saved my Ethan and kept our love alive. I want you to know how much we both appreciate it. I would have lost Ethan if not for all of you." He and Ethan raised their glasses. Again there were smiles as the glasses rang out.

Bruce looked at Peter and smiled. "If not for this event, I may never have found what I lost with Peter years ago. I now know I care for him more than anyone and I have all of you to thank for bringing us together again. You are all special men to me and I truly love you all for it. Thank you for being here and being part of my life." He raised his glass. The sound of crystal rang again.

Hank cleared his throat. "Okay, guys. But I think I'm really the lucky one here. If not for all of you, I would never have found myself. I'd have continued through the rest of my life, being afraid of who I am. But worst of all, I would have remained alone. Not anymore. Peter, Bruce, Ethan, Shawn, you have shown me that love truly can be shared by two men. Even you, Mario, and you Mike, two straight guys, supporting me in being me and helping me take that next step toward being whole." He looked at Jake. "And now, to be able to share time, joy and happiness for the days I have left with the man I have loved all my life but was so afraid to express it. And let me tell you. One day of real true love and happiness with someone is worth more than a lifetime of loneliness. Thank you, guys. I love you all the rest of my days for the greatest gift you have given me." He turned to Jake. "Jake. I love you." He raised his glass. Again, there was the sound of clinking crystal.

Jake smiled. "What can I say? I have always believed the Fates work in mysterious ways." Jake shook his head. "I now know I was put with all of you to help me in the same way you helped Hank. There are no words that can express my gratitude for that. If this had not happened, I, too, would have lived the rest of my life alone, never knowing and always wondering. Thank you guys from the bottom of my heart. And by the way, Hank and I may be old enough to be fathers as well as grandfathers to all of you boys but I have to tell you, last night proved there's a furious fire burning in both of our hearts and we're not going to let it go out. Now, I know I love and am loved by an amazing man." He smiled at Hank as he raised his glass. The glasses touched again.

Ethan looked at Jake and Hank. "Seriously. I think it's wonderful. You both now have a chance to love and be loved. You're being handed something special on a silver platter. And I don't say 'silver' in reference to age, either."

Hank shook his head. "We get it guys. You're right. As Jake said, we're not going to let it burn out. We do have a second chance and I'm glad for it. And we owe it all to all you guys."

Peter spoke again. "Now, just a comment. You two don't necessarily have to move in with one another or anything like that or hold hands while walking down the street. But. You can share the things that are the truly important things in life. You are both good men and you deserve love and happiness. I see many more years of joy, love and happiness for you both."

Ethan jumped in. "Hank, you and Jake are good-looking men! Neither one of you look your age. And I can tell even with your clothes on, you're both incredibly buff. No fat there. And you're both in good health. I can see you sharing many years together, too."

Everyone set their glasses down and clapped and smiled with approval. They grabbed their glasses again, raised them up, clinking them together for the final time with all of them calling out. "Hear! Hear!"

Shortly, Jake looked at Hank. "Well, I guess it's time for us to hit the road. I have to get to the office tomorrow morning. And seriously, I need to get some rest."

Hank responded. "I have to agree. These have been some weird-ass days. Don't mean to be a party pooper but I am also exhausted."

They shook everyone's hands as well as 'man hugs', thanking Ethan for the meals and concert. "Guys, it was great to meet you all. If you're ever back this way, please, let us know. Would love to see you all again."

Hank and Jake headed to the door.

As they headed to the car, Ethan called out. "You two come to dinner on Friday evening. We'll expect you both around six-thirty. And we won't take 'no' for an answer."

"Sounds good." Hank called back.

Peter took Jake's hand and shook it. "I will contact you about the journals. I'll be in touch."

Again, all gave big 'man hugs' then watched Hank and Jake drive off. They all went back in and sat in the great room.

Mario turned to Peter. "So, what's on your agenda now?"

"I have another archaeological dig, coming up in about a month. I think that will give Bruce enough time to move in with me." He gave a big grin and turned to Bruce, whose face lit up red. "Why don't you and Mike come stay for a few days? Bruce and I can show you Boston."

"That could be fun." Mike agreed.

Mario turned to Bruce. "And what are you going to be doing?"

Bruce shook his head. "I'm finally going to write that book." With a big grin on his face, he looked at Mario. "And don't worry. I promise I WILL spell your name right. I will spell everyone's name right."

Everyone clapped their hands and made sounds of approval.

Shawn wanted everyone to know. "Ethan has another concert, coming up next month and will be back on his schedule. I know he'll be at the keyboard, working on his programs. I'll be checking to see if any new clients have shown up for me with the company. So, I'll be back to work soon as well."

"Guess we'll leave tomorrow morning." Bruce suggested.

Mario spoke up. "Well, I have to say it. If I hadn't been involved in this whole damn thing, I'd never have believed it. Even if a damn priest had told me about it."

"You've got that right." Mike agreed.

Ethan raised his hand as if in a classroom. "I have one question. Will I ever know the whole story?"

Shawn immediately jumped in. "I will tell you one of these days when I think you're ready to hear it and if you really must know it." He turned to Peter. "Do you think it's okay to do that?"

"Down the road perhaps." He looked right at Ethan and spoke emphatically. "I want you to remember this. There's no reason for you to know the whole story. But should you ever start to hear anything about it, remember. What happened was not your fault. Do you hear me? It was NOT your fault. You were only the unfortunate recipient of a terrible, terrible curse. That's very important to remember. Do you hear me?"

Ethan spoke rather like a scolded child. "Yes. Yes, I will remember."

There was a moment of silence before Mario commented. "I don't know about you all but I am exhausted. I know it's early but I'm turning in." He stood up. "I'll see you all in the morning."

Mike agreed. "Mario's right. I think I'll hit it, too. See you all in the morning." He headed for the stairs behind Mario.

"Ethan and I will have breakfast for everyone before you all leave tomorrow morning." Shawn reassured everyone.

They all headed to the stairs and their rooms.

As Peter and Bruce began to get in bed, Bruce looked over at Peter. "I really hope Ethan never finds out the whole damn story. It would be a shame for him to feel guilty. And you know he would."

Peter turned to Bruce. "Not to worry. He will never ask anyone about what happened."

Bruce twisted his head. "But how do you know?"

"When I had him under in session, I gave him a suggestion. After we all leave, never to ask ever again. That's how I know. And I'll let Shawn, Mario and Mike know this when Ethan isn't around, so they will have no concern down the road. I'll call Hank and Jake and let them know, too."

Bruce smiled. "I'm glad. I really am. That was kind and good of you to do it."

Peter looked right at Bruce. "It's interesting you should play that old Rosemary Clooney song tonight. If you only knew how many times I have played it, thinking about you. I also want to thank you again for getting in contact with me. About this case. If you hadn't, I might not have found you again. I know I said it the other night but I really had no idea how I felt about you until I saw you that day in the hallway of the hotel. I knew instantly you were the one and you always had been."

Bruce smiled. "I never knew how much I missed and cared for you until that same moment. I don't ever want to lose you again."

Bruce turned out the light and they both kissed in a passionate embrace. He knew his life was going to be filled with love and happiness and shared with an incredible and amazing man.

Soon, all was quiet and they were asleep.

THE END

Printed in the United States
by Baker & Taylor Publisher Services